The SAINTED

a Chris Pella Novel

iBooks
Habent Sua Fata Libelli

iBooks

Manhanset House
Dering Harbor, New York 11965
Tel: 212-427-7139
bricktower@aol.com • www.ibooksinc.com

Library of Congress Cataloging-in-Publication Data
The Sainted, a Chris Pella Novel
Medico, Michael p. cm.

1. Fiction—General 2. Fiction—Thriller 3. Fiction—Horror
Fiction, I. Title.

978-1-59687-436-7, Hardcover

December 2015

First Edition
First Printing

The SAINTED

a Chris Pella Novel

Michael Medico

Dedication

To my wife, family and friends
The joys in my life

"In this holy flirtation with the world,
God occasionally drops a handkerchief.
These handkerchiefs are called saints."
—Frederick Buechner

"They say there's a heaven for those who will wait.
Some say its better, but I say it ain't
I'd rather laugh with the sinners than cry with the saints.
The sinners are much more fun…"
—Billy Joel

"Oh, no they're not."
—Chris Pella

Preface

Gracciano-Vecchio, Italy, 1268...*The midwife found her way through the dark streets on a mission to greet the newest citizen of her small town. Donisa saw there were no lights coming from the houses and the small shops along the way. Even though it was dark, she knew the streets better than most. After all, she grew up in Gracciano-Vecchio.*

How she loved this town and the beautiful regions of Toscana. Gracciano was a small, sleepy town compared to Montepulciano with its monastery and brothels. She made the sign of the cross at the mention of these houses of shame, but these regions had been home her entire life, and she was happiest here. Her family, the Zacci's, have been farmers and shopkeepers for more than six generations, and Donisa had roots that she was thankful to the Lord for. As she hurried through the muddied paths, thoughts of her past and her family made her smile. How they treasured her and how they made sure she was cared for and blessed with an abiding love of family, the land and of life itself.

As Donisa turned the corner, the de Segni Mansion, with its balconies and beautiful gardens, came into view. It was by far the grandest home in all of Gracciano Vecchio, and the de Segni family was well known in the region as devout and benevolent. Senor de Segni's wealth was great but so was his faith and charity, and he was held in high regard by the entire town. When Donisa arrived at her destination, she knocked on the door...as late as it was, she knew the whole household would be up, eagerly awaiting her arrival.

"How is Senora de Segni doing? Is she almost ready?" Donisa asked the young maid.

"Senora is in labor, and she has been asking for you," was her reply, but before the maid finished, Donisa was rushing to the senora's room.

At the door, she was greeted by Senor de Segni—a tall, ruggedly handsome man whose nobility was apparent, and he commanded great respect from all who knew him. He was pacing the floor in anxious anticipation. He looked worried, and his concern for his wife was evident in how he greeted the midwife.

"Where have you been? Do you not know how much pain my wife is in?"

Of course she knew how much pain the Senora was in. Hadn't she delivered more than thirty beautiful children into God's world alone and an equal number that are surely in Heaven and into the arms of the Blessed Mother? What of her own six children...the miracles in her life.

"Senor de Segni, please do not worry. Your wife will be fine, and your baby will light up your home as no other could! Now leave me to my work, and let me get her ready."

It was the custom of the time that the men would wait outside the birth room, but Senor de Segni was not one to be ordered outside, especially at a time like this.

"I will not leave. I will be here at her side, and I will welcome my child into the world."

Donisa knew there was no arguing with this man, so she set about the business of bringing new life into this house. As she opened the door to the bedroom, the midwife saw that Senora de Segni was lying on the bed waiting for the moment of her child's birth. Donisa observed that Senora de Segni was a beauty in her own right. The Senora was born of a family that owned many tracts of land surrounding Siena and was betrothed to her husband in what seemed a marriage of wealth to wealth. As it turned out, however, there was a bond between the two that was as immediate as it was unexpected, and for these past eight years, they lived in happiness with an enduring love that grew stronger each day.

The room that the Senora rested in was as warm and inviting as one could hope for and, given the family's means, not unexpected. A fire was lit, and the warmth came in waves and seemed to defeat the chill that is part of the Toscana weather in early spring.

As Donisa entered the room, she quickly came to the side of Senora de Segni and held her hand. When she turned, she saw that it was the midwife and gripped her hand tightly, "I am so happy to see you, Donisa" the Senora said in obvious pain, "I feel that the child will be coming very soon!" Donisa had a sixth sense when it came to all things related to childbirth, and she said,

"The child will be here within the hour."

The blanket, cloth and water to clean the baby were made ready and the Senora was made as comfortable as could be expected, given her situation.

With her husband by her side, the entire household prayed, and as they prepared for the blessed event, a stillness settled over the house.

The peace was broken by the first painful screams of labor, which came one after the other. The Senora held tightly to Donisa's hand, as she tried to free her body of the child in her womb. The sweat on her brow was wiped away by the midwife, and Donisa's comforting words and exhortations seemed to ease the apprehension that the senora was surely feeling. Senor de Segni, who had been quiet until now, seemed to turn frantic and asked,

"Is there any comfort I can give? Will she be well?"

Donisa could only guess what dread and anxiety he must be feeling for his wife, and she tried to assure him that "all is well and going as God planned. We must be calm and have faith." A cry came from his wife that tore at his soul. She screamed in extreme pain, but the scream was soon overtaken by a fountain of tears and a joyous cry that signaled the birth of a child...a beautiful baby girl.

Donisa began to weep as she cleaned and wrapped the beautiful baby and handed her to her waiting mother. Both the Senor and Senora looked lovingly at the infant who appeared awake and gazing at them...they were complete... they were a family.

It was at this moment of absolute joy for the new parents that a heavenly sound filled the air unlike any sound that anyone in the household had ever heard. With that sound, there appeared a bright light that poured through every window like liquid gold, and it soon filled the room and totally surrounded all who were there.

The light seemed to come from above and below—from all sides as it slowly encircled the house, illuminating each room, making them as bright as any glorious summer day. The light radiated warmth but no heat, and one could look into the light and not be blinded. Senora and Senor de Segni were terrified for their child and for themselves. They wanted to flee but suspecting it was a sign from the Lord, they began to pray.

At that instant, bright burning torches appeared around the bed where the mother and baby lay. It was a sign–a sacred sign.

Donisa knew, the parents knew, that they had brought into the world a blessed child, welcomed by divine lights...a child of God, and her name was Agnes.

Chapter 1

Huntington, NY, 2013...They, whoever they are, used to call it the "Gold Coast." All along the North Shore of Long Island, financiers, industrialists, entertainers and your run-of-the-mill rich folks built large estates, and they have called this beautiful setting home for decades. But even the rich have their problems, and over the years the large estates have given way to smaller but stately homes and later–with all the trimmings and taxes that go along with status these days–subdivisions of multimillion-dollar "McMansions."

My name is Chris Pella. I live in the town of Huntington and while not the toniest place among the moneyed, the town does have its charm and a fair share of people with enough wealth to live life on their own terms. Huntington, sometimes called "The Little Apple" is located on the Long Island Sound with beautiful vistas of the surrounding communities all the way to Connecticut. The area also encompasses affluent towns of Lloyd Neck and Lloyd Harbor, Huntington Bay, Cold Spring Harbor, Dix Hills and many other communities rich and poor, large and small.

Huntington Harbor and the area around it is a combination of New England tradition and North Shore style plus easy access to some of the best sailing around, and that's where I live. Power and sail boats alike cruise the waters of the Sound (as locals call it) mooring to swim, fish, water-ski or just party. You can take your boat right up to *Prime* and have the privilege of paying a premium for a drink while enjoying a spectacular view of the harbor.

The "downtown" itself has become somewhat of a magnet for upscale restaurants like Honu for tropical exotic tastes, Mac's for great steaks or Buenos Aires for food with a South American flair, but if you're feeling a bit more casual there's always the Golden Dolphin Diner, Finnegan's or Mundays. I enjoy eating out, and while my metabolism helps keep my weight down, my wallet tells me how often I can indulge.

I was never a real culture nut, but Huntington has the Cinema Arts Center for the independent and international film crowd, The Paramount for a whole variety of contemporary music, the Heckscher Museum for fine art lovers and so much more. The town has become sort of a mecca for entertainment and dining, and if you don't believe me, try and find a parking spot on any weekend night.

There are many parks, beaches, ice-skating rinks, country clubs, health clubs, golfing and even parades...well, you get the point. It seems there are more great things to do *per capita* than any town that I've ever been to, and it became my home. I love where I live, I like the people, and given that I started out as a nice Italian boy from the Bronx, I feel pretty lucky to have landed here.

I am an only child and was named in honor of St. Christopher. As the story goes, St. Christopher was crossing a wide river when a small child asked to be carried across. St. Christopher lifted the child, but when he put the young boy on his shoulders, he found the child to be unbelievably heavy. The child, according to the legend, was Christ carrying the weight of the whole world. I know his sainthood, even existence, has been called into question, but my folks loved the name and the legend of St. Christopher, and so do I.

I'm single, 32 years old, and considered good-looking by the women I date. I also like to think of myself as a "good guy"...certainly no Saint Christopher, just a good guy—maybe that could be my epitaph. I live in a two-bedroom condo that I furnished in a traditional way, as I consider myself a traditional kind of guy. I dress in what I call "preppy chic," and I love those shirts with the horses and alligators and the red, white and blue logos. So you don't get the wrong impression, I make sure I only buy stuff on sale, and I really know how to get great deals on clothes. Lord and Taylor, Macy's and Bloomingdales seem to know what I am looking for because just as I think I need some new clothes, I get mailings with little cards that give me an "extra 20%" off the sale price... not too shabby.

Two holdovers from my childhood: I attend Mass every Sunday, and I say a prayer every night before going to bed. It seems old-fashioned in this secular world, but it affords me a kind of peace that I couldn't imagine getting from the latest edition of "Dancing with the Stars" or "American Idol."

I was born in the Bronx, and I never completely lost the accent – I lay it on thick when I get the opportunity. Once I met a woman, Emily, from England and after some small talk, asked her out. On our first date she told me she loved the way I spoke and that most of the people in London loved New York accents better than, say, Southern accents. She said that it was especially sexy. I never thought of myself or my accent as anything more than what it was…and that was anything but sexy. Still I took the compliment in the spirit that it was made and, later that night, had the best sex I'd had in a long time. I guess it pays to have a sexy voice.

I'm of Italian descent and growing up Italian definitely has its perks. From the food, to the holidays, to the sense of family, I take pride in my heritage. I owe that to my parents, who I often think about in the fondest of terms.

They are both gone now, but the memories of Mom and Dad are vivid and full of the experiences, large and small, that shaped the way I act, think and live my life. My parents, Anthony and Gilda, were born here, but both sets of my grandparents were from Italy and settled in America when they were very young. Mom and Dad went to school here and learned English because it was important to their parents that their children were brought up as proud Americans. My grandparents considered living in this country very special and that we should be grateful for this place. My grandparents also made sure that both Mom and Dad learned to speak Italian and to take pride in that tradition. Speaking Italian came in very handy when my parents and grandparents wanted to chat about private matters without me understanding what they were saying. Eventually, I learned to speak Italian, so Mom, Dad and I were able to have some wonderful conversations over the years.

Jokes seemed to be funnier in Italian – I remember a porcelain ashtray in our home with a joke that said *Il serpente che punta la mia suocera morì di avvelenamento*, which I'll translate as I assume that many of you may not speak Italian: "The snake that bit my mother-in-law died of poisoning." Anyway, the joke could lose something in the translation, but it always got a laugh from the old folks in my family.

I grew up in a real Italian section of the Bronx, and in my mind's eye and nose I can still see and smell the cheeses, meats and breads from the stores along Arthur Avenue. Each Sunday my father and I would buy the feast our family would enjoy after Mass at the Immaculate Conception Church. My dad, Anthony (who never liked being called Tony), would buy the special *granna padana*, a cheese that would fill the air of Ferrari's Italian Deli with an aroma that would make our mouths water. There were spicy Italian sausages and crusty semolina bread, large ripe tomatoes, sweet roasted peppers and salty cured prosciutto – antipasti that would be served and eaten before the family sat down to the "real" dinner.

For dinner, what else but pasta with a thick, rich sauce that was so good you took bread and lapped up all that was left. My mom started cooking at 7 a.m. on Sunday because the sauce or "gravy," as some called it, would need to cook at least six hours. She would add the meatballs, beef braciola and sausages, then cook the sauce for another two hours so the flavors would intensify. I still use Mom's recipe for the sauce and, when I finally sit down to eat, I think that she'd approve.

After our trip to Ferrari's, my father and I would go to the bakery next door and buy cannolis, éclairs or sfogliatelle for dessert. Our Sunday meals became a tradition, one that gave us time to catch up as a family, much of the time along with our extended family, and speak of all that was happening in our lives. The Sunday meals helped me to understand my folks, their lives and dreams, what they expected of me, and what they expected of themselves. It was at these dinners that I learned about our family history, how my parents met, how grateful they were to have one another and how much love they felt for each other even after their passion subsided. Sunday meals were a time to slow down, eat to our hearts' content and count our blessings. The Pellas weren't rich by a long shot, but you couldn't tell by the food on the table and the happiness we felt in each other's company.

As a young boy, I'd watch the old men playing bocce in the park and the women sitting on the stoops of their buildings talking, laughing, all the while never realizing there was anything more to life than what they enjoyed every day. I guess this way of thinking and the genuineness of these people help form a positive attitude about life even when reality hits you with a brick. For me, though, the greatest influences on my way of thinking were my parents. I really loved my mom and dad. They were great parents and, as corny as it seems coming from a guy my age, I tried to make them proud. They were generous, tough, funny and filled with so much love for me that it was kind of special and embarrassing at the same time.

My dad never graduated high school because his family was poor and he needed to go to work. At first he was hired to do menial jobs and worked as a laborer. As he became more skilled, he was given more responsibilities and ultimately became a foreman on a number of construction projects over his lifetime. I'll always remember that his hands were like sandpaper, his knees wracked with arthritis and the lines on his face were the road map of a tough, hardworking life. While he could have complained, and he had every right to, he never did. It was what he needed to do to provide for his family and make a better life for me. It was America's immigrant credo that their children would have a better life than they had, and he made sure of that.

For Gilda it was different. Her parents recognized that she was a bright child and, although it would require great sacrifice, they made sure she would graduate high school and onto college. When the time came, she went to City College and received her degree in biology, embarking on a career as a laboratory technician. My mom had a keen mind and a structured, analytical way of thinking that made her the perfect person for her vocation. She loved working in the labs, running tests and analyzing the results, but always questioned those results until she was satisfied that they were valid and proper. For her it became a way to help doctors help patients, and she was very good at her job. Even when she met Dad, fell in love and got married, she continued to work–up until I was born, when they both decided that she would quit and become a full-time mom. Gilda and Anthony did this at great personal sacrifice, and I believe it made all the difference in my life.

My dad never went further than the tenth grade when he had to quit school so he could work to help support his family. This was a lifelong regret for him, and it was for this reason that he worshipped at the altar of education. Unfortunately for me, because of his passion for education, it was preordained that I would have to go to college.

I was a good student but the thought of going to four more years of college after graduating high school gave me nightmares. I hated everything about college, I hated the classes, I hated the professors, I hated the books, I even hated the cafeteria – but I loved my parents more, so after four years I graduated from the State University in Buffalo with a liberal arts degree, a business minor and a 3.1 GPA. Okay, maybe "hated" is too strong a word, but I was dragged kicking and screaming through college, and when I got my degree I swore I would never step into a classroom again!

But at my graduation, I made sure that Mom and Dad got front row seats to the ceremony and, when I received my diploma, I saw my father beam with pride. Anthony and Gilda are gone, but those memories are like an elixir. The memories warm, comfort and even help cure the loneliness I feel now that my folks are in the Lord's hands.

Once out of school, I set about doing what every 21-year-old does: looking for a job, having as much fun as I could and trying to find my place in the world. But life has a way of throwing you curveballs, and much of what I would experience seemed to be preordained.

Chapter 2

I tell you all this because you may want to know a little about me and my life, and I think you should also know that I can communicate with the saints.

What I am saying is that they talk to me, and I talk back to them. They teach through the stories they tell, and I listen. They reveal visions, and I learn. And miracles…yeah, even miracles I witness while staring and gaping in total amazement.

I know that you think all this saint talk sounds crazy, but you've got to believe that it's been like this most of my life. It started from when I was about fourteen, and it's been like that until now. From the time we moved to Long Island, I've had this gift. I don't think it has anything to do with Long Island being the center of some heavenly repository of saints…I think it's just me. Some may call this "special talent" a curse but for me, it is definitely a gift. Imagine having St. Peter let you know whether you're making it through the pearly gates or having St. Joseph show you how to build an armoire.

Just kidding. It's not like that at all.

It happens like this…I can be doing just about anything. I can be having a cup of coffee, reading a book or looking at beautiful pleasure crafts from my home overlooking the Huntington Harbor, and these visions will come to me. I am still in the present, where everything seems to freeze in time. My surroundings change, and I am transported to wherever or whenever my saints want to take me.

As a fourteen-year-old kid, I guess I could have been out playing ball or trying to imagine what it would be like to kiss Joanie behind the backstop at the Mill Dam ball field, but that wasn't in the plan. What was in the plan? Adventures. Some were wonderful, some terrible, but they all were life altering for me. I would not have given up the journey for all the treasure on earth.

It started like this. Winters can be tough on Long Island, and as the weather one year got very cold, I got really sick. My mother kept me home from school one day, and I lay in bed with the most horrible fever, cough and sore throat that you can ever imagine. I could have overplayed my condition, especially because I didn't like going to school, but I didn't have to because I was really sick. You know the kind of sick I'm talking about—light-headed, chills and sweats…the whole ball of wax, and I had it in spades.

Mom was very concerned about my condition, and she had to go to the store to pick up the medicine our doctor prescribed. Since I was fourteen, I guess she felt that it would be okay to run out for a little while, so reluctantly, she left me alone with strict instructions that I stay in bed. Mom had a lot of rules, but this one was easy to obey because every time I tried to get up, I collapsed back into bed, so that's where I stayed.

As I lay there in bed, the entire room began to spin. I was overcome by dizziness and nausea. I thought that it was the sickness that made me so disoriented, but that wasn't it at all.

While I was in this state, I received my very first vision.

In the vision, my room was transformed into an ancient expanse in what appeared to be a desert country. I was in a small town surrounded by a flat, sandy vastness with outcroppings of rocky hills in the distance. In the midst of this expanse, I found myself standing outside a large mud and stone building. It was one of a number of smaller and larger dwellings and shops where the people were going about their business.

I had never seen anything like it—well anything like it outside of books about ancient times.

As I gaped around at all that I was seeing, something drew me to walk inside the building behind me. As I went inside, I entered a very large room. The room was sparse, with little in the way of decorations. It was more like a place where people worked, not lived. In the room, there were many cots set up along the long walls on both sides. On each cot, people were being treated for what seemed to be all kinds of problems, sicknesses or wounds.

I looked out the window, and I saw a group of soldiers dressed in what looked like ancient Roman uniforms. But this was not Rome, or at least not the Rome I saw in the movie *Gladiator*. The soldiers were patrolling the marketplace that was next to this building while the people looked to be shopping for cloth, spices, food and other basic items.

I noticed that the shoppers in the market took great pains to avoid the building I was in. They would walk by looking away, covering their mouths. It was obvious that I was in a hospital, and you could tell the people outside were consumed by fear of catching any of the illnesses being treated here.

Two other things became obvious to me. First, nobody seemed to notice I was among them. Second, I no longer felt sick.

In the ancient hospital, there were two physicians brothers, twins actually, treating their patients. The men hurried from one person to the other shouting instructions at the nurses and aides and giving comfort to the sick wherever they could.

"Get water for this one; he is burning with fever!" shouted the one doctor, as he wiped the brow of the man who was vomiting. The doctor and a nurse were busy cleaning the man as best they could. The meticulously thorough cleaning looked to be more of a treatment than simple bathing, and both the doctor and nurse kept at it.

"Bring me the mint…bring me the mint!" shouted the other twin doctor. He was comforting a woman holding her head in agony. He took the mint, placed it into a bowl and began to crush the leaves. He then made the woman breathe in the aroma of the mint. You could see her pain subside, the mint bringing her some measure of relief.

My initial wonder turned to confusion. Where was this place? Why was I here? Who are these men?

All the people in the entire building focused on their tasks and took direction from both doctors. This frenzied activity went on until a nurse suddenly screamed, "He's dead, he's dead!" At the sound, the twin physicians came running to the bedside of a dead black man. All activity stopped. A hush came over the room. In death, the man's careworn face seemed to be at peace. The doctors said a prayer over his body, now free of pain, wishing him eternal rest and heavenly rewards. All of those present in the room, doctors, nurses, aides and patients alike stopped and joined in prayer for this man. Then the doctors did something that literally shocked me into the realization of what was about to happen.

The doctors began to cut off the left leg of the dead man.

With a long, sharp metal instrument, the doctors began their work. They took great pains to assure that the leg was cleanly severed and done with minimal damage to the bone and the skin surrounding the hip. Working with great concentration on the amputation, the doctors took care to be sure that the leg was placed on another table, washed and covered with a clean white cloth.

The dead man was carefully wrapped in a shroud of sorts, and when the nurses finished, one of the doctors said,

"Prepare him for burial."

After that, the doctors turned their attention away from the dead man to their next patient. Lying in a bed next to the dead man was another man writhing in agony, and his screams echoed through the entire chamber. His leg was infected with sores that had become ulcerated, and the infection covered most of the skin. Immediately, the twin physicians began to prepare this man for another operation of some sort.

Ancient medical tools were laid out to perform the procedure that was still a mystery to most in the room, including me. The doctors began preparing an herbal compound, mixing it with what they called a "spathumele." The mixture smelled horrible, but that didn't stop the doctors from their work. The mixture was placed into a bowl with mint and hot water, creating a steamy herbal liquid, but I didn't know for what purpose. With bowl in hand, the nurse began to wipe the man's head and allow the steam to be inhaled. In a very short time, his screams lessened, and he seemed to fall into a semiconscious state.

"Cosmas, have you cleaned the body and leg well?" said one doctor.

"I have, and I am ready to begin," said his brother.

"Continue to wipe the man's brow while we are preparing him for what is to come," commanded Damian to the nurse.

As the nurse continued to wipe the sick man's forehead, his cries stopped, and he seemed to drift into a stupor. As the man fell into this state, the doctors started to pray.

"Lord, we beseech you to grant us the wisdom and skill to save this man and Your intersession and strength to guide our hands so that we may help in this his time of greatest need. We ask this in the name of Your Son, Jesus Christ."

With that prayer there was a collective "Amen" from the doctors, nurses and some of the patients.

The doctor called Cosmas picked up the first tool, a long gleaming knife or scalpel of sorts, and he began to cut off the man's ulcerated leg. The patient let out a muted cry, but the nurse continued wiping the forehead, administering the herbal mixture and soon the man fell into a restless state of unconsciousness.

With all due speed, Cosmas finished cutting off the ruined, infected left leg from the body. Although it was a cool day, both Cosmas, Damian and the nurses assisting them were covered in sweat. The twin doctors worried about the bleeding, knowing that the danger to their patient was greatest now.

"I need to stem the flow of blood, but I do not want to alarm the nurses" Cosmas whispered to Damian.

With that, Damian picked up a clean linen cloth that was on the table with the other instruments and sprinkled some dried, crushed herbs onto the bandage.

"I have the cloth with yarrow, and I will hold it in place."

As Damian placed the cloth onto the hole where once there was a man's leg, the bleeding slowed dramatically. As he administered to the man, Damian frequently changed the cloth, but after the fourth time, the bleeding had practically stopped. The crisis had passed.

When Cosmas and Damian were done, with great care, they disposed of the amputated leg in a sack made of a brown woven material. The nurses then lifted the man off the cot, quickly changed the bloody bedding and placed him back onto the cot. He had fallen completely unconscious, and he had trouble breathing, but the need to continually wipe his brow was over, at least for the moment. Cosmas then carefully lifted the amputated leg they had taken from the dead man and placed it onto the clean cot next to the wounded opening on the unconscious man's hip.

"We are ready. Let us start."

Damian and Cosmas took the leg, positioned it where it needed to be and with that, they began to graft the black man's leg onto the white man.

"Take pains to assure the bone is in place and prepare the sutures," said Cosmas. For hours, both doctors worked tirelessly as they sewed the new leg onto their patient, taking time to be sure that all was going as expected. The nurses were busy going about all their duties to help the doctors, but you could feel that they were in awe of all that was going on. The gathered mass sensed, on some level, that something miraculous was taking place. All the while, both doctors continued to pray, which seemed to calm and reassure all who were taking part in this surreal scene.

The doctors began stitching the new, healthy leg onto the man. Damian and Cosmas turned toward me and stepped out of their bodies. The hospital room faded and became no more that a haze with the doctors still taking care of the man, but their spirits were now standing in front of me.

A halo appeared around the heads and bodies of the men, not only the type of halo you see in paintings or books. These also a glow that encircled their entire bodies.

Damian looked straight into my eyes and asked, "What do you see in this place you are in?"

At first I didn't know, or maybe didn't want to know, who he spoke to. I turned behind me to see if anyone else was there.

"You, I am speaking to you."

With that, I pointed at myself and said, "Who, me?"

"Yes, you…we have known you were here from the start. You were summoned here, so that we may tell you of what is required of you."

I immediately started rattling off everything that was on my mind "Who are you guys? Where am I? How did you do that? Is the guy going to be all right? Why do you have the bright light around you?" The questions came out as fast as I could think of them.

"I am Damian, and this is my brother Cosmas. You are in Cilicia, and it is nearly 300 years after the death and resurrection of Jesus Christ. We have been given an honor of which neither of us is worthy. We are called saints, saints of the Holy Church, and in life we looked to do the Lord's work as doctors serving those sick and in need of help."

Cosmas then said, "The man has been given a miracle, he will live and walk again, and it was only through the blessings of Christ that it has come to pass. We still need to know, what is it you see in this place?"

I was dumbfounded. I was talking to someone who lived more than 1,700 years ago, and they are asking me questions.

"Uh, I don't know. A hospital, I guess."

With that answer, the brothers looked at each other and smiled. Damian said, "It is far more than that. It is a place for hope, for renewed faith, for charity, for life and yes, even for death. It is where we have found what was required of us."

Cosmas also explained, "We are all here in this life with a purpose. Our purpose is to help the sick, to comfort the dying and to serve the Lord. Do you know your purpose?"

I didn't know what to say, so all I said was, "No."

"Christopher"...he knew my name. I couldn't believe that he knew my name.

"Yes, Christopher, I know your name, and I know why you are here."

"Why? Why am I here?" I said.

Damian then said, "You were brought to this place to see us, so that we may let you know what is required of you...your purpose."

He continued, "You are here for the same reasons the hospital is here. Throughout your life, you will be called on to serve the Lord by helping people to ease their pain, find hope and comfort, renew their faith and deliver justice so that they may find the peace of the Lord through His Son, Jesus Christ. You will be asked to perform works for the good of those truly in need, all in service to our Lord."

"But I'm just fourteen, a kid, what do I know? Who will listen to me?" I stammered and became anxious at what was being said and overwhelmed by the spirits of the brothers. I know now that they were truly great men, but back then, they sounded like my high school principal.

Cosmas and Damian looked at each other, and in an instant, the room disappeared. I was transported to a place that seemed to be floating on a cloud. Everything was bright white and for the first and only time, I became frightened. The twin brother saints stood before me, and as they raised hands in prayer, there appeared all around them hundreds, maybe thousands of apparitions.

Damian seemed to know that I was scared and said, "There is no need to fear what you do not understand. What you see are our sisters and brothers, those who have gone before you and have been given their reward in heaven, the gift of God's peace and eternal love."

Cosmas continued, "These saints in Christ all have a bond, they all have had their faith tested, they have given themselves to the Lord and they all understood their purpose...why they lived and what was expected of them."

Damian and Cosmas then each moved aside, and I saw a vision of St. Francis of Assisi. He spoke to me, "You will go into the world and see happiness and trouble, life and death, good and evil—you will be expected to help in any way you can. You will help those in need. There will be times you will confront the true nature of evil, but know that you will not be alone. We will be there with you." Sts. Francis, Cosmas and Damian all smiled at me, and the vision melting into a bright glow and, with that, it ended.

I was now back in my room, staring at the ceiling, sick as ever. My first vision was over, and for the first time, I was overwhelmed by all that had just happened. I couldn't fathom the meaning of it all, and I reckoned that it would not be my last visitation.

Me, Chris Pella, a fourteen-year-old kid, experienced visions of ancient times, witnessed an operation that was impossible—miraculous, even—spoke to Sts. Cosmas and Damian, was transported to a gathering of saints and told of my purpose in life...imagine that.

Chapter 3

So far, I have communicated with 176 saints—saints from the earliest Christian times, some more contemporary, some female saints, some male saints, and they all were very real to me. The saints would come to me in all types of visions, and in them they would speak to me.

Some of the visions are simply reflections of the past to help me understand who I am and my place in the scheme of things, but others are quite more profound. Each of the saints I have met have three things in common: their holiness, their abiding faith in God's plan and His Son, Jesus and that they have suffered or persevered to one degree or another for their faith. Some have been martyred in the vilest and cruelest of ways, while others passed in relative quiet—all the while offering up their lives or suffering as penance for some real or imagined sin.

Consider St. Fabius. He was a Roman soldier that lived in the third century. St. Fabius refused to carry a Roman banner because it used pagan symbols. He was given a chance to "get his mind right" so to speak, but he refused. He was chastised by his commanding officer and was given no alternative but to submit to this idolatry. When St. Fabius refused this command, he was promptly marched out in front of the troops and put to death. In those days, the Romans specialized in particularly nasty and painful forms of deaths…so he was martyred because of his faith.

You've got to admit, that took some balls, but when I asked him why he chose death over life, St. Fabius told me that he didn't have a choice. He said that his belief in his Lord was absolute. What mattered in the end was that this was the only option left for him. Choosing death over denying your faith—that's a saint for you.

You also need to understand that Christians, especially Catholics, are big on saints and even have designated "patron" saints for just about everything—from all types of illnesses and handicaps to occupations like "marble workers" and even protection against plagues caused by "rats." For the uninitiated, Patron Saints are selected by the church and, by virtue of their example and accomplishments, these saints are chosen as the protectors or guardians over many different areas of life.

So now, let me introduce you to St. Barbara. St. Barbara is the patron saint of the US Field Artillery…that's right, US Field Artillery. St. Barbara lived in the fourth century and was brought up as a heathen by her tyrannical father, Dioscorus. St. Barbara's father built a tower where he forced his daughter into total seclusion. While in this lonely desolation, St. Barbara gave herself to prayer and study and was converted to Christianity in secret.

When Dioscorus found out about St. Barbara's conversion, this totally pissed him off—my words not hers. Dioscorus became so infuriated over her conversion that he denounced her in public. She then suffered many indignities and was brutally tortured. In the end, St. Barbara was beheaded by her own father, who actually acted as the executioner. This is where it gets really miraculous. As she lay dead, St. Barbara's soul was released, and it was carried to heaven by the angels. Further, God became so angered by what her father had done, He brought His wrath down, swift and devastating. The skies opened, and Dioscorus was struck down by bolts of lightning, relegated to eternal damnation as his punishment. I guess you can see why St. Barbara is the patron saint of the US Field Artillery.

St. Barbara is a wonderfully gentle soul who seemed to be embarrassed by all the attention she's received since her passing. When she told me her story, my mouth must have dropped because she started to laugh at me.

"What's so funny?"

"You cannot yet know what it is that God has planned for you," St. Barbara said. "He may have trials and torments far worse than I was ever made to suffer, so you will need to be strong even as you face your own death."

She wanted me to know that what mattered most was her faith…her love…even her forgiveness of what was done to her by her father. That quality seems to be a characteristic of many of the saints that I've met …they are happy, at peace and just can't see what all the fuss is about.

No matter where or when these visions came, even if I was visited in the middle of the night, I was never frightened except once, which I told you about. This may be hard to imagine for a kid of fourteen, but it's the truth. The gift that was given to me was all the saints that I've known and interacted with never made me feel I had anything to fear. When I had a saintly vision, I would be overcome by a sense of puzzlement or unease, but as I delved further into the visions, my thinking became clearer, and I experienced an overwhelming sense of awareness and wonder. It was only after these visions were gone that I would be weighed down by what I was told or what I was required to do and the significance of it all. I guess I could have told my parents, but for some reason, I felt that this gift had to be kept a secret.

What was also weird was that I seemed to have some sort of understanding of what these saints were saying. It was not always clear at first, but I was able to apply this ability no matter what language the saints spoke, when they were alive or how abstract or involved their message was. They tried to make it simple to understand even if I didn't get it all at first. I was made to comprehend that it was all part of the gift, God's plan, so to speak, and I still marvel at each and every experience.

I began to read all I could find about the saints, their lives and their works. I would go to the library in town, and while other kids would be checking out books on sports or cars or dinosaurs or science fiction, I'd be checking out copies of *The Encyclopedia of Saints* and *Butlers Lives of the Saints*. The librarian, Mrs. Stemple, always looked at me in a strange way, and one day her curiosity must have overcome her. She said to me, "What a wonderful young man you are, reading all these books about saints. I'm sure your parents are very proud." She then walked around the counter of the library and pinched my cheek and gave me a motherly hug and smile. I didn't know what to say especially since my best friends Danny and Dennis were watching this and cracking up in the corner. Then, as luck would have it, Joanie walks by and smiles at me at the same time Mrs. Stemple pinches my cheek. So now Joanie starts to crack up, and I can't wait to get out of there.

"Shit, why does this always happen to me?" I said under my breath—then I say, "Thank you, Mrs. Stemple, these books are for a report I'm doing for school, and my parents are proud of me." What else could I say? I exited the library with all due haste. The last thing I wanted was for Danny and Dennis to see what I was reading. I was so embarrassed; plus, I didn't want to see Joanie and have her think I was some kind of religious dweeb, so I took my books and bike home and stayed in my bedroom most of the next day. Over the next four years, I kept reading as much as I could about the saints and their lives.

As it happened though, over the next four years, I would have other visions that would help me understand my gift. Some of these visions, though, can come at very inopportune moments, and I'd like to share one that happened on the night of my Senior Prom.

Chapter 4

I attended St. Anthony's High School in Huntington. Joanie is now my steady girlfriend, and I invite her as my date to the Senior Prom. The day came when I finally got to take her out way past midnight. Joanie and I were both nearly eighteen, and we were very excited. At the time, I had a 1975 Buick Skylark convertible. Very hot! It had a 350 cubic inch 5.7 liter V8 and was painted in beautiful royal blue with a white convertible top, white interior and used pair chrome mag wheels that cost me $200. I washed and waxed the car and put one of those pine things on my rearview mirror to get rid of my gym shorts smell…it looked and smelled great…and I was ready!

I picked Joan up at her parent's house just up the road from where I lived. John and Josephine were wonderful people and because they were Italian, I felt right at home. While Joan was getting ready, John took me aside for "the talk" that I was expecting. He told me about not drinking, how to respect his daughter and that he trusted me. Translated to English, this meant that if I did anything other than kiss her, I was a dead man. I looked respectfully at him, nodded in the appropriate way and assured him that I had nothing but the best of intentions regarding his daughter. Although, I pondered, we may have had different definitions of the word "intentions."

When she finally came down the stairs, my jaw dropped in amazement. She looked beautiful, and I couldn't believe that I was taking her to the prom. I had bought flowers that she wore on her wrist, and it matched the color of her dress perfectly. In truth, it was my mom who called her mom and got the color, and she went out and bought the flowers. Who cares, anyway—we were ready!

Joan and I went to the prom and had a great time. We met our friends, laughed and got really close when we danced, but we had "to leave room for the Holy Ghost," as we were told by the priests and nuns who were chaperoning. After the prom ended, Joanie and I met a group of friends and continued to party for hours. We drove to a club out in the Hamptons and tried to get them to serve us beer, but that didn't work, so we settled for soft drinks, fried clams, pizza, burgers, loud music and a lot of fun.

Just before dawn, Joanie and I decided to go alone to Fleets Cove beach in Huntington and see the sunrise. We were listening to the waves as they crashed onshore and found ourselves gazing into each other's eyes. I reached for her across the front seat, and we began to make out. As it became more intense, I reached down for her breasts, and I began to think to myself, "Oh boy, this is it! I'm gone get laid!" It was kind of like the old Meatloaf teen anthem, *Paradise by the Dashboard Lights*, "I remember every little thing as if it happened only yesterday!"

We both settled, in various stages of undress, into a comfortable position in the back seat. I was fumbling to find the hooks on Joanie's bra that would finally reveal what I had only dreamt about up to now. It was at this exact moment that I heard a voice…

"Must you shame yourself in such a manner?"

I jumped off Joanie and scrambled to find out who was there. Joanie jumped up too and asked,

"What's wrong…what's the matter?"

"Are you so weak that you must reject the virtue that should guide your life?"

"Oh my God, who are you?" I said.

"I'm your girlfriend, remember?"

"Not you…uh, I mean, who's out there?"

"Did you hear something? Is there someone out there?" While Joanie looked up and down the beach, a vision of St. Bernardine of Siena overwhelmed my senses.

"I am Bernardine of Siena, and I have come to save you from yourself and help you reflect on what you were about to do."

"I looked, and I don't see anyone up or down the beach. What did you see?" Joanie sounded like she was getting nervous, so she locked the door of the car and turned to me.

"Suppose I don't want to be saved from myself?"

"What the hell are you talking about?" Joanie said, clearly concerned.

I had done some research over the years since my first vision and I tried to become familiar with as many saints as I could.

"Aren't you the patron saint of advertising?" I asked.

"Patron saint? Advertising? What the hell are you talking about? Are you okay?" Joanie said, clearly freaked out by now.

Now I am fumbling with my shirt and trying to zip up my pants, and Joanie appears to be on the verge of a full-fledged panic attack, thinking that there was someone outside the car door. I tried to calm her down but hysteria was now taking hold.

"Take it easy. I thought that I heard the police outside speaking to me, and I got a little panicked."

"Police! Where? Where are the police? Oh! My God! My mother! Oh, no my FATHER!"

St. Bernardine responds, "I am humbled to have been chosen as a patron of iconographers—advertisers, in your words."

He then allowed another vision to come. It was the fourteenth century, and I was in a medieval hospital.

> *A young St. Bernardine came to the door of the hospital and rushed inside. He seemed to know that the plague raging throughout his beloved Siena was creating a desperate situation. In the city's hospitals, many of the townspeople were dying each day, and St. Bernardine and his coworkers were trying to help relieve their suffering. Many of the workers in the hospital were not immune, and some of them were also falling ill and dying. The conditions were wretched,*

and as more and more people were falling ill, there were fewer people able to help them.

"Why are you showing me the hospital?"

Joanie jumps up, "WHAT HOSPITAL? AM I GOING TO GET SICK? WHAT DISEASE DO YOU HAVE?"

By then I didn't know if I was talking to Joanie or St. Bernardine. It was a stupid question to ask, but I asked it anyway.

"Why aren't I speaking to the patron saint of virginity?" I said sarcastically.

It was then that I thought that Joanie would punch me out.

"I am a VIRGIN you idiot! I thought that this was our night. I didn't realize that I would have to deal with a nut job!"

I knew there was no way out of this, and I wanted to tell her about my vision, but reality got in the way as I tried to explain, "I am not a nut job, Joanie. I know this sounds crazy, but you have to believe..."

St. Bernardine then interrupted me and said, "St. Catherine of Siena was not chosen for this vision. It is I who was asked to intercede in this your hour of need."

"Need...need? Are you kidding what I need is..."

"What you need is a shrink and a cold shower! I'm outta here," and with that, Joanie zippered up her dress and slammed the car door. I tried to call her back, but she was so sure I had become totally insane that she wouldn't even turn around. Joanie walked to her home, which was conveniently across the street and down the block from the beach.

So here we are...the Buick, St. Bernardine and me all together. I tried to summon the strength to deal with this, but all I could say is,

"Look what the fuck you've done!"

Immediately I knew I had made a mistake because St Bernardine was not to be talked to in this way.

"I will not listen to blasphemy and indecency from you. Do you not realize what might have happened? How could you, in a moment of weakness, commit an act that may have caused that young girl to bear your child? What of your lives, your plans, your hopes and dreams? Are you both to be so encumbered at such a young age?"

I felt my anger, along with my libido, fall sharply, and when I was able calm myself, I asked,

"Is this what I can expect throughout my life?"

"Did you not see the hospital and all who were sick and dying? What do you think those people expected...what was their fate? They all had dreams, they had desires, and they had family they loved. All those people had hopes for happiness, and what they received was not what they expected. What you can expect is that God's will be done. With that, the vision of St Bernardine disappeared, but his words still lingered.

I took my shirt, pants, what little was left of my dignity, started the Buick and left Fleets Cove Beach.

What became of Joanie? Well, we are still good friends. She married a guy who works in, of all things, advertising. They have two sons, really good kids, and they live about a mile from where I do. I see Joanie from time to time in town. Every now and then, she will smile at me, shake her head and laugh...a little.

Chapter 5

As you've gathered, I can see the saints, I can hear them, I can touch them and I can even speak with them. I ask them questions as I try to understand the meaning of the visions and messages given to me. They speak to me directly or in parables, quote the scriptures and they even make me privy to their lives and miracles. Though I can attempt to describe what I've seen and heard, words will never be adequate.

As with all these visions, they are meant to teach, inform and inspire. The saints themselves can't always intercede; they leave that mostly up to me. They are like coaches who can give me the pointers, but when it's my turn at bat, I'm alone at the plate. What sometimes makes it very hard is that I can't discuss this with anyone because if I did, I'd probably be locked up in some asylum, strapped to a chair, blubbering about Michael the Archangel coming to release me from the torment.

There is this one person who I can go to, though, and I'll introduce him to you a little later.

So here I was, a kid of fourteen, heading into puberty at breakneck speed, and that's when I got to speak with my first saints, Cosmas and Damian. Believe me, you don't forget your first saints.

It was with St Augustine of Hippo that I had one of my most disturbing and life changing visions. It would be impossible to describe the man and his life without writing a book by itself, so I'll give you the much-condensed Wikipedia version:

> *"He was a Latin-speaking philosopher and theologian who lived in the Roman Africa Province. His writings were very influential in the development of Western Christianity.*
>
> *According to his contemporary, Jerome, Augustine "established anew the ancient Faith." In his early years, he was heavily influenced by Manichaeism and afterward by the Neo-Platonisn of Plotinus. After his conversion to Christianity and baptism in AD 387, Augustine developed his own approach to philosophy and theology, accommodating a variety of methods and different perspectives. He believed that the grace of Christ was indispensable to human freedom, and he framed the concepts of original sin and just war.*
>
> *When the Western Roman Empire was starting to disintegrate, Augustine developed the concept of the Catholic Church as a spiritual* City of God *(in a book of the same name), distinct from the material Earthly City. His thoughts profoundly influenced the medieval worldview. Augustine's* City of God *was closely identified with the Church, the community that worshipped* God."
>
> *He is revered by Catholics, Anglicans, various Protestant denominations especially Calvinists as well as the Eastern Orthodox Church.*

Not bad for a guy who is the patron saint of brewers. Oh yeah, I should also mention that his mother was a saint, St. Monica. Imagine the pressure!

He doesn't like talking about the early part of his life because in his younger days, he liked to live life in the fast lane, so to speak. He and his friends spent a lot of time drinking and partying until he saw the futility of it all. After that, he managed to completely turn his life around. People who struggle with addictions also turn to St. Augustine for inspiration.

Remember when I told you that most of these visions left me in a state of calm and clarity? Well, this was not one of those times. Even though he died in 430AD, it was St. Augustine who introduced me to Satan back in 1995 by quoting from the prophet Isaiah, complete with a vision of the fallen angel and of hell itself:

> *"How art thou fallen from heaven, O Lucifer, who didst rise in the morning? How art thou fallen to the earth that didst wound the nations? And thou saidst in thy heart: I will ascend into heaven, I will exalt my throne above the stars of God, I will sit in the mountain of the covenant, in the sides of the North. I will ascend above the height of the clouds, I will be like the most High. But yet thou shall be brought down to hell, into the depth of the pit."*

To say that this particular vision was so shocking is to vastly understate how distressed I was. The horror of the vision, the finality of hell, the purest evil embodied in Satan should have driven me to madness, but that was not the purpose of the vision. St. Augustine helped me understand the meaning of this journey of the mind and soul.

After what seemed like hours, I told St. Augustine, "I think Satan is the biggest fool of all time. He had it made, God's love, and he blew it."

I was shown this vision for a purpose that St. Augustine was quick to point out. It was a warning of the possibilities.

"It was pride that turned him against God…it was pride that condemned him to the fiery depths…it is this pride that makes him seek the souls of men."

I can tell you one thing for certain—hell is "hell." I guess it would be hard for anyone to grasp the reality of the situation, but there I was in the middle of a vision so overwhelming and profound that it changed my life forever.

Pretty heavy stuff for anyone, at any age, to understand.

I've come to know St. Augustine pretty well through these and other visits and visions. I've even learned that he likes to stroke his beard. He could use a bit more time in the sun. When he's counseling me, all I can say is that he's about the smartest saint you would ever want to know. On the flip side, he can be a little pedantic, you know, boring at times—and too academic for my tastes, but he's a saint, and I guess he earned the right to live eternity on his terms.

I am a sinner, and I know it. I have always been haunted by what St. Augustine showed me in the first of his visions. It seemed to me that this came close to the biblical vision of hell, and I was sure that this was what was waiting for me when I bought the ranch. I imagined myself in the fiery pit, devils dancing while impaling me on long, pointed spears, surrounded by all the other sinners getting what they deserved… again words fall far short of what I am trying to describe. It wasn't really like that Hieronymus Bosch painting, but I still imagined that I was the centerpiece of it all, and that always gave me pause to reflect on St. Augustine's warning.

In subsequent visions, St. Augustine did give me some reason for hope, knowing that I'd never make it to Heaven on the first try. There is a place called purgatory, and he quoted from his own book, *The City of God:*

> *Temporal punishments are suffered by some in this life only, by some after death, by some both here and hereafter, but all of them before that last and strictest judgment. But not all who suffer temporal punishments after death will come to eternal punishments, which are to follow after that judgment.*

I was not prepared for this vision of purgatory. It was not a place, but more of an unimaginable state of despondency. I was engulfed in all-consuming despair. What I was consumed by was a vast nothing, a surrounding darkness that settled over me and weighed down my soul with a sense of self-loathing, combined with a sense of hopelessness and helplessness.

It was only at that point of complete and utter desolation that I perceived a small tear in the fabric of my despair. I was able to see a light, radiance more than mere brightness. In an instant, momentary joy lifted my hopelessness, and my spirit gave rise to the anticipation and promise of what could be.

I guess I can try to say something funny now, but this is the hope that I held onto for the last fourteen years.

Chapter 6

As the saints were not in a position to support me, I needed to support myself. I own and operate a collector coin shop, and I've expanded to include an online coin collecting site, social sites like Facebook and ebay, where I sell and trade in these treasures. My father loved to collect coins, and I inherited his passion for collecting. So for me, owning my store combined a hobby that I've loved since childhood and a way to make enough to support myself. I must admit, though, I'll never get rich unless I find a hoard of gold coins, or somehow I get a hold of a 1933 The Saint-Gaudens Gold Double Eagle Coin.

It was the perfect occupation for someone who never really cared for accumulating wealth—collecting, trading, buying and selling old coins were all that I ever wanted to do.

I operate the St. Aloysius Gonzaga Coins and Currency. I know it sounds weird; after all, what does a saint have to do with coins? Well, it seems St. Aloysius was born into wealth and gave it all up. He is the Patron of Christian Youth and is a model of selflessness to a very materialistic generation. So here I am, a guy selling money and not caring if I make much of it...you get it now?

Anyway, it is a small shop on Main Street in the village filled with mostly US coins, collectible tokens, medallions, paper currency, books about coins and various holders. It's about what you would expect to find in a coin shop. As I hold some of these treasures, I often wonder how many other hands held them, what did their owners buy, did the money do some good or did it corrupt? Over the years, the store has become a kind of gathering place, usually for the older guys that like to collect coins and trade stories. I'd always have coffee out for them, and I'd enjoy just listening to them tell of their collections, their amazing finds, their families and their lives. Some of the men even take their kids and their grandkids here to pass on the love of coin collecting. Sometimes it sticks, and sometimes, it doesn't. All in all, St. Al's is a happy place, and I enjoy the time I spend here.

Owning the store also gave me freedom, freedom to delve into the meanings behind my sainted visions and the mysteries that often seemed to come along for the ride.

My saints became my friends—yes, even St. Bernardine is a friend.

Throughout my life, I have taken these signs and visions and attempted to interpret them in order to get a sense of their true meaning. The saints—I guess you could call them heavenly advisors—allowed me to see what they wanted, prodding me to find the inspiration to heed their message or do their bidding. Oh, I really don't mind, but it's sometimes difficult to know what to do, or how to act, when you are told of things in verse, parables, disturbing visions and obscure metaphors.

My experiences with the saints, the puzzling visions and messages turned me into an amateur detective of sorts. I attempt to work on clues given to me by the saints, along with their expectations that I use these communications. These visions help me learn and understand how to solve problems, unravel crimes and even intercede in affairs of the heart. This exercise is at once frustrating and immensely satisfying.

Take St. Jude, for example—yes, *that* St. Jude, one of the twelve Apostles. He visited me while I was in the Golden Dolphin Diner having lunch one Saturday. Now St. Jude lived at the time of Christ, and talk about anxiety, one of the original Apostles wanted to communicate with me!

In between bites of Greek salad with grilled chicken, St. Jude appeared to me in what could be considered one of the holiest of visions.

The room was long and narrow. The men were seated at the table, and all awaited the word that was their last hope. There was wonder and reverence, but there was also fear. What would become of these men? Who *among us will have the courage to follow the man from Galilee? What would Jesus want them to do?*

My eyes were wide, my mouth was open and I was totally immobile. I was there, at the Last Supper, and I was at a loss to know what it all meant. I tried to ask, but St Jude held out his hand to let me know there was another vision to come:

For Jesus had been telling the unclean spirit to come out of the man. It had seized on him a great many times. They tried to secure him with chains and fetters, but he would always break the fastenings, and the devil would drive him out into the wilds.

Jesus asked him, "What is your name?" He said, "Legion" –because many devils had gone into him.

I asked St. Jude to help me understand because I couldn't fathom what this all meant.

"There is evil in this world, and you can never know from where it comes, even from those you know. It may sometimes be found in the hearts of men but always in Lucifer. You will be needed to seek out the most heinous malevolence, battle it for the innocent and restore faith in the Father."

"I know there is evil, but how can I fight something so evil?"

St Jude replied, "You are much stronger than you can ever know. Your strength comes from God, His heavenly angels and all the saints. You will never be alone."

The mental picture suddenly vanished, but after all these years of signs, sermons and visions, I knew my work was just beginning.

Chapter 7

Why did this four-year-old girl feel terror...why could she not enjoy this beautiful day God had given her? She loved to walk with her Momma through the beautiful fields on their way to the market like they did every week. The women of the household always followed them, as was their custom, and it gave Senora de Sengi a quiet moment with her beautiful Agnes.

They would buy food for their table—vine ripened tomatoes, the vegetables of the season, a cask of wine and more. On the way home, they would pick flowers that Agnes would give to her father that night. Flowers were something the Senor loved, and he always made his little Agnes feel like she was the most precious thing in his life. It was a truly wonderful day.

So why should today be any different?

They passed the hill overlooking the casa de putana near Montepulciano. The sun was high in the sky, but it gave no warmth, and little Agnes became more and more frightened. Her Momma saw the fear in her child, and she became frightened herself. The sun's light slowly began to disappear as the darkness moved across the sky. It appeared like an impending storm, only this was no signal of rain to come. All saw a growing darkness that ungulates with movement and with it their terror grew.

Agnes' mother grabs her and looks up to see hundreds and hundreds of huge black crows gathering like an ominous sign of approaching evil. The crows seem to form a giant gapping mouth that looked to swallow both of them. The shrieks from the crows were painful to hear like those of a demon seeking to terrorize all who were there.

The Senora grabbed ahold of Agnes, and she and the women all started to run, but there was no shelter to be found. As Agnes' mother ran, she fell and the child tumbled out of her arms. The crows swept down, and Agnes was helpless to defend herself against the vile blackness that swarmed around her head. The Senora and the women screamed and beat their hands trying to save the child, but they couldn't stop the onslaught.

The crows cut and clawed Agnes with their talons and beaks and kept attacking the child who was helpless to defend herself. It was only until the women were able to beat back the crows with sticks and rocks that Agnes was free of the violence that could have killed her.

Agnes' mother and the women ran to comfort the child and clean her of the wounds to her small face and body. What they found, however, was a little girl without one scratch or wound on her body. How could this be? Why is this little girl free from any harm? What miracle is this?

While tears flowed, the women tried to purge the image of what could have happened to the poor child. Agnes looked past her mother, past the women who she knew loved her, looked past it all and whispered to no one, "il Diavolo."

Chapter 8

I guess this is as good a time as any to introduce you to my Uncle Al.

Chief Spartaco "Al" Barese is a veteran police officer with 34 years on the job, 20 years in the Suffolk PD. He is my mother's younger brother, and he was named Spartaco (aka Spartacus) by his father, my grandpa, who loved to read Greek and Roman history. As a matter of fact, each time Grandpa would read some classic when my grandmother was going to have a baby, their child would get the name of some god, goddess, one of the legendary heroes or heroines or ancient characters he was reading about. I have Aunts Inez, Aurora, Flora and uncles Orpheus and Spartaco. As the family history tells it, Grandpa had a change of heart when my mother was born, and she was named Gilda after the character in the opera *Rigoletto*. As far as Uncle Al was concerned, he never went by his birth name—and be warned, you take your life in your own hands by calling him Spartacus or Spartaco, so everyone just called him Al.

Chief Al Barese has been the lead investigator on a number of violent crimes during his career, including murder. You may remember the

"Parkway Murders" back in 1997. Uncle Al was a detective at the time, and it seems that there was a serial killer that would leave his victims and their broken cars in the woods off random exits on the Northern State Parkway on Long Island. As time went on, the murders became more and more violent, the local politicians were putting more and more pressure on the police as the general public became increasingly frightened.

Detective Al Barese was working on the investigation and became part of the team of decoys to act as stranded motorists in need of help. He believed that this was the way to trap the killer, and as a volunteer, he needed to be out at night to help with the effort. Well, it was all planned. Uncle Al and other officers would pretend to breakdown near different exits to see if they would have any luck. There were well-trained back-up teams, and the units were prepared for anything. Uncle Al, using a different car each night, would appear stuck along the side of the parkway with his emergency flashers on. Night after night for nearly one month, he and the other decoys had no luck at all.

The press was relentless in questioning the competence of the police department and took every opportunity to slam their lack of progress in the case. The constant negative drumbeat on TV and in the papers was very frustrating, and it was beginning to affect the morale of the men on the force.

It was a Thursday in late April that Uncle Al was on his way to the next stakeout when his car really did breakdown. He cursed and yelled at the crumby piece of crap he was driving and called his commander. He told him what happened and that the team should use another officer as the decoy. Al then made a call to the tow truck company that had a contract with local municipalities, and he was towed into the repair shop.

After waiting for about an hour, the tow truck showed up, but Uncle Al was still so pissed off about the car that he couldn't take any solace in being rescued. He drove back to the repair shop with the driver, fuming about what happened, and the driver unloaded the car in one of the empty bays in the garage. The driver, who was also the mechanic, told him that it would only take about 30 minutes to fix the problem, so Al could wait if he wanted to. Uncle Al took a seat in the waiting room and poured himself a cup of coffee under a sign that said, "For our

Sleepy Customers." As Al opened a two-year-old copy of *Hot Rod Magazine*, he began to feel tired, and his eyes became heavy. He lay back in the chair and closed his eyes.

The next thing he remembers was waking up in a dizzying state and being dragged down a hallway to the back of the garage. When he tried to resist, he realized that he had been drugged and could no longer summon the strength to fight back. The driver, who was dragging my uncle, dropped him at the end of the hallway. As Al looked up, he saw the tow truck driver walk over to a toolbox in the corner of the garage where he picked up a tire iron.

What happened next is still unclear but it seems that the tow truck driver didn't realize that Uncle Al was a cop. Knowing what was about to happen, Al managed, and he doesn't know how, to reach for a gun he always carried in his ankle holster when he was on the job and undercover. In a half-conscious state, he raised the gun to confront the tow truck driver who had turned, now facing Uncle Al.

"Police, stop now! Put down the tire iron, and get on your knees with your hands behind your head."

The driver became enraged and ran toward my uncle. He had the tire iron raised and was about to bring it down across Al's skull when he fired a shot that blew a huge hole right through the driver's chest. The tow truck driver stood for a moment, looked down at the gaping hole in his chest and dropped dead. The killer had already murdered ten people, and thank God, Uncle Al wasn't number eleven. The heroics of Detective Al Barese became a sensation for about a week in the press and on TV. He became a celebrity of sorts, and all his buddies on the force took pride in him bringing the killer to justice and honor back to the work they do. This is what put Uncle Al on track to become Chief Detective. Although you would think these kinds of violent and perverted acts would become business as usual, he really never got used to it.

Throughout his career, Uncle Al was a stickler for details and his "by-the-book" style was instrumental in getting convictions in some high profile cases. He was steady, knew the facts inside and out and no defense attorney could shake his confidence. Many defense attorneys tried, unsuccessfully. He gained a reputation as a skillful, expert witness. All in all, Uncle Al was a prosecutor's best friend and a genuine asset to the police department where he commanded and got the respect of everyone in his unit.

After Dad died, Uncle Al became a second father. He was always there for me, helping when I needed advice, helping me move into my condo, spending the holidays with me and just being there for the everyday problems we all have. All in all, he is a great man.

Some days Uncle Al would come by the shop, or I would meet him near police headquarters in Yaphank. We'd get lunch, talk, laugh and sometimes cry.

When my mother died, I tried to keep it together. After the wake was over and all the people were gone, I looked at Mom's sweet face, and I became overwhelmed. She laid there in her favorite dress, but there was no joy on her face—only silence in death. A lifetime of love was placed in a casket, and I had to say goodbye.

I tried to hold back the tears, but it was Uncle Al who broke down first. A man, fifty years old, 6' 1", 210 pounds and tough as they come, with a personality big enough to match his mouth. He wept like a baby. He loved and cherished my mother, and when she died, part of him went with her. I remember trying to understand what he was going through and comfort him, but we just hugged and cried together because it seemed the right thing to do in honor of her memory and our loss.

Uncle Al made sure that he continued to be an important part of my life. He's a bachelor, and because of his job and the risks that went along with it, he never thought he should get married. He's good-looking, very funny and has had plenty of girlfriends. I'm sure that the thought of marriage crossed his mind, but he never took the plunge. Anyway, I suspect he felt closer to my mother's memory when we were together, and I always felt safer when he was around.

By the way, Uncle Al is the only person in the world that knows I communicate with the saints. He can't see or hear what I see or hear, but he believes everything I say because of what we've experienced together.

The first time that Al and I worked together was merely by accident. The granddaughter of my friend Fred, one of the men who always came to my shop, went missing. Tina was his only granddaughter, and she was the light of his life. When she was little, he would bring Tina into the shop, and all the guys would make a fuss over this pretty, little girl.

Her grandfather beamed with pride. Through the years, we saw less of Tina, but Fred kept us updated, and it seemed that all was well.

Only recently, we became aware that Tina was going through a difficult time. Her parents divorced a year earlier, and at 14 years old, she took the news very hard. Her grades dropped, and she began to cut classes so she could hang out. Tina had gotten into trouble with the police on a few occasions, but the transgressions were minor, and she was able to evade any real punishment.

Tina was now 16 years old, so when she went missing overnight, her parents assumed that it was another effort at rebellion—usually she was just sleeping over at a friend's house. Tina had gone missing before, but never more than overnight. Her parents called all her friends and the school office, but no one had seen her. Now more than 24 hours had gone by, and Tina's parents became frantic, so they reported the missing girl to the police. Given her past issues with cutting school and staying out all night, the police made the assumption that this was just another attention getter and that Tina would show up soon. The police met with the parents, took down all the information and did their reports. A missing person's bulletin would be issued, but there was little that would be done in the following 24 hours.

My heart went out to Fred, whom I considered a good man and friend. I tried to keep his spirits up, but his heart was broken. I could see the fear in his eyes and hear panic in his voice as he spoke of Tina and what trouble she may be in. He asked, no, he *begged* me to talk to my Uncle Al to see if anything more could be done to find Tina. I knew that Al was overloaded with work and that this was not the type of case his department took on, but I promised Fred I would ask.

I picked up the phone and dialed the Suffolk County PD. The operator picked up and said, "This is the Suffolk Country Police Department, how may I direct your call?"

"Hi, can I speak to Chief Detective Barese please."

"One moment please," she said.

He picked up, "Chief Detective Barese here."

"Hey, Uncle Al, remember me? It's your favorite and most handsome nephew in the whole world." I always said this to get him to smile.

"Favorite nephew? You don't sound like my favorite nephew. Leo is my favorite nephew. He calls his uncle all the time, makes me special meals and he even spends an evening with me from time to time. HA! Favorite nephew, indeed!"

"Hey Unc, Leo never calls you, he never cooks you a meal, he never tries to see you and God forbid he should spend an evening away from that skank of a girlfriend."

"Wait, hold it." Uncle Al seemed puzzled. "You say Leo never did any of those things for me?"

"Yeah!"

"Then who am I speaking to?" Al asked.

"It's me, your loving nephew Chris."

"...And you did all those things for me?"

"You bet I did, and I even let you pay for dinner when we go out."

"Ah, then you can't be Chris, you must be my favorite nephew, Tommy!"

"Cut it out, Uncle Al."

"Okay, Okay. How are you Chris?"

"I'm good. How are you?"

"Well, aside from a few unsolved murders, a $685 car repair bill, no vacation in three and a half years and local asshole politicians that should stick to taking bribes and not interfere in my business, I'm doing great!"

"Glad to hear things are going so well, but I have a problem."

"Shit, I knew I shouldn't have picked up the phone. I just knew it. What now, you want me to fix a speeding ticket or something? No way. You do the crime, you do the time. That's the rules, and that's what I say."

"Seriously, I need your help." I must have sounded really concerned because Uncle Al became worried:

"Sorry Chris, what happened...what's wrong?"

I explained what Fred told me and that Tina had disappeared, and the family was frantic. I told him that he was the only one I could turn to, and I heard a heavy sigh over the phone.

"Chris, you say this kid has done this before, and you know that it's almost certain she's done it again."

"Listen, I know that you are probably right, but she has been missing far longer than any time before and with all the crazies out there...well, I don't want to imagine what could happen."

"But Chris, this is not my department. We have a whole unit that works on cases like this, and they will be happy to…"

I interrupted. "Uncle Al, the family has called, and all they get is lip service from the guys on the other end of the line. I know they mean well, and I know they are very busy, too, but Tina could be in real trouble."

"Alright, let me see what I can do, but I am not sure how much I can get done."

Appealing to his vanity, I said, "Are you kidding, the man who single handedly solved the Parkway Murders and used the killer for target practice can do anything! That's my Uncle Al!"

"There's one murder I won't want to solve…it's called the 'Coin Shop Owner Murder,' and I personally know the killer and the killed. Now get off the line, so I can do some work."

"I love you."

"I love you, too."

Chapter 9

Nearly four days had passed, and we heard nothing about Tina. Fred had stopped coming to the shop, staying at home depressed and despondent about his missing granddaughter. I tried to call him, but he didn't have the energy to speak and would merely acknowledge my call and hang up.

Of course I checked with Uncle Al, and he had to acknowledge that the more time went by, the more chance that the worst could happen. He had seen it before, kids that went missing and wound up as prostitutes or drug addicts or both. Their lives would be ruined even before they had a chance to live. Al had seen it too many times, and he was afraid it could have happened again with Tina.

As Chief, Al Barese had a lot of sway over the officers in all the various departments, and he felt sure that whatever could be done was being done, but he liked to check with each person in his department working on the case.

"Hi Dan, this is Chief Barese."

"Hi Chief, I know why you're calling and no news on the Tina Staley case. I hear from her parents every day, and I have to deliver the same message. It's like she's disappeared, and there isn't a clue to be found." Now Dan Orello was very good at his job. He's a twenty-four year veteran of the force, and he is about a thorough as you can get. As a matter of fact, Uncle Al depends on Dan to help make sure that everything is done right. All the "i's" are dotted and "t's" crossed before a criminal is brought to trial, and he takes the stand.

"I know you're doing everything possible. But this case has me worried, and I keep thinking what it would be like if this was my daughter. I guess it's good that I never got married..."

"Hey Chief, everyone knows you are personally involved with this case, and they want to get it resolved. Everything that can be done is being done. Take my word for it."

"You know I trust you with my life. Thank everyone for me."

"Will do," and with that, Dan hung up.

The next time I spoke to my uncle, he gave me the usual update. I gave him the usual "I love you," and we both hung up.

It had been a slow day at the shop. It was nearly 5 p.m., so I closed up. The evening was warm and being outside felt good, so I decided to walk home. The walk was about a mile, and it was very pleasant, so I took my time. I passed the usual shops and found myself in front of my favorite bookshop, Book Revue. They have a huge selection of new, used, rare and autographed editions, and it's the kind of place I can get lost in. I don't mean that it's so cavernous you can't find your way out, but it's just so wonderful that you find yourself lost in the pages of the books you pick up.

I always wander over to the remainder table where I can get great bargains on books. It may take you a few visits, but eventually, you will find books that suit your taste or mood or inclination. On this visit, I found a slightly used hardcover copy of *The Girl Who Kicked the Hornet's Nest* for only $3.95...wow, this was a deal. I read the first two novels in the trilogy and enjoyed them immensely and grabbed it as my own.

Book Revue has these little reading nooks where you can sit down in a comfortable chair and read to your heart's content. It was there that the vision came. My comfy reading nook turned into a small dark room where there was a bed—no, more like a cot and kneeling on the floor was a woman. She had her head bowed in prayer.

"Jesus Christ, Lord of all, You see my heart, You know my desires. Possess all that I am. I am your sheep: make me worthy to overcome the devil."

She did not acknowledge my presence, as the saints usually do, so I remained silent out of respect for her moment in prayer. Then I heard the laughter of men and women and what sounded like the sex moans. Because I am, in fact, a spirit while experiencing these visions, I am able to walk through walls and doors or any other solid surface. I walked through the wall out into the hallway. In truth, I've never been to a brothel, house of prostitution or whatever you want to call it, but take my word for it, this was a brothel. Men and women walked around half-naked, chasing each other from room to room.

I am watching all this while standing by the door where I'd seen the woman pray. It was then a drunken Roman soldier came staggering up to the room. He flung open the door and immediately grabbed the praying woman and tore at her clothes. Forgetting for a moment that I was unseen, I jumped at the soldier in hopes of saving the women from being raped. As I jumped, however, the room disappeared, and I found myself falling, and when I landed I looked up and smiling down at me was the woman who was praying. It was St. Agatha. She was surrounded by the same glow I had seen on all my saints before, but she was holding something in her hands. I got up off the floor and stood before her. She was holding a tray, and on the tray were two human breasts...hers.

In life, St. Agatha experienced many torments and tortures, but she always remained steadfast in her faith. In this vision, St. Agatha allowed me to see her suffering at the hands of Quintianus, a Roman Prefect at that time. He wanted to possess this woman, but she had pledged her virginity, her life and her soul to the Lord. She refused all his advances. With that, Quintianus subjected St. Agatha to further suffering when she was sent to prison after the brothel. In prison, one of her tortures was to have her breasts cut off, and I was dumbfounded at the horror of it all.

If you had seen this cruelty, you would be as grief stricken as I was for this beautiful person.

The vision continued as St. Agatha spoke to Quintianus: "My courage and my thoughts be so firmly founded upon the firm stone of Jesus Christ, that for no pain may they be changed. Your words be but wind, your promises be but rain, and your menaces be as rivers that pass, and how well that all these things hurtle at the fundament of my courage, yet for that, it shall not move."

I didn't know what to say, but I didn't have to say anything as it was St. Agatha who stepped out of her body and spoke to me first.

"My suffering is of no consequence now because I live with the blessing of the Lord, and He is all anyone needs. But it is you who are troubled, and I know what it is that troubles you."

As I looked at her, I was grateful that St. Agatha knew what I had to say, but I said it anyway,

"I am troubled, but not for myself. My friend's granddaughter is missing. She's so young, and I know that she is in danger. Can you help me find my friend's granddaughter?" I stopped speaking since I was trying to suppress a tidal wave of emotion.

St. Agatha said, "You must look for the way to her salvation in the darkest of corners where light refuses to go."

I didn't know what St. Agatha meant by these words. I've often had moments with the saints where the messages were so cryptic that I would need to take time to just think. As I was contemplating what was meant by all this, St. Agatha held out her hand, and I touched it.

My breath was taken away, and I gasped and immediately I saw Tina. She appeared to be strapped to a bed unconscious, but somehow I knew she was alive. She was in a dark, filthy room with half-eaten food laying all over the floor and cockroaches climbing all over the furniture, the bed and Tina. There was something else, small glass and plastic vials, along with needles all over the floor.

St. Agatha allowed me to be brought into Tina's horror, but she held out hope,

"In the depths of despair, there is always hope, and the child clings to the hope of deliverance from evil. It is in the Lord that you must place your trust, and it is in the Lord that you will find salvation for her."

The connection between Tina and St. Agatha's words wasn't initially apparent to me. The enigma of the message, the vision and the ghastliness of Tina's situation made me pause, and then I finally made the connection. Prison…brothel…torture…St. Agatha turned away. Her body became like beams of light, and she disappeared.

In the next instance, I found myself seated in a brown leather chair with the book on my lap. I jumped off the chair, dropped the book and ran to the sidewalk outside Book Revue. I knew I had found an essential clue to help find Tina, and I knew that I needed to call Uncle Al. I dialed his number on my cell and the phone rang:

"Chief Barese here."

"Uncle Al, I know where she is. I mean, I know where I think she is. I mean, I know where she could be. The place…" I was rambling on and on, speaking faster than my mind could process the words.

"Whoa…take it easy, Chris. What are you talking about?"

"Tina, I'm talking about Tina. I think I know where she is."

"How the hell do you know where Tina is?" Now Uncle Al was getting nervous. He knew I wasn't one to make up stories, and I never lied to him…never, well, almost never.

"I just know—not the exact place, but I know where she is."

"Okay, calm down, where is she?"

"She's being held captive in some kind of a drug den or brothel."

"A drug den or brothel? Is this some kind of joke? A drug den or brothel!" I could almost see Uncle Al leaning back in his chair rubbing his eyes and thinking he should have become a tailor like his father.

"Chris, how could you possibly know that she is in a brothel or, what did you say, a drug den?"

"I just do Uncle Al. I know she is there."

"Listen I need to have a little more to go on than coin shop intuition. Which is it, a drug den or brothel? Where is this drug den or brothel and the question of the day…how do you know?" Uncle Al's a cop, and he won't give up. I knew he wanted to hear something from me that would make sense to him. I couldn't tell him the truth, so I lied to him for the first and last time in my life.

"I got an anonymous phone call, and the person said that Tina was being held against her will by some real bad guys, and that if we don't get to her soon, something very bad will happen." I spoke fast because I knew that Uncle Al would know I was lying if I slowed down.

"First, why did the person call you and not her mother or father? Did you speak to a man or a woman? Why didn't this person say where this supposed drug den or brothel is located? How do you know this person is being held against her will? Chris, we can't just mobilize the Suffolk County PD and send them on a wild goose chase."

"Unc, this isn't a wild good chase. The call was from a woman and she didn't say where the place was, but she told me Tina was in grave danger. I guess Tina might have mentioned my name, or maybe she had a card from the coin shop. Maybe she knew her grandfather was my friend. I really don't know why I was the one she called." I couldn't believe how convoluted things were getting, and I knew Uncle Al was suspicious.

"Listen Chris, you can try, but you can't bullshit a bullshit artist. What's going on here? I need to know, and I need to know now." When Uncle Al says now, he means *now*.

"Do you trust me?" I said in the most sincere, straightforward way I know how to.

"Of course I trust you Chris. You know that."

"You have to trust me this time without knowing how I know. Please, Uncle Al, Tina is in trouble, she is being held against her will in some really nasty place and I know she is in great danger." I didn't know what other way I could say this but I ended by telling him, "I'm sorry I lied to you. I never will again."

"Okay Chris, I believe you, but now I need to make the department believe me, and I need to have proof. Let me get back to you."

"I love you." He hung up before I could say, "I love you, too."

Chapter 10

First thing in the morning, a meeting of all the detectives working on the case was called in Chief Barese's office. There were four detectives in all, two worked out of the missing persons unit and two out of homicide. Among the assembled squad were two women and two men, and they all sat down, coffee in hand, listening to what the chief had to say.

"Last night, I received an anonymous phone call. It was from a woman who said she knew where Tina Staley was." This information was passed along in the most serious voice that Uncle Al could muster, and as he looked around the room, he saw each of the detectives look at each other excitedly.

Detective Christina Shannon, the second most senior member of the team, was in her late 30's, very pretty, small in stature, but you wouldn't want to mess with her because she was tough, and she didn't take crap from anyone. She was sitting next to Dan Orello, and she was the first to speak. "How do we know this is real and not some phony lead by a deranged pervert?"

"She had information that only someone who saw Tina would know." Uncle Al lied.

Up to this point, the police had treated Tina's case as just another missing person. There was no formal police announcement asking for help finding her, nothing in the press or TV reports asking for the public's assistance, no photos on milk cartons or anything like that. Al told Detective Shannon that the caller told him about the small scar on Tina's chin, her age, what she was wearing, the onyx ring her Dad bought her, her high school ID card, the works.

"The caller had information that no one else would know other than the family and us."

"Where did this anonymous caller say she was?" Detective Christian Oliver asked. Now, Detective Oliver wasn't what you'd call a "by the book" cop. He had great instincts that had been honed over a stellar career, and he was the one person who was most like my Uncle Al.

"She said that she was being held captive in some kind of drug house or brothel. She wouldn't say where it was, but she did say that she'd been there about a day. I know this sounds highly suspect, but I believed her, and I think it's worth following up."

"Do you think she might have been one of the other hookers or addicts that called? Maybe they got religion?" Detective Oliver said.

"Could be, I don't know." Al admitted.

Detective Avery Michaels, the other woman on the team, said what everyone wanted to avoid saying, "You know Chief, Tina may be drugged up, even dead by now. These people play pretty rough, and a 16 year old kid is no match against these gangs of depraved scumbags. They'll kill her and think nothing of it."

"I know that's possible, but until we know for sure, we have to follow this lead. Any other thoughts or questions?"

"Have you considered that she might be there of her own free will? She could have been taking drugs all along, and now she's being pimped to support her habit." It was a possibility that no one wanted to contemplate but someone had to.

"You're right, it is a possibility, but Tina has no history of taking drugs. Her parents have had her tested. Besides she is still a little kid in my eyes, and we have to see if we can find her. In the end, we'll know one way or the other." A sad and sobering thought, but Uncle Al was, above all, a realist.

Detective Dan Orello offered an action plan: "I'll get working with vice to get a list of known drug and whore houses in the area and beyond, and I also get a list of known pimps and hustlers. We also may want some of the beat cops to start questioning these guys when their paths cross."

"Good idea, and let's keep this low profile, but I want a report every day with an update on the status of the investigation. Are we all clear?"

"Yep," responded the team, and they all left.

After everyone left the meeting, Uncle Al sat back and started to think about our conversation last night. He was always a thoughtful man, and his instincts were kept sharp after so many years on the job. He picked up Tina's file and read it again. She was a problem kid, and she got into trouble, but she didn't appear to have anything that would point to her living on the edge. Lots of kids have problems, but they don't all turn into addicts or prostitutes—someone usually turns them. Who could be trying to turn Tina?

Uncle Al immediately picked up the phone and dialed the coin shop.

"St. Aloysius Gonzaga Coins and Currency," in the usual way I answered the phone.

"When you got the information on Tina, did this person mention any other name or hint at someone or something?"

"I really don't remember. We only talked a minute or two and I..." I thought of Quintianus the Roman Prefect who brutalized St. Agatha.

"Listen, try to think. It's very important. Was there anything else that could help us get to Tina?"

How could I tell Uncle Al what I knew or how I knew it? I knew what I knew because of my vision, and I couldn't tell him that.

"Chris, come on, speak to me. There has to be something else."

"Well, there was something, but it didn't make sense to me, and I thought that it was gibberish."

"Listen, anything that was said, even gibberish, can be a clue. What did she say?"

"She told me something that sounded about like 'Quintianus' or 'Kintianus' or something like that." At least I had gotten that much out, and I hoped that Uncle Al could make something of it...what, I didn't know.

"Kintianus or Quintianus? What the hell is that supposed to mean?" Uncle Al said to himself, more than me.

"I don't know, it sounded so weird that I didn't think it meant anything, but I'm sorry I didn't mention it to you sooner."

"Okay, let me think about it, but if you come up with anything else, call me right away."

"I will, and I love you."

But Uncle Al had already hung up.

I sat back in my chair behind the counter, and I didn't know what to do. I couldn't let him know what my life had become...about the saints...the visions. I felt helpless, but I knew that my uncle was in charge, and that always made me feel better. Just then the phone rang, but before I had a chance to say St. Aloysius Gonzaga Coins and Currency, I heard a voice say,

"I love you too," and he hung up.

Chapter 11

We were in day four of Tina's disappearance, and I was concerned because I hadn't heard from Uncle Al. I know it was just overnight, but I needed to have something to hold onto that would help calm my nerves.

I called Fred again. When he picked up, I said, "Don't hang up Fred; it's me, Chris."

"What do you want?" It was a vacant greeting from a man who was in the depths of depression.

"I won't even ask how you're doing, but is there anything you need? Can I get you something, help in any way?"

Fred just said, "No."

"I wanted to call and let you know that Al and his team are still working on Tina's case. They've got 4 detectives looking into all possibilities, and I know they will find her. I know she will be safe...I just know it."

"How can you know she's safe? How can you be so sure? She is my angel, my princess, and she's gone. I can't imagine where she is or what might have happened to her. I don't know what I'd do if anything happened to her." I could tell that he was on the verge of a breakdown. Tina was his pride and joy, and she loved him equally.

I remembered a story he told of the first time he took her out on his own. Just Grandpa and Tina, and they had a whole day together. She was nearly three at the time and a wonderfully happy, playful little toddler. Her mom was concerned about all the things that moms are concerned about, but Fred assured her that Tina was in the best of hands, and he would make sure she was safe. So Tina's mom packed up a diaper bag with, of all things, diapers and diaper wipes, a change of clothes, sippy cup of apple juice, bag of Cheerios, a sweater in case it got cold, another bag of healthy snacks and a toy for when she was in the car. So with Tina in one arm and the diaper bag in the other, off they went.

Bright sunshine, a summer breeze and giggles galore—the whole day was wonderful. Grandpa and Tina went to Heckscher Park and fed the ducks and swans stale bread. Sure, it was against the rules, but it made Tina so happy that she would giggle every time the ducks put their heads in the water and grabbed at the bread with their beaks; anyway, it wasn't that much bread. Later they walked over to the playground, and Fred put Tina on the swing and pushed her higher and higher, and with each movement of the swing, she would laugh louder and louder. Fred thought that he had never been happier in his whole life.

Next he took Tina for a lunch of chicken nuggets and French fries, and later they went to a make your own yogurt place where he bought Tina a vanilla cup with rainbow sprinkles. Spoiling Tina became Fred's hobby, and every time they went out together, he bought her a toy, and this time was no exception. They stopped at Toys Galore and she found a mermaid doll that she loved, and Fred got it for her. Tina hugged it and named it "Annabelle," which was actually the name of her neighbor's dog.

The day went by in a flash for Fred. When he took Tina home that evening, he told her that they had made a memory. She gave her grandpa "the biggest, tightest hug he ever got," and it became a day he would never forget.

All the regulars in the coin shop loved to hear Fred tell the story, to see his face light up and hear him laugh. He was a great guy. Now that he was in such pain, all of us wanted to help, but we felt helpless.

I spoke to Fred in as calm a voice as I could muster, "Can I bring you over some pasta? I made sauce the other day, and I think you'll like it. What do you say, Fred?"

"I'm not hungry," he said in a voice so low that I didn't know what he said.

"What did you say, Fred?"

"I'M NOT HUNGRY!" He yelled, dropping the phone in tears. When I heard this, I said, "I'm coming over now."

I closed the shop, jumped into my car and drove over to Fred's. He lived in a small house in a cul-de-sac about fifteen minutes outside of town. Fred's wife, Carol had passed away a few years earlier after a short but painful battle with pancreatic cancer. After Carol died, Fred sold their home and moved into a smaller place. He always liked to say he did it because he was lazy and didn't want all the yard work around the house, but we all know it was because of the lifetime of memories he had with Carol and the loneliness he felt each day he walked through the door.

I parked my car in his driveway and ran up the front stairs. I knocked, but there was no answer, so I rang the bell but still no answer. I tried turning the doorknob and found the front door was open. I went in.

"Fred? Fred, it's me Chris. The front door was unlocked, and I came in. Are you okay? Where are you?" There was no immediate answer, and I became worried.

"Fred? Come on, Fred, speak to me." I needed to find my friend, but even if I did find him, what would to I say? How can I help make him feel better?

"In here," a hollow voice came from the small sunroom that faced his back yard. I rushed to the rear of the house, and I was shocked by what I found. Fred, who was always a healthy, robust figure of a man, seemed to have withered away in only four days. Fred liked to wear stylish clothes. He was kind of a fashion plate, and he liked to dress the part. This was my mind's picture of Fred, but this was not the Fred I am now looking at. He looked gaunt and unkempt, his hair was a mess, he hadn't shaved in days and the clothes he wore were wrinkled. It looked like Fred had slept in them, what little sleep he got.

Out of fear for his health and sanity, I said, "Fred, I am so sorry for what has happened, but you have to try to keep it together for Tina's sake. She would not want you to do this to yourself." I tried to reason with him, but he did not want to listen to me or anyone else.

"Just leave me alone." It was a pathetic cry from a man who seemed to have lost all hope.

"Fred, there is always hope. You have to believe that, and I know that the police will have some news for you and your family very soon. Just have faith." I didn't know what else to say.

With that, Fred tried to struggle to his feet. He held onto the edge of the couch and turned toward me. There was menace in his eyes and a vacant stare—this was not the Fred I knew. This was a totally distraught man. In his weakened condition, he rose to his feet and took one feeble step toward me.

"Faith? You say I have to have faiiiiiiii . . ." with that, Fred fell into a heap on the cold tile floor.

I panicked, "Fred? Fred? Oh my God, Fred! Are you okay?" But he wasn't okay. He was unconscious, with a deep cut from hitting his head on the tile floor. I immediately ran to the phone and called 911.

The operator answered: "911, do you need police, fire or ambulance?"

"Please, I have an emergency; my friend is passed out on the floor. He has a cut on his forehead, and he's bleeding. Please come and help him."

The operator asked for Fred's address, and I gave it to her. She also asked, "Does your friend have any other injuries?"

"Not that I can tell."

"Does he take any medications?" She continued.

"No, not that I know of."

"Do you know if he's been drinking alcohol?"

"No, I don't think so. Please hurry, he could be really hurt."

The 911 operator said, "The ambulance is on its way, and they should be there in the next three minutes." She told me to hold on the line until the ambulance arrived, and within thirty-seconds, I heard the sound of sirens.

Before I go on, I'd like to say a few short words about the Huntington EMS and all the other EMS workers around the country. These men and women are amazing. Many of them are volunteers who work all shifts, they give up personal time and they take courses to sharpen their skills. These skills have saved countless lives, and every time you see an EMS worker, you should go up and shake their hand and thank them for all they do.

The ambulance pulled up to Fred's house, and two people got out. They maneuvered the stretcher up the steps and into the sunroom where Fred lay on the floor. After they did a cursory examination and took his blood pressure, they carefully lifted him onto the stretcher, buckled him in, wheeled him through the house and out to the ambulance. He was considered very dehydrated, so the crew administered a saline drip and hooked him onto a portable monitor in the ambulance. They asked me pretty much the same questions that the operator asked while they secured the gurney in the rear of the ambulance. Once they were sure the patient was safe, they turned on the siren and rushed him off to Huntington Hospital.

I wasn't allowed to ride in the back of the ambulance with Fred, so I hurried into my car and followed the ambulance to the Emergency Room. I parked and ran to the admission window where a nurse was stationed:

"My friend Fred Klein was taken here to the ER, and I want to know when you will have any news of his condition."

"Mr. Klein was just admitted, and he will need to be examined by the emergency room physician. I won't have any news for a least an hour, so please take a seat, and I will let you know as soon as we hear anything." She was obviously used to dealing with people who were anxious family members and friends, so I hunkered down for the long wait.

While I was waiting at the hospital, I decided to let Uncle Al know about Fred. I went outside to make the call.

"How's he doing, Chris?"

"I won't know for a while, but he was in pretty bad shape when I found him. They're examining him now."

"I hope he'll be okay. Give him my best, even though he probably doesn't want to hear from me."

"Fred is so down, he doesn't want to hear from anyone. I know, in his heart, he appreciates everything you're doing."

"By the way, I'm glad you called. I thought that I would let you know that your gibberish may turn into something, and we are checking it out." Uncle Al, being circumspect also said, "It might be nothing but my team will follow up, and I'll keep you posted."

"Are you kidding me? Uncle Al, you can't leave me like this. What happened? What's the lead? Tell me, I promise I won't tell anyone else. I swear!" I hoped that I could appeal to his sympathetic side, especially since I was the one who talked him into taking this on.

"Chris, you know I can't reveal confidential information about an ongoing investigation."

"Come on Unc, I've been worried about this from the start. Look at what's happening to my friend. I promise, pinky swear, that I won't tell a soul. I'll even pay for our next dinner, unless I can't afford it—then you can pay." I said this all in my best impersonation of an Eagle Scout.

"Chris…"

"Please, you've got to tell me."

"Shit, okay, but if you say a word about this, I'll cut off your penis, and there'll be no more British women for you…ever. Got it?" I know it sounded like a joke, but he meant it.

"My solemn word."

"That word us, 'Quintianus' is not a word. It's a name or a root of a name. It comes close to a name that belongs to a scumbag named Heriberto Quintana. My team took that name and ran it through the criminal database, on up popped Quintana. I must admit, it was like finding a golden egg."

"Heriberto Quintana? Who is he? Where is he?"

"He's a real lowlife drug dealer. He gets young girls and boys hooked on heroin or crack and pimps them out to whatever pedophile has the money. He chooses young girls, runaway kids, kidnaps them and forces them to take drugs. By the time they're hooked, there's no way out. He literally turns them into sex slaves, turning tricks and making him a lot of money; oh, he's a prince alright. Heriberto Quintana operates here on Long Island, where he's the head of a particularly vicious gang, MS-13."

"MS-13, I've heard about them. Is that where you think Tina is?"

"Well, we can't be sure, but a lot of the pieces seem to fit, so we're going to follow up. By the way Chris, good going on that lead, you may have given us important info in this case. Let's hope."

"Hope"… that's the word I used with Fred, but now there is really room for hope, and I started to have some myself. "Thank you, St. Agatha," I said to myself, but Uncle Al was still on the phone.

"St. Agatha? Who the heck are you talking to?"

"Sorry, Unc, it's a little prayer I say when I want to give thanks."

"Well, don't thank St. Agatha yet because we still need to find Tina, and we still need to get the scumbag, excuse me, alleged scumbag, who may be holding her captive. I'll keep you posted, and remember, call me with anything else you can think of, and don't say a word to anyone. Okay?"

"Okay and Uncle Al, thanks. I love you."

"I love you, too."

I returned to the waiting room, and in about a half hour, the doctor came out. He must have seen me jump up, so he approached me,

"Hi, I'm Doctor Raymond Thaler. Are you the man who found Mr. Klein?"

"Yes, he was at home, and when he tried to get up, he fell. He's been in a terrible state of depression." I went on to tell him about the events surrounding Tina's disappearance and how devoted Fred was to her.

"How is he, Doctor?"

"Are you a relative?" the doctor asked me.

"No, but I'm a close friend. All of his friends and family are concerned, and I think they are on the way here now."

"Well, I can only give the family the complete details on his condition, but I can tell you that he is lucky you found him in time to get him to the hospital. We are treating him for severe dehydration, hunger and a serious concussion from the fall."

"Will he be alright?"

The doctor seemed to choose his words carefully: "It'll be touch and go for a while, but I believe he will recover. My fear, though, is that if he continues in this depressed condition, he may just fall back into the same state, and the next time he may not be as fortunate."

"What can I do to help, Doctor?"

"There is really nothing anybody can do. We have him sedated, and I'll know more in the next 24 hours."

"Thanks for all your help, Doc. Please, let me know if there is anything I can do." With that, I left the hospital and went home.

Chapter 12

I was worried, nervous and excited at the same time. Maybe it was nothing, but I didn't think so, and St. Agatha had shown us the way. Her suffering at the hands of Quintianus and Tina's suffering at the hands of Heriberto Quintana was too coincidental to be circumstantial.

At 2 a.m. I was sitting up in bed thinking about all that had happened, about Tina, about Fred, about Uncle Al, and I couldn't sleep. I got out of bed and went down to the kitchen for something to drink. I poured a glass of orange juice, and I sat down at the kitchen table with the vision of St. Agatha, Tina's personal horror, Fred's condition and my call with Uncle Al—all kept going over and over in my mind.

If I couldn't go to sleep and I needed to think, maybe I should get out of the house and just drive around? This seemed like a good idea at the time because it was 2 a.m. on a weekday, and not many people would be around. I started the car and took off going south on Route 110, a main thoroughfare on Long Island. I had the radio turned to a classic rock station, and they were playing the 70's Asia classic "Heat of the Moment," and I began to sing along. I'm sure you know what it's like when you get behind the wheel with no particular purpose and no particular place to go…you just drive, and that's what I did.

I was deep in thought, accompanied by more classic rock, when I finally looked around to determine where I was. It seemed that I had been in the car for more than 45 minutes, and I was now on the South Shore of Long Island, in a squalid and run down part of town. Looking around and noticing that most of the storefronts were dark, I saw a woman was standing in the shadows. She looked up and down the street, and before long, a car pulled up to the curb. The driver opened the window. A short conversation took place, she opened the door and they both drove off.

It was pretty easy to guess what had taken place. I thought it would be wise to make a hasty retreat, so I made an illegal U turn and started back going north on Rt. 110 to Huntington. As I was stopped at a light, I saw a small group gathered on the corner, two girls and a man. They were arguing, but about what, I didn't know. I assumed that the women were hookers, and the man was a customer. I opened my window to try and hear what they were talking about when I heard the blast of a horn. The light had turned green, and there was a Dairy Barn truck behind me, and the driver was trying to make his deliveries. I immediately put on the gas and moved to the side. I'm sure he thought that I was a "john" because he gave me a dirty look as he passed.

I shut off the engine and turned off the lights. I don't think they noticed because they continued to argue. All I could make out was ". . .no fuckin' way" and "I'll cut you bitch…" and other expletives that seemed to be a natural part of their vocabulary. Then, in a flash, the guy hauls back and throws a punch at one of the young girls. She fell to the sidewalk. I was about to get out of the car when I saw the man pull out a knife and threaten the other woman. He reached down and grabbed the dazed and bleeding girl by the hair and began dragging her down a narrow alley. The other girl followed both of them, and I could hear her sobbing and pleading with the guy, who I now guessed was their pimp, not to hit her friend anymore.

I didn't know what to do, and I was about to call the police when I thought of Uncle Al. Now, you have an idea of how much I bother the man, but this time it's after 3 a.m., and I'm sure he's sleeping. He will probably promise to strangle me when I wake him up. I said, "What the heck!" to myself, and I called his number.

"Ugh…what the hell time is it? This better be important"

"Hi Uncle Al, it's me Chris!"

"I'm gonna strangle you, you worthless piece of shit…"

I innocently said, "Did I wake you up? What time is it?"

"It's 3 a.m., and yes, you did wake me up."

"Listen, Uncle Al, just hear me out." I told him that I couldn't sleep, and that I had driven down to the South Shore. I told him about the hookers and the pimp and all about what I had seen.

"I'll call the vice crime unit and get them down there to check it out, and I know what you're up to, so you better get home now. These people are dangerous, and they will kill you no sooner than look at you."

"What do you mean, you know what I'm up to?"

"You know what I mean, Chris. Out at 3 a.m.—prostitutes…pimps… Tina! You're out looking for Tina. Let me tell you something, son . . ." Al only calls me "son" when he's serious, ". . . You don't want to be there even if Tina is with these scumbags. The minute they think she's a threat to their business, they will kill her and leave body parts throughout Jones Beach parking lot just to make a point."

"But I wasn't even thinking that this might be where Tina is. I swear I just was driving in my car."

"Well, that's good, now turn on the ignition, put it into drive and get the hell out of there. You hear me?"

"Yeah, I hear you. Thanks Unc, I love you."

"I have no idea why…God only knows…but I love you, too."

Chapter 13

I sat in the car, my hand on the keys, but I didn't start the engine. I guess, subconsciously, I could have been thinking about Tina and the possibility that she was in this area, but it never actually crossed my mind until speaking with Uncle Al. I kept thinking about whether I should follow the two hookers and the pimp to their place of business. What should do when I get there?

The police were coming, and I decided that if God and the saints were on my side, how could I lose? So I got out of the car, locked the doors, after all it was a bad neighborhood, and walked towards the alley. The alley was a long, dark walkway with holes in the blacktop and garbage all over. I stayed close to the wall on the right side of the alley as I made my way down. I could see no light from within the doorways that lined the alley and all the windows with iron bars were dark, too. I was about to turn back, thinking they had gone through the building and out another exit, when I heard the squeak of rusted hinges from a metal door that led to the alley.

I looked around for a place to hide, and I found a small dumpster. It stunk of spoiled food and rancid grease. I nearly gagged because the smell was so sickening, but it seemed preferable to getting my throat slashed, so I crouched down and tried to hear what they were saying. Whoever was at the door lit a cigarette and began talking in Spanish to another man standing alongside him. As I speak Italian and took high school Spanish, I was able to get some of the meaning in the conversation,

Man 1: "Why (unintelligible) hit (unintelligible). She's a top earner and when (unintelligible) about this he'll slit (unintelligible) throat."

Man 2: "How can I get (unintelligible) shit all over me. She (unintelligible) big problem for a (unintelligible) her out."

Man 1: "(Unintelligible) my friend, it is you (unintelligible) the problem."

The conversation continued for a few minutes with both men saying much of the same thing. One recurring part of their talk was the reference to someone who must be the leader of this gang. It seemed they both were afraid of what might happen. After the one guy was finished with his cigarette, he dropped it on the ground, crushed it with his shoe and they both went back inside.

I got up from my hiding place behind the dumpster and went over to the door where the two men had been talking. I tried the doorknob while whispering to myself,

"You must be the biggest asshole in the world to try to go inside and see what's going on. Are you some kind of idiot...Uncle Al is going to kill you if those guys don't kill you first." I said this believing that the door would be locked but as luck would have it, it was open.

I remembered the rusted metal hinges so I slowly turned the knob and carefully opened the door, as I didn't want to make any loud noise that would bring these dirt bags out of their hole. I opened the door that led into a small space, lit by only be a single 30 watt bulb. It was still too dark, and I couldn't see who were in the rooms beyond the entryway.

I closed the door but left it slightly open, so I could make a quick run for it if I had to. As I made my way down a short hallway, I heard some talking in one of the rooms ahead and slowly walked towards the conversation. I found the opening between the rooms where I heard people talking. There was a large pile of cartons on one side of the entrance, so I hid behind them and peaked out of a space between the boxes to see what was going on.

A girl was sitting on a half-broken chair speaking to one of the men that were in the alley. The hooker started screaming, "Look what you did to my face! My jaw is swollen! My lip is cut! Who's going to want me now? You're a piece of shit, you know that, a piece of shit!"

"Listen baby, the only reason I hurt you is because you don't respect me. How can I do my job without the respect of all of you?"

The girl cursed the man, and then she began to cry uncontrollably. I sat watching this and was shocked to see that the girl could not have been older than sixteen, the same age as Tina.

"You see baby, you call me a piece of shit, and then I can't get no respect from the other girls. I tell you it's not right. You got to know who is in charge here. Now baby, let me make it up to you. I got something you want."

He reached into his pocket and pulled out a dirty syringe. The pimp took a spoon and a vial of something, pouring the contents of the vial into the spoon and started to heat it up with a cigarette lighter. The contents go from solid to liquid in just about a minute, and he fills the syringe with the fluid. The girl, who had been sobbing, now is just whimpering as she stares at the needle.

"Please, I need it. I need it."

"No problem, you'll get it, but I gotta know."

"Please, I need it now. Please, Ernesto!"

"You get what you need when I get what I need."

"Please...please..." she was pleading and on the verge of hysteria.

"Come on baby, what do you say to me? Come on, say it."

"I'm sorry."

"You don't sound like you mean it."

"I mean it. I'm sorry."

"Baby, this is really good stuff, and I know that you need it, but I'm not hearing that you're really sorry."

"Please, I'm really sorry that I didn't respect you, Ernesto. I mean it. I'm really very sorry for causing you trouble."

"Well, that is much better baby. See it doesn't take much to please me. Now come here, and let me make you happy."

With that, the girl got up from her chair and began walking towards Ernesto. He had a big smile on his face as he held out the syringe. Just as she reached out, he pulled the needle back and started to laugh. He held it out to her again, and again she reached out, but at the last second, he pulled it back. Ernesto kept doing this, laughing every time she tried to grab the needle. The poor girl started to cry as she slumped onto the floor while Ernesto kept laughing at the poor hooker's sorry state.

While I was deciding what I should do, the decision was made for me. I felt the tip of a knife press against my throat, and as I slowly turned, I was facing a short Hispanic man whose arms and neck were covered in tattoos.

He yelled out, anger filling his voice, "Ernesto!"

With that, Ernesto looked up from the girl on the floor, and he went pale. The syringe fell out of his hand, and it was immediately picked up by the girl. She took the needle, plunged it into her arm and crawled over to the couch where she crumpled into a ball of human misery.

"Heriberto, what are you doing here? I thought you were at the warehouse. What's going on?"

Heriberto pressed the knife a little harder on my throat and said to me,

"Get up now."

I had been on my knees, but I got up in a standing position. Heriberto pushed me out from behind the boxes into the room.

"What…who the hell is this?" Ernesto was as shocked as I was scared.

"He's the cabrón who got in here while you were fucking off."

"Heriberto, I swear that I was…" He stopped because he knew that he was in trouble and lying would only make it worse.

Heriberto pushed me into the room, and I tripped on the legs of a chair and fell onto a stained rug that covered the floor. What had I done? Uncle Al was right, somehow I wanted to find Tina, and that clouded my judgment. With a man named Heriberto in the same place, I figured that he would have Tina, and she could be somewhere nearby.

Heriberto looked over to the couch and asked Ernesto, "What have you done to my property?"

"Heriberto, she was giving me a hard time. She stole money from me, and I needed to get her straight and…" but Heriberto cut him off.

"You needed to get her straight? My property—and you needed to get her straight?"

"But she gave me no respect; I can't let her get away with that shit."

With that, Heriberto walks over to Ernesto and within six inches of his face, he says, in the most menacing tone I have ever heard,

"You have to earn respect." And in an instant, Heriberto plunges a knife, twice, into Ernesto. Ernesto stares at the knife and the blood coming out of his chest and stomach, and he falls to the floor, dead. My mind was spinning because I was now in the middle of a situation that I knew I could never get out of.

"Manulo! Manulo! Get in here now!"

A few seconds later, the other man that was in the alley with Ernesto comes running in, and he stops in his tracks.

"Heriberto, what happened?"

"Ernesto and I had a little difference about the meaning of respect. I won the argument. Now I want you and Julio to get rid of him. Do you understand? NOW!"

"Sure…sure. I get Julio and we'll…" Manulo's voice trailed off, and he hurried out of the room.

Heriberto turned towards the unconscious hooker lying on the couch. He shook her, hard, then harder, then violently, but the girl wouldn't or couldn't wake up.

"Puta!" he shouted at her, but he got no answer. He turned to me. Heriberto still had the knife in his hand as he took three steps to where I lay on the floor. He was standing over me and said,

"Get up."

I didn't have much of a choice, so I boosted myself off the floor and stood in front of this man, a man who committed murder right in from of me.

Heriberto was staring down at Ernesto's body and said, "Ernesto was a good friend of mine. Did you know that?"

Like a jerk I answered, "No, I didn't."

"What the fuck! Who asked you maricón?"

He turned to me and continued his intense stare, so I thought it would be better just to keep quiet. My mind is racing, trying to think of what I should do next. I guess I could try to jump Heriberto, but he was so fast with the knife that I knew I wouldn't have a chance. Just ask Ernesto. I was beginning to panic, but just when I thought I had no chance left to live, Manulo and Julio entered the room.

"We are here to take him out to the van."

"Well, get him the fuck out of here. What do you want, my permission? And you better not get any blood on the floor of the van, do you understand?"

"Sure, Heriberto, sure we understand. We'll wrap him in an old blanket." And with that, they dragged the body out toward the door to the alley.

There was total silence in the room when Heriberto finally spoke,

"I think I'll introduce you to Juliano, eh? I think you will like him. Well, do you want to meet Juliano?"

I didn't know what to say for fear of making him angry again, so I only said, "Yes." I figured that it would buy me some time in hopes that Uncle Al called the police, and they were on the way.

"Oh yes, I am sure you will like Juliano, and he will like you." A big smile came over Heriberto's face, and he chuckled. "He will ask you about things like life, death, food, why you are here."

"Why are you here?" Heriberto asked with mock puzzlement.

I didn't know what to say, but I knew I had to come up with something. "I heard that you have young girls here, and I wanted to… " with that, he took a fist and slammed it across my face. The punch was so powerful that it knocked me off my feet.

"You want young girls. You've got some cojones. How do I know you're not a cop or someone's big brother looking for their sweet little cono."

My face was bruised, and it began to throb. I think that he may have given me a black eye because that began to hurt, too.

"Do you know who I am? I AM HERIBERTO QUINTANA, and I will bring down all the forces of hell on you. DO YOU KNOW WHO I AM?"

He was screaming at me, or just at the world, but I remained down on the floor waiting for things to calm down. Manulo and Julio came back in the room and looked at me on the floor and then back to Heriberto. Both men had blood over their hands and shirts from dragging Ernesto to the van.

"We got him into the van, and we're going to dump him in the canal."

"Wait, I want you to take this *ojete* upstairs. Put him in the room at the end of the hallway. We are going to have a party later, and Juliano is coming with some gifts. What do you think *ojete*, do you want to party with Juliano? Answer me, you piece of shit."

All I could say was,"Yes."

"Oh, I'm glad because the last thing you want to do is make Juliano sad that you will not party with him."

Manulo and Julio smiled at this as they emptied my pockets of car keys, wallet, pocket change and all. They both grabbed me by the arms and started to drag me up a flight of stairs. The building was a real dung heap, and I heard the crunch of vials and other garbage as they crushed under my feet. The men took me down a dark hallway with doors on both sides, a few were open and some closed. I tried to look inside the doors that opened to the rooms, and I saw some unfortunate girls, kids really, that were just lying on filthy beds, fast asleep probably due to their drug induced states.

We reached the end of the hallway when Manulo let go of my arm to open the door. As he did, I looked over to my left and saw Tina. It was the exact same room that St. Agatha showed me in her vision. Tina appeared unconscious, but I knew that she was probably drugged, and she was in no position to help me or herself.

Manulo opened the door, and they both threw me into a dark space that was no cleaner than any of the rooms that I saw. They locked the door and left. As I lay on the floor, a rat passed over my feet. I jumped up and ran to a corner of the room where I hoped there were no other rats, roaches or any other vermin. I was in some pain from the punch and confusion over the circumstance that I found myself in when I received a vision.

My rat and roach infested prison was transformed to a large house that was located in a small town in the province of northern Galilee. I was in the home of someone who appeared to be very wealthy, and all those present in the room were looking at the woman supplicated to Christ.

> *She was very beautiful and very proud, this young woman kneeling at the feet of Christ. In life she was a sinner, and her sorrow for what she had done knew no bounds. It was like a ponderous weight on her soul, and as she knelt at the feet of Christ, her tears flowed. She wished, she pleaded, for His forgiveness and anointed His feet with oil.*
>
> *Christ was filled with such compassion for the woman that He laid hands on her head. In an instant, the seven demons that had tortured her poor mind and body were exorcised.*

The vision evaporated and with it, the form of St. Mary Magdalene stepped out of the place and spoke to me,

"You must look to save this girl. Like the Lord struck the demons from me, He will strike the sickness from her, and you will be His source."

How could I save Tina? I was a prisoner myself, and even if I did get to her room, how would I get her out of the building? I also thought of Juliano, who was this man, and what will he do to me? I knew I didn't have much time, so I asked St. Mary Magdalene,

"What can I do? I am a prisoner myself. Tina is unconscious, she could be drugged, and she may have been raped. How can I do this by myself? I need your help. Please, help me, show me the way." The vision continued:

> *Christ stood before all. Mary and the assembled looked at the man from Galilee in solemn reverence, and Christ spoke, "Many sins are forgiven her because she has loved very much." Then he turned to Mary, and He said kindly, "Your faith has made you safe; go in peace."*

"Can you understand that if the Lord could forgive the worst of sinners, He can forgive us all? She is loved, and you will find a way so she can be saved. It is His will."

I was overwhelmed by the vision of Jesus Christ Himself. I was trying to fathom what I had seen, what the words meant and why I was so privileged. I was deep in thought when the vision of St. Mary Magdalene vanished, and the door to the room crashed open. I looked up. In walked Heriberto with a well dressed and very handsome looking man that I assumed was Juliano.

Heriberto was the first to speak: "Ah, we hope you are enjoying your stay with us. Juliano is here as I promised, and we want to be sure you are comfortable." As he said that, the gang leader smashed his foot down onto the head of a rat that was crossing the floor. The rat exploded into a mass of guts, brain and blood and Heriberto yelled,

"Mire lo que le hizo a mi pantalón!"

"Now, Heriberto, don't worry about your pants. It seems that you are making our friend nervous."

With an exaggerated bow, Heriberto said, "Oh, please excuse me. I didn't realize I made you so nervous. I wouldn't want you to feel unwelcome." His voice made my skin crawl.

I needed to try and make some kind of effort, so that they would not harm me. "Please listen, I only wanted some action. I didn't mean to barge in. Please, I didn't see anything, and I won't tell anyone. Just let me go."

Juliano smiled. "Of course we'll let you go. But I understand our friend Heriberto promised you a party. I love parties, don't you?"

"All I wanted was some action. Please, just let me go."

"I wouldn't dream of letting you go before we have had our party, and I will be sure you get all the…what did you call it? Action, that's it, *action*. I will be sure you get all the action you want."

The horror of the situation was growing, and it was apparent that Juliano and Heriberto had no intentions of letting me go. In fact, they had great torments in mind.

"Heriberto, I think it's about time we introduced our guest to some of our protégés."

"Yes, that's a good idea. After all, that is what he came for." He turned to me and said, "Come my friend, I want to introduce you to a new arrival."

With that, Juliano motioned to Manulo and Julio as they entered the room. Manulo tied my hands behind my back, and both men grabbed me by the arms and led me out of the room. I didn't have far to walk when they pushed me into Tina's room. I was surrounded by the four men. As they stood me at the edge of her bed, Heriberto began to taunt me.

"The little puta is just waiting for you. I hope your cock gets good and hard because she likes it up the ass."

"Now Heriberto, don't be so crude. Our friend, what is his name? Oh, yes, it's here on his license, Christopher Pella, said he wanted some action, and it's within our power to accommodate his desires, is it not? And, yes, we did promise him a party, didn't we?"

"Si, we can give him what he wants."

Juliano turns to Manulo and Julio and says, "Boys, if you would please leave the room. I am sure our guest would like some privacy." They left the room.

"Oh Christopher, there is one thing I failed to mention. After this is over, we will need to have a real heart to heart talk. It wasn't at all good of you to sneak into our home and disturb our tranquility. Heriberto was so upset that he had to kill poor Ernesto. I feel that in all good conscience, someone will need to take responsibility. In the meantime, consider this our gift to you."

Tina was lying there still unconscious as Heriberto pushed me onto her bed. He began to unbuckle my pants. I kicked and yelled at him to stop. He just laughed at me, at the position I was in and continued to try to take down my pants.

Then we heard a commotion coming from the room on the floor below. Muffled sounds—but I could just barely hear what was said:

"Police, drop your weapons, and put your hands on your head!"

I heard gun shots and screaming and a scuffle of some sort. I recognized the loud voices of Manulo and Julio who must have been in the midst of all this. Juliano looked unconcerned as he turned to Heriberto.

"Would you please go downstairs and see what the fuss is all about. I'll wait here with our guest until you return."

Heriberto pulled a gun from under his shirt, checked to see if it was loaded and left the room. Now Juliano and I were alone, except for the unconscious Tina. He looked at me with a cold, hard smile and started to pace along the front of the room.

"I do believe that the authorities have found our little home away from home. Don't you think?"

"I think you're a fucking lunatic, and in about two minutes, you're going to find out what the word 'payback' means. Look what you've done to Tina, just look at her." For the first time, I was thinking that I just might get out of this.

"Oh my word, such anger. All I did was give you what you wanted. You are most ungrateful. I am sure Tina would have loved you to be her first, shall we say, experience."

I began to yell out to the police downstairs, "Hey! Come upstairs! I'm here with a lunatic who kidnaps kids and gets them hooked on drugs!" I kind of sounded like a poster child for Americans against Perverts, or some such group, but I screamed it out anyway.

I then heard the first shots and screams of pain coming from some of the people downstairs. Some of the screams seemed to be in Spanish, so I assumed that the police had the upper hand, and Manulo and Julio were out of commission. Juliano was just standing there, looking at me and smiling as I tried to get myself off the bed.

"I know who you are."

"What . . . well, bully for you. You've got my license."

"I know who you are. What you are. What you do. I know you came for this pitiful creature."

I immediately became frightened and started to think. He couldn't know about my coming for Tina, how could he know about my secrets? No one knows about my gift, my visions and my saints.

"You think you can stop me with your pathetic, little visions? You do not know the real power, the real force of genuine evil." Juliano began pacing the floor of Tina's room.

"I may not know the real power of evil, but I do know the real power of good."

"Very clever Christopher, but you have never had to face ultimate evil, and I will delight in helping you understand its true meaning."

There was no response to this madness except for the next vision. Tina's room now became transformed, and Juliano and I were transported to the holiest of places. We are in a cave, a crypt, St. Mary Magdalene is on the floor, and she is weeping. With that Juliano, stopped pacing and became visibly frightened,

"What have you done to bring me to such a place?" He asked no one in particular.

St. Mary Magdalene's spirit rose out of her prostrated self and stands before Juliano, speaking to him:

"The Lord is risen, and it is an abomination that you are even able to see His empty tomb."

Juliano looks at her and then turns to me and says, "Beware, for I am the Beast." He then transforms himself into a demon so hideous that I immediately had to cover my eyes from the horror.

St. Mary stared him straight in the eye and began to pray: "Our Father who art in heaven, hallowed by Thy name. Thy kingdom come, Thy will be done . . ." and before The Lord's Prayer was finished, Juliano shrieked in rage and vanished.

St. Mary looked at me and said, "The young girl is troubled, but let her know that she is loved. As Christ loved me, He loves her, and she will find peace. Her family loves her, and she will know happiness in their care." St. Mary Magdalene smiled at me and disappeared.

Chapter 14

"Help us…Help us…we're upstairs. There's a young kid, and she's hurt, help us!" I screamed at the top of my lungs. A team of police officers ran into the room, guns in hand, ready for the worst. As they saw me lying on the bed, they might not have realized that my hands were tied because they looked at me with utter revulsion.

"Stay where you are, you piece of shit! Keep your hands behind your back, and don't move." It seems that I had been called piece of shit more times in one day than ever before.

As my hands were still tied, I had little choice, but I tried to get up anyway: "Please, help me. Tina needs help, and my hands are tied."

"I said stay where you are, and don't speak."

One of the officers came to the side of the bed where I was lying and said, "What are you doing here? Are you one of the pieces of shit that prey on young girls?" His was angry. I needed to explain why I was in this place.

"My name is Chris Pella, and this is Tina Staley. She is the granddaughter of one of my friends, Fred Klein. I was trying to find her. You can ask my uncle, Al Barese, he's the chief…"

The cop cut me off: "You know Chief Barese?"

"I do. He's my uncle, my mom's younger brother, and he can vouch for me. I swear it's all the truth, just ask him."

The cop went silent: "He's here now."

"Great, you can go and ask him. He'll let you know that I'm telling the truth."

The cop just looked at me and said, "He was part of the fire fight, and he's been shot. It looks pretty serious, and the ambulance is on its way."

"Uncle Al, shot?"

What had I done? The man, who was like a father to me, was lying on a filthy floor in some drug-infested slum, and I was responsible. I started to choke up. The police officer saw that I was so upset that he came over and untied my hands.

"Can I see him? I need to see him."

"He's downstairs. I'll take you to him."

As he untied my hands and helped me to stand, I asked, "Can someone please help Tina and the other kids here? They have been beaten, drugged and molested."

"Sure, we've already called the hospital and child services. They will be coming here to take charge of these kids."

We left the room. Officer Terry Ray, which was written on his nameplate, started to lead me down the steps. As we walked, I saw the police looking in the rooms where the young kids were. We walked down the long hallway, and I asked him,

"What happened to Heriberto Quintana? He was the one who ran this place and gave the kids drugs. He also murdered Ernesto. I don't know his last name, but Quintana stabbed him right in front of me."

The officer looked at me and said, "You've had some night. I don't think you'll have to worry about Quintana anymore. Quintana came into the room and began firing. He shot Chief Barese, but before he could get another shot off, your uncle used him for target practice. He's something, your Uncle Al."

All I could say is, "He sure is."

"You know, he's the one who called us and told us about these parasites and to be sure we came with back up as it could get violent. As a matter of fact, he was here before we arrived."

I thought to myself that Al must have suspected that I wouldn't go home, and that I would be in danger. Like I've told you before, I always felt safe when he was around.

As I walked into the room, I saw the body of Heriberto Quintana. His eyes were wide open. He was dead. There were policemen all over the place keeping order, and there were other men in white coats taking care of the wounded and looking for evidence, or something of that sort.

I looked over to the couch and saw the poor hooker who had been beaten by Ernesto. She was laying face down on the couch, and she was bleeding from a wound near her neck.

"What happened to that poor girl, Officer Ray? Is she dead?"

"I'm afraid she is. In the firefight,she got up off the couch in front of Quintana, and he shot her. Did you know her?"

I wanted to answer, but the next thing I saw was Uncle Al on the floor. He was lying there, bleeding from a very serious wound to his shoulder, just above his heart. My body and mind began to tremble at the site. Laying here is the guy who asked my father what his intentions were towards my mother before they got married. It was a hilarious story and became a legendary tale in our family. Laying here was the bravest man I knew, a man who embodied the essence of doing what is right and proving it every day. Here is the guy who loves me like a son, and here he was dying because of me.

I fell to the floor, kneeling beside him. I started to cry. What would I do without him? I grabbed his hand and held it tightly while he was being administered to by a medic onsite.

"Uncle Al, it's me, Chris. Can you hear me?" I needed to hear his voice and have him know that I was there.

The medic who was working on his wounds looked up and said,

"Are you okay? Your face is bruised, and it looks like you've got a black eye. Do you need help?"

"No, no I don't. Chief Barese, my uncle, how's he doing?'

"Chief Barese has lost a lot of blood, and he's unconscious. He's been very seriously wounded, and I'm trying to stem the flow of blood. He's already lost a lot, and there is little more I can do here. He'll need to be taken to the Emergency Room where they will determine his condition and chances for survival."

Chances for survival? I couldn't fathom the meaning of those words because I couldn't imagine life without him. It almost didn't matter that he couldn't hear me because I needed to tell him everything that was on my mind and in my heart.

"Uncle Al, I love you. I am so sorry that I didn't listen to you and leave this to the police. Please forgive me. Please don't die. I need you around; I need to know you are there for me. Who will I spend Christmas with? Who will yell at me for waking you up at 3 a.m.? Who will pay for our dinners every month? You can't leave me; we have too much more to do together." There was frenzied activity all around, but all that mattered was Uncle Al. I was helpless to do anything for him.

In an instant, all the people in the room seemed to freeze in time except for Uncle Al and me. I looked up to one of the most glorious sights I had ever experienced.

> *St. Michael the Archangel was floating above me. He was surrounded by a brilliant, white light. He hovered in the space just below the ceiling. Michael the Archangel held a sword in his right hand, and he was carrying a shield on his left arm that was inscribed with the legend, "Quis Ut Deus," which is Latin for "Who is like God."*

Uncle Al was still unconscious, and although I was aware of all that was happening, I couldn't move. My whole body felt weighed down as I watched in wonder. Then, we were both transported to a place in the ancient Near East. It was a sacred place, the *Michaelion* at Chalcedon, built by Emperor Constantine in the fourth Century. Constantine had built this sanctuary to honor this as a sacred place in veneration to Michael, the prince of angels, and his powers heal the wounds of the faithful who come to pray.

In the *Michaelion*, there was a clear pool fed by a spring where Michael the Archangel hovered above the water. Michael dipped his shield into the spring, and it filled with the healing waters. My body became light, and I floated up and was there, face-to-face, with the Archangel. He motioned me to hold out my hands, and when I did, he filled them with water from his shield.

I stared down at my hands and looked up at Michael. Words would not come, and all I could say was, "Thank you."

I floated back down to where I was kneeling next to Uncle Al. I instinctively knew what to do. I took the water and poured it from my hands onto his wound. When I finished, I looked up to see St. Michael surrounded by the Heavenly Host of Angels and in one massive exodus, they flew towards the light.

I was back in the present, kneeling alongside Uncle Al, with the people in the rooms going about their tasks. The medic looks up at me,

"What the hell? This is the strangest thing…"

Then something incredible happened. Uncle Al looks up at me and says,

"When I get out of the hospital, I'm gonna strangle you!"

I couldn't believe it—well, actually I could. I looked down at Uncle Al and smiled at him saying,

"How could you strangle your favorite nephew?"

"Favorite nephew? Leo's my favorite nephew," and he smiled back.

The medic seemed to be in shock.

"He was nearly dead just a minute ago. What the hell happened? I've never seen anything like it."

I said, "Maybe it wasn't as serious as you initially thought."

"Are you kidding? The wound nearly severed his shoulder. I just can't believe it. One minute he's bleeding like a sieve, his blood pressure is dropping like a rock, he's unconscious—and the next thing is that he stops bleeding, and he's making jokes with you. This can't be. It's impossible."

"Well, all I know is that you got him back, and that's all I care about." But all the medic could do was to shake his head and look bewildered.

As all this was going on, the ambulance arrived, and they started to evaluate his condition. Once that was done, they loaded Uncle Al onto the stretcher, hooked him up to the I.V. and wheeled him out. He looked very weak, but he was alive. I was right beside him, holding his hand when he said,

"What happened in there?"

"We found her Unc; we got her out. We got Tina and some other girls and boys that were being held in this rat hole. They are being cared for by the medics and child services."

"I mean what happened in there?"

"Oh, you were shot by Quintana, Heriberto Quintana. You remember. He's the scumbag that you identified from the gibberish I gave you, you know, Quintianus. He killed a low life and a poor girl, who was strung out, and you were able to shoot him before he killed anyone else."

"Chris, I mean what really happened? I've seen enough bloodshed to know that I was a goner, and I need to know. I mean to me, what happened to me?"

"What does it matter? All that matters now is that you are getting help, and they are taking you to the hospital. I am just so thankful that you are alive and will be fine."

"Chris, I have to know the truth. I don't know what happened to heal my wound, but it wasn't some iodine and a *Finding Nemo* bandage.

Why do I have this nagging suspicion that you know something about all this?"

I was looking down at Uncle Al, and he was looking back with those piercing eyes. Even though he was in a weakened state, he knew a lot about telling the truth, and he knew I promised never to lie to him again. As we got closer to the ambulance I said to him,

"Listen, this isn't the time or place to speak. They won't let me ride in the ambulance, so I'll follow you back to the hospital. When they allow me into your room, we can talk. How's that?"

"Okay, but remember your promise, and remember I can tell when you are lying."

"I'll remember."

Chapter 15

I looked around and found my wallet and car keys, and I ran towards my car. When I got there, I found the trunk lock jimmied—my spare tire, some tools and a beach blanket were missing. I smiled and thought, "So much for locking the car." Who cares, Uncle Al was going to be fine. I just knew it, and that was all that mattered to me.

I started the car. Thank God they didn't steal the engine, and I drove to Huntington Hospital. It was far from where Uncle Al got shot, but they had an excellent trauma unit, and the doctors and nurses were very familiar with treating all sorts of serious injuries. As the ambulance pulled into the parking lot outside the Emergency Room, the medics opened the back door and rushed Chief Barese into the care of the waiting physicians.

I drove close behind the ambulance, so I arrived less than a minute later and ran up to the nurse's desk:

"Hi, I'm Chris Pella, Al Barese's nephew. I know that he just got here, but is there any news about his condition and what is being done? He was shot, and it looked serious. Is there any word yet?" The nurse sensed that I was very nervous and rambling on, so she tried to assure me that Uncle Al was in good hands and getting the best treatment possible.

"Dr. Scanlon is the attending Emergency Room physician, and he and his staff have years of experience with cases very much like Chief Barese's. I know you are worried, but be assured that he is in the best of hands." She smiled a smile that can only come from years of practice, and I thanked her and sat down in the waiting area.

After about an hour, I heard someone say my name. It was a doctor, and he said, "Mr. Pella, are you Mr. Christopher Pella?"

"I am. Please, call me Chris. Do you have any news about Chief Barese? I'm his nephew, a family member, you can tell me about his condition, right?" I felt that I needed to say I was family because of what happened when Fred was in the hospital.

"I have to tell you this—with what happened to your Uncle and what we can determine now is that he is about the luckiest man alive."

I wanted to jump for joy, but I needed to know, "What do you mean?"

"Well, in all my years of practice, I have never seen a wound as large, and potentially life threatening as his, begin to close up and heal so fast. His recovery is truly miraculous. The entire staff is looking at your Uncle as some kind of super hero."

"Well, we do refer to him as 'Ball Breaker Man,'" but that's just among our family and friends."

The doctor laughed and then said that they were performing some more tests, but it would be at least another couple of hours before I could see him. I thanked the doctor and asked him to thank his staff for their work. Then Dr. Scanlon walked away, and I sat back down in my chair for the long wait.

I looked up at the clock, 9:12AM. I remembered that Fred was in the same hospital, and I wanted to bring him the good news. Visiting hours had started at 9 a.m., so I went to the front desk and asked the senior citizen volunteer working there,

"I'm here to visit Fred Klein. Can you please tell me his room?"

"Well, let me see. Oh, here it is, he's in Room 497. You just take the North Elevator to the fourth floor and follow the signs."

I thanked her and went to see Fred. When I got to his room, I poked my head into the opened door. Fred was lying on the bed and appeared to be asleep. I didn't want to disturb him, so I just stood outside waiting for him to wake up. As I stood there, I must have looked like a lost soul because this nurse walks up behind me and says,

"I hope you didn't hurt that guy's fist when you smashed your face into it." She said this with the most appealing laugh I had ever heard.

I turned to see a stunning young nurse standing there with a chart in her hand. She tilted her head and grinned at me,

"So what happened to you, Rocky? Do I need to call the doctor or the police?"

"Uh, I uh, I, what do you mean? "I stumbled over my words because I had never met anyone so beautiful in my life.

"I uh, I'm here for Fred. I mean, I'm here to see Fred. I mean, I'm here to talk to Fred. I'm his Fred—I mean friend."

She laughed again and said, "Just wait here. I'm going to take his vitals, and if he's up to it, I'll let you see him for a few minutes only. Understand?"

"I will…I mean, I do."

"You have a lot of trouble speaking, don't you?"

"Not usually." And that was the truth.

Another smile and she walked into the room, closing the door. I was dumbfounded because when you consider what I'd been through, Uncle Al and Fred both in the hospital, and I now meet the most beautiful girl in the world…I had earned the right to have a nice and peaceful nervous breakdown. As I was pondering a vacation in the psychiatric ward, the nurse opens the door to Fred's room,

"Okay Rocky, you can go in, but only for ten minutes. If you try to stay any longer or make him upset, I'm going to kick your ass, which seems to be pretty easy given the way you look."

"My ass? Oh yes, my ass!" I replied, having regained some of my composure. "I mean, thank you, and if there is anyone who will be kicking my ass, I promise it will be you."

"Very good, now don't be long. He needs his rest." She turned and began to walk away when I said,

"By the way, what's your name, just in case I have to send you an invitation to kick my ass?"

She turns to me and says, "My name is Elizabeth. What's yours?"

"I'm Chris, I mean Christopher, Christopher Pella."

"Well, what is it, Chris or Christopher?"

"Everyone calls me Chris. Are you Elizabeth, Beth or Liz?"

"Everyone calls me Beth, Beth Della Russo, pleased to meet you." She held out her hand, and I shook it.

Oh my Lord—beautiful, smart and Italian. My mother must have something to do with this. "Well, it's a pleasure meeting you Beth Della Russo, and thanks for talking good care of my friend. He's been through a lot."

She gives me a curious look and walks away.

I turned the knob on Fred's door and looked inside. He was lying on the bed, eyes open with that same hopeless look on his face. I walked into the room and stood in front of his bed.

"Hey Fred, how're you doing?"

He looked up at me and didn't answer.

"I've got some good news for you."

"What news can be good except that you found Tina?"

"Well, that's it Fred, we found Tina! We found her!"

If ever there was a person that completely transformed in an instant, it was Fred. His eyes went wide, and he pushed the switch that lifted his hospital bed up so he could better see me.

"What? What did you say? Mother of God, did you say you found Tina?"

"I did Fred. That's exactly what I said."

"My baby, my love, you found her?"

"That's right. We found her."

Now Fred starts to yell and scream, tears running down his face. So I join in because this kind of happiness is contagious.

Once she hears the commotion in Fred's room, Beth comes running in. She looks at Fred and looks at me, and I could see that she's getting angry.

"What the hell is going on? Didn't I tell you not to get him upset? Now you get hell out of here!"

Fred immediately interrupts, "No, no, this is wonderful news. This man gave me the greatest gift I could ask for."

"What do you mean?" Beth said.

"He found my Tina! He found my granddaughter!"

Beth looks at me, slightly less suspicious than before and she says, "Okay Rocky, what the hell is going on?"

"Listen, I was going to tell Fred all that happened to Tina. It's a pretty frightening story, and I don't know if Fred wants me to tell it, given all the sordid details."

Fred looks at me and says in as serious a voice as I've heard him speak, "You found my Tina, I need to know what happened to her, and Beth can listen if she wants to. Don't hold back anything because if I have to help her, I need to know." It was a very brave statement coming from this man. He had to listen to the depravity and degradation of someone he loves very much.

Beth had been staring at me very hard, but her look seemed to soften as I began to tell my story.

I first looked at Beth as if to give her background, "Fred is my friend and his granddaughter, Tina, was having a hard time dealing with her parents' divorce. She would rebel and stay away from home and became a source of great worry to them. When Fred became despondent after hearing Tina went missing, I tried to help..."

I went into the complete details of her nightmare. I told them both about the drugs, the hookers, the filth, the pimps and the murders. I told them of my capture by the drug dealers and of my Uncle Al and his investigation. I told them how he called the police and how he got shot killing the bastard who would have ruined Tina. I didn't mention Juliano, how could I explain this demon, this consummate evil? However, I did tell them about Heriberto Quintana, Ernesto, Manulo and Julio, and how they will never bother these kids again. For nearly half an hour Fred and Beth sat there in silence, and I ended by saying,

"Tina is being taken to the hospital where she will receive the best of care. She was lucky that when these dirt bags kidnapped her, they hadn't had time to hook her on drugs, but some of the other kids were far less fortunate."

Fred had tears in his eyes and said, "Chris, come over here." I went to the side of his bed, and he reached across and hugged me. It was one of the most emotional encounters of my life.

"It's over, Fred. The nightmare is over. Tina has people who love her, and that will get her through this. She needs you, and you need to get better because you are her rock."

"How can I ever thank you?"

"You can thank me by getting better for you and for Tina. Can you do that for me?"

"I can, and I will." With that, Fred collapsed back into the hospital bed, exhausted but delighted and fell asleep almost immediately.

Beth touched my shoulder and whispered, "Come on, Rambo. We need to leave Fred to get some rest." I smiled at her, and we left the room.

Outside in the hallway, Beth spoke first, "That was some story, Christopher Pella. You really made a difference in both of their lives. I don't know if I should have been listening, but I'm glad I did. You're quite a guy."

"Hey, if you think I'm quite a guy, you got to meet my Uncle."

She smiled that beautiful smile, "Where is he? I have to meet him."

"He's being given tests in the emergency room, but I'm hoping he will be in a room of his own soon."

"Don't worry about that. We'll be sure he's well taken care of." She started to walk away, but I didn't want her to go.

"Uh, hey Beth, I need to ask you something."

She turned to me with a shit-eating grin and said, "What do you want to ask me, Rocky? Or is it Rambo?"

"Uh, well, I wanted to know maybe, if you have the time, well when you have the time…" but she interrupted me:

"Yes, I will go out with you, but no fooling around on the first date, agreed?"

"Agreed!"

With that, she wrote her number down and handed the piece of paper. She turned and walked down the hall. I also turned and walked away—six feet above the floor, metaphorically speaking.

Chapter 16

I knew I should have only been thinking about Uncle Al, but thoughts of Beth kept coming across in my mind. I don't understand how I could be so taken with someone in such a short time. I kept looking at the piece of paper she gave me with her phone number, and I resolve to call her as soon as my face healed or when I got home, whichever came first.

The waiting room had become more crowded since I'd went to see Fred, so there were no more seats left. I stood by the window hoping to hear some news about Uncle Al. About an hour passed when I heard the phone ring in the ER admitting office. A different nurse looked out of the glass window and said,

"Are you Chris Pella?"

I said I was, and she handed me the phone, "Don't be too long. This is an Emergency Room, and we have emergencies here."

"I won't be long. I promise. Hello?"

"Hey, you heroic asshole, come up to room 495. Wait until you see the room I got!" It was my uncle, and I was never happier to hear his voice.

"Please refer to me as the handsome heroic asshole."

"Just get up here!"

I handed the phone back to the nurse, who looked like she was ready to put me in the corner for a time out, and thanked her. I ran to the North Elevator, which was becoming my personal favorite, and pushed the button for the fourth floor. The doors opened, but I didn't need to read the sign again. I knew exactly where the room was.

I rushed down the hallway but didn't see Beth at the nurses' station, so I just went into room 495. On the bed, like he was king of the hill, sat Uncle Al. In the room, there was a large hospital bed, private bath and shower, a large flat screen TV and sound system, flowers on his nightstand, paintings hanging on the wall, two nurses trying to comfort him, two police officers standing there eyeing the nurses and there was Beth watching over all this and smiling.

The first thing I said was, "You got all this just for being shot? What is the world coming to? I can't believe that my uncle is turning into the biggest sissy on the force. Ladies and officers, all I can do is apologize for his contemptible behavior. Please, don't let this get back to the Suffolk County PD before I have a chance to tell them myself. Oh, by the way, can someone come over here and rub my back? It really hurts!"

The nurses laughed, and they left the room.

"Really Beth, thank you and the entire staff for taking care of my uncle. I am more grateful than you will ever know."

Beth smiles at me and says, "Well Rambo, I guess you're going to be buy me the dinner of a lifetime. What do you say?"

"Agreed!"

She turned to Uncle Al, "Listen Chief, you may be feeling better, but you had a serious wound. The doctors are only letting you stay in this ward because they expect you to rest without half the force in your room." She turned to the police officers: "Okay guys, get out of here. If you have to stay, there's coffee in the waiting area."

"Yes, ma'am. Goodbye, Chief. We were all worried, and we're really glad to see you're doing better." Uncle Al thanked them both, and with that, they left the room.

"Now it's my turn to leave, but remember that you need rest, even from family, so you've got ten minutes with Chris, and then I want him out of here. Capisci?"

"Si, capisco bennissimo. Now Chris, say goodbye to the nice lady."

"Goodbye, nice lady."

Beth left the room, but as she did, I noticed her back was almost as good as her front, and I smiled. Uncle Al seemed to notice, and he said,

"She is very, very nice, beautiful, smart and Italian. Your mom must be pulling some strings in heaven."

"Funny, I was thinking the exact same thing."

I walked around the side of his bed, and I sat down. "I am so sorry Unc, I know you told me to go home, and I know that I should have. Now you are here, and it's my fault. Please, forgive me."

"Hey Chrissy, don't be so maudlin. If I was dead, I'd really be pissed off, but I'm alive. The doctor's can't believe it. Quite frankly, neither can I."

"What did he say, the doctor that is?"

"Well, according to them, I'm a walking, living, breathing miracle. They think that I have some special healing powers that allowed me to recover so quickly. Are they right, Chris?"

"No."

"What do you mean?"

"I mean that you're a great cop and a great uncle, but you don't have any special powers."

"Agreed. So what happened to me? Why am I alive when I should be dead, and what do you have to do with all of this?"

"Uncle Al, I am going to tell you a story. It's a story of a young kid who experienced something so miraculous that he had to keep it secret for more than seventeen years."

"Go on. I'm listening."

I had tried to come up with a way of telling Uncle Al all about my saints and visions. The last thing I wanted was to have him think that I was some nut who fantasized about saints and visions. This was going to be the most difficult conversation I'd ever had, but I needed to tell him the truth, so I took a deep breath and began.

"One day this kid got sick, and while he was laying in bed in complete misery, he had a vision, his first, and that changed his life."

"What was this first vision?"

"He met Saints Cosmas and Damian."

"You mean while he was so sick, he had hallucinations of meeting Saints Cosmas and Damian? By the way, who are Cosmas and Damian?"

"No, I mean he was transported back in time to the fourth century A.D. where he met these saints, twin brothers who were physicians working in someplace called Cilicia. He spoke with them, saw them work, and he saw them perform a miracle."

"What kind of miracle?"

"They cut the leg off this black guy and put it on this white guy."

Uncle Al smiled at me and said, "I hope the black guy didn't mind."

"No, he was dead."

"Chris, you know I love you, but this is crazy talk. What does this have to do with my injury?"

"Please Uncle Al, you need to hear this. So please let me finish the story."

"Okay Chris, sorry I interrupted."

I took another deep breath. I needed time to figure out what I was going to say next.

"This kid was awestruck by what he had seen. When Sts. Cosmas and Damian first spoke to him, they actually stepped out of their bodies, faced him and began speaking."

Uncle Al asked, "What did they say?"

"They told him that he had a purpose in life, and that there were things he was expected to do."

"What kind of things?"

"Oh, different things—like helping people in need, fighting evil, stuff like that." I felt weird talking this way because it trivialized the true meaning of the gift I received and the special relationships I had with the saints.

"Listen Uncle Al, I can't put into words what was said and the true meaning of all this, but this is the only way I know how."

"Okay, so this kid has a vision, meets two saints, gets instructions on his purpose in life. What happens next?"

"Well, actually, he meets other saints."

"Really, how many?"

"176."

"A hundred and seventy-six, huh?"

"Yes, but that doesn't include the ones he saw in the gathering of saints."

"Really, how many were there?"

"He couldn't say. There were too many."

"Okay Chris, time for a recap. Cosmas and Damian, 300 A.D., black leg onto a white guy, purpose in life, 175 … no, 176, fight evil, lots more at the gathering. Did I leave anything out?"

"Well, there was his prom night, and he was trying to get laid, but St. Bernardine of Siena made him stop." I sounded like a complete idiot.

"St. Bernardine…getting laid?"

"No, St. Bernadine wasn't trying to get laid, he was. I mean the kid was."

"Chris, let's stop this nonsense and get to the truth. This is about the sorriest fairytale I've ever heard."

I had to continue, so that I could make him understand why he was still alive.

"Uncle Al, in order for you to know the truth, you need to listen to me and try not to jump to any conclusions until the story is over."

"Okay, I'm still listening."

"What I'm going to tell you next is about the hardest thing I've ever had to say in my life." I gulped and blurted out,

"I am that kid."

"Oh, so now my nephew has visions of saints? How long has this been going on?"

"My first vision was when I was fourteen."

"Who else knows about this?"

"No one. You're the first person I've ever told."

"Well, Chris, I truly feel honored." I knew he was being sarcastic.

Uncle Al turned away from me and just stared out the window. I know that he needed time to process all of this, not that he believed me, but he need time to figure out what he could do to help me. Here I was, someone he loved like a son, with a story so crazy that he would need to confront the possibility that I had lost my mind and needed real help.

"I'm sorry, Chris, this is a lot to lay down on me, and I need time to think about what you told me."

"I know, Uncle Al. Maybe I should come back later. My ten minutes are almost up anyway."

"That's a good idea. I'm a little tired, and I need to get some rest. In the meantime, let's keep this to ourselves, okay?"

"I've kept it to myself for more than sixteen years, a few hours more won't kill me," I said, smiling.

I hesitated a bit, but I said it anyway, "I love you."

"I love you, too. No matter what."

Chapter 17

When I left the room, I didn't have any particular place to go. I went across the hall to check on Fred, but when I opened the door, I saw he was asleep. I left him in peace. I walked down the hallway, but I didn't see Beth at the nurses' station, so I walked to the elevator and pressed the down button.

I got off in the lobby, and I saw a sign for the cafeteria. I hadn't eaten in a while, and I was very hungry, so I made my way there. It was just before lunch, and the line was short. I ordered a turkey and bacon wrap on a whole wheat tortilla with a side salad and iced tea. The cashier took my money, and I found a quiet table in the corner to eat and ponder the situation.

I took a few bites of the wrap, which tasted pretty good, and drank some of iced tea while I sat there alone with my thoughts. I told Uncle Al my secret, and I knew I needed to convince him I was telling the truth, but how? How can I tell him about finding Tina? How can I tell him that he was saved by a miracle, a miracle carried out by Michael the Archangel and so much more? I was sitting there feeling miserable about the situation when someone stopped at my table.

A woman stands there, and asks, "Aren't you Chris Pella?"

I look up and answer, "Yes, I am. I'm sorry, but I don't seem to recall..."

"I'm Cathy Staley, Tina's mom."

I immediately rose: "Oh, Mrs. Staley. Please, sit down. I'm sorry I didn't recognize you. Have you been to see Tina? How's she doing?"

"I just saw Tina, and she seems to be better. But she still needs to be tested, and the doctors are detoxifying her now. She'll be kept in the emergency room for a while, but they assured me that she will be fine."

"That is wonderful news. I'll be sure to stop by when she can have visitors."

"Chris, I was up to see Dad, I mean Fred, and he told me about what you did to find Tina. I ... I, I don't know what to say, how to thank you.

My baby girl in that horrid place—I shudder to think what may have happened to her if you didn't help." Tears were rolling down her cheek, and she began to sob.

"Cathy, Tina and Fred are getting the best of care. Their love for each other, and your love for them, will get you all through this. I am just so grateful that they are okay."

Cathy responds, "So am I. So am I," as she wiped away her tears.

"I know why Tina was rebelling. I know Mr. Staley loves her, too, and that both of you will be great comfort in the weeks ahead."

"Jack and I will be sure to not let our personal problems get in the way of her recovery because she will need all the support she can get. Tina is all that matters now."

"Tina's lucky to have you, Jack and Fred. If there is anything I can do, please, let me know."

"I will. Thank you from the bottom of my heart." I got up as Cathy stood up. She stood there and looked me straight in the eye, gave me a hug, kissed my cheek and walked away.

Given all that had happened, all the people I saw made it feel like I was on a roller coaster of emotions. I sat back down and picked up my turkey wrap to take another bite when someone else came and stood at my side. I looked up and there was Beth holding her lunch tray. I couldn't be happier than to see her right now.

"We haven't even gone on our first date, and you're cheating on me already?"

"Well, I've got to keep my options open; after all, I am Rocky or Rambo, and my reputation is important."

"I guess I'll have to sit right here and make sure that no one else gets to you before I have the chance." So she sits down opposite me.

"I'm not so sure. What if something better comes along?"

"Well, that works both ways, buster. You know there are a lot of handsome doctors in this hospital, and few of them wouldn't mind getting on my better side."

"Hey, all of your sides look great."

Beth smiled that fabulous smile, and I knew that I was sunk. I loved looking at her, hearing her talk and wondering what it would be like to be with her. She must have sensed that I was preoccupied by something, so she asked,

"Who was that woman?"

"That was Tina's mom, Cathy. She was in to see her daughter and Fred, and she recognized me."

"That poor woman. She must be going through her own personal hell given all that happened to Tina."

"Once she puts this horror and pain behind her, she'll be able to see a bright future for her daughter. Isn't that what every parent wants?"

Beth looks at me, but all she can say is, "Wise beyond your years."

"I wish I was. Come to think of it, if I'm so smart, how come I'm not rich? Huh, Elizabeth Della Russo, how come I'm not rich?"

"Well, God may have different plans for you."

I must have gone pale, so Beth quickly said,

"Sorry, Chris, I didn't mean you were going to die or anything like that."

"No, I'm sorry. For some reason, I just thought about all that happened today, and I hope that God hadn't planned to make me do that again."

Beth laughed, and we sat together in comfort eating our lunch and getting to know each other a little better.

"Hey Rambo, this doesn't count as a date, got it? I'm expecting something better than this spinach salad. Comprendere?"

"Si, io comprendere."

As Beth got up from the table, she said to me, "Bella, Grazie per un buon pranzo."

"You're welcome, and I promise the dinner will be nicer."

I was totally captivated, and my mother must be in her glory.

Chapter 18

I waited for a few hours before I went back on the North Elevator up to see Uncle Al. What was I was going to say? I tried not to think about his reaction. I guess if I were him, I'd have the same dread and worry. I got to the door of room 495 and went in. I saw Uncle Al sitting up on the bed, and I rushed to him,

"What are you doing? You've been seriously wounded, and you have got to lie down."

"I feel fine."

"Well, feeling fine and being fine are two different things. Come on, lay back down, and here, let me help." I put my arms around his shoulder, and he leaned back onto the bed.

"Chris, we will get through this together. I know you must be confused, but you have to believe these are hallucinations. They're not real. I know someone who can help find just the right doctors…"

"Unc, it figures you would think I was crazy. While I was out, I was thinking of ways to convince you that I am telling the truth. The fact is that I know what has been happening to me is totally unbelievable." I felt I had to say it, "Do you trust me?"

"Of course, I do. Chris, you're my…"

"I mean trust me enough to let me finish what I was going to say, if not for my sake, for Mom's?"

He looked at me, "You play dirty, but yeah, I'll listen to you, not just for your mom's sake."

"Thanks, I appreciate it. So where was I, oh yeah, the prom. I'll tell you the complete story someday, looking back, it was really funny, but for now I want to tell you about Tina, and how I found out she'd been kidnapped."

I went on to tell Uncle Al about my vision of St. Agatha outside of Book Revue and how when it was over, I ran to the street to call him.

"Remember when I tried to lie to you about how I knew where she was?"

"Yeah, I remember."

"Well, I knew it because I saw the room Tina was in. St. Agatha showed it to me along with all the degradation and depravity she had to endure in her time. I saw St. Agatha being raped. I saw her prison, and I saw Quintianus."

"You saw Quintianus; he's a real person?"

"Yes, more that 1,500 hundred years ago, and when you asked me if I could remember anything, I gave you his name."

I continued, "When I told you that I went for a ride last night, and I wasn't trying to find Tina, I was telling you the truth. I really was out for a drive to kind of clear my head. It was either divine providence or dumb luck that I happened to stop in front of the house where Tina was being held captive."

"Go on."

The terrors of the day came flooding back into my mind, but I had to get the story out. "I snuck inside and hid behind some boxes, but I was caught by Heriberto Quintana—about the craziest person you will ever hope to meet, except for me, of course." I lowered my head. When I looked up, I hoped Al would be smiling. He was and said,

"What happened then?"

"Well, for starters, he gives me a black eye and does this to my face," I said this pointing to my bruises.

"Quintana kills one of his guys, Ernesto, for beating up this young hooker. He then tells these two other guys, Manulo and Julio, to drag me upstairs and lock me in a room. On my way to the room, I looked over and saw Tina. Unc, she was in the exact same room that St. Agatha showed me in her vision—the exact same room!"

Should I tell Uncle Al about Juliano? I was really in a dilemma as to whether I should tell him about Juliano, but I decided not to. Saints were one thing, demons entirely another.

"I stayed in this rat and roach infested shit hole for a while before they came back for me. I didn't know what to do, and I was sure they were going to kill me. I had another vision, this time it was St. Mary Magdalene. Uncle Al, I was there. I was at the house where she wiped the feet of Jesus with her hair and anointed them with oil. Uncle Al, I saw Jesus."

"My God, Chris." Uncle Al looked totally dumbfounded and worried.

"I know. I know you think I'm nuts, and I don't blame you, but I swear on all that is holy, I am telling you the truth. Her message was that Tina was innocent, she was loved and worth saving, and that I was the one that needed to help her.

At this point, there was no way I could stop telling my story, so I continued, "I also had Tina on my mind, trying to figure a way to get us both out of there. The door opened, and Heriberto and the two guys, Manulo and Julio, dragged me into her bedroom. They tied my hands and threw me on the bed where they wanted me to rape Tina. Heriberto heard a noise downstairs and sent Manulo and Julio to see what was going on. When they didn't come back, he pulled out his gun and left the room."

I paused to take a breath and said, "I think you know what happened next because you were there, and I wasn't."

"Is that it? What about my wound? What about how it was healed? Which one of your saints did this miracle?"

"It was St. Michael, St. Michael the Archangel."

"Wait, you mean the same Michael the Archangel that drove Lucifer into hell? That Michael the Archangel?"

"I'm afraid so."

"Chris, can I speak?"

"Sure you can."

"Chris, we need to get you help. I love you, and I want you to get the help you need to stop these visions, or hallucinations, or whatever you want to call them. Chris, you can't be seeing saints."

"Why?"

"Because it's impossible. That's why."

"By whose standards is it impossible?'

"By everybody's standards, that's who."

Uncle Al was getting agitated, and I didn't want to see him get upset: "I don't want to upset you. I really don't. I only told you these things because I know you need answers to why you healed so fast. Do you want me to stop telling you the story, or should I continue?"

"What else is there to say?"

"Well, I can tell you how he did it. Don't you want to know?"

"At this point, sure, tell me. What harm can it do? I'll ask for the padded cell next to yours, so we can be together."

I started to break into a smile but stopped. "You were laying on the floor, blood pouring out of your shoulder just above your heart. I was kneeling next to you, frightened by not knowing what I would do without you around."

"It was then that St. Michael appeared to me in a vision, and when I have these visions, everything and everybody around me seems to stop in time. First, you should know that St. Michael is not only a fierce defender of God and His entire domain, but he is also known for his healing powers. Oh, and by the way, he is the patron saint of police officers."

"I knew that."

"St. Michael took me to this place, the *Michaelion;* it's a holy place, a sanctuary where there was a clear pool of water. He took his shield..."

"He had his shield?"

"Yes."

"Did he have a sword, too?"

"Yes, he did. Can I continue?"

"Yeah, sure."

"He took his shield and dipped it into the water and filled it part of the way up. He then motioned for me to cup my palms, and he poured some of the water into them. I took the water and poured it onto your wound. When the vision was over, your wound was healing. I know all of this sounds so incredible and so impossible, but it's the pure and simple truth."

"What can I say? What can I do? How can this be possible? Chris, just think of what you've told me and the impossibility of it all. I ... I don't know how to react to all this because I love you, and I don't know how to help you."

I saw the grief on Uncle Al's face, and we sat there in silence, trying to find the next words to speak to each other when all froze in time and a new vision came.

The doctors looked at St. Camillus and told him that the wound to his leg wound never heal. As a novice in the Capuchin order, he took the news with great sadness, for he was told he may never be professed. When he heard this, he lifted himself off the bed and vowed that his fervor would not be diminished, and he promised to his savior, Jesus Christ, that he would care for the sick the rest of his days.

The vision changed, and I was transported to a time and place years later.

The streets near the harbor of medieval Rome were filled with bodies of the dead and dying. St. Camillus saw the ship at the dock and knew what he must do. The friar roamed the deck among all the poor souls where he said prayers over the dead and gave the living comfort while they waited for death. The bubonic plague was a curse, but it was not for St. Camillus to understand why. All he needed to do was to try and help. The pain in his leg was getting worse, but it was his penance, his cross to bear. After all, was Jesus not made to suffer greater torments?

I saw the glow, which I had come to know well, surround St. Camillus as he stepped out of his earthly body and presented himself to me.

"The truth is hard for some to accept. It was true in the time I was alive, and it is still true in yours."

"I have tried to tell my uncle in the best way I know how, but to him, it seems impossible, and I can understand why."

"I have seen the suffering in death, and I did not understand why. It is faith that needs to guide him, and you must try to help him understand."

"But how can I help him?"

"He has also known the pain of someone he loved dying. He was given trials where his faith was tested. When you speak of these things, he will understand."

"What things? I don't know what you are talking about, and I need to know. Please, help me know what to say."

St. Camillus looked at me and knew my dilemma. None of the saints could reveal themselves to anyone but me, and Uncle Al needed to understand that. He had to have faith that I was telling the truth, even though he could not see what I saw.

"Your uncle will need to reach down into his soul for a memory and image that he has buried there, long ago."

"What image? What are you talking about?"

"The death of his father and what he was asked to do."

"Wait, what about Grandpa's death? What did Uncle Al have to do? I need to know, what did he have to do?"

"He had to do what was right, and he did."

"What do you mean—He had to do what was right?"

St, Camillus held his hand up as if to say there was no more he could do or say. I would need to figure it out myself. With that, the vision of the saint and his surroundings slowly disappeared.

I found myself back in the hospital room with Uncle Al. He was still deep in thought. I tried to remember all that was said, all that was shown me, and somehow come up with the meaning of it all. While I was sitting there thinking, it came to me, everything I was told came together.

Uncle Al, who had been silent up to now, says, "Chris, listen to me. I will do everything in my power to…" but I cut him off and said,

"How did grandpa die?"

"Chris, come on, we need to discuss this."

"Uncle Al, how did grandpa die?"

"Chris, what the hell does Grandpa's death have to do with what's happening to you."

"Uncle Al, how did grandpa die?"

Al seemed to know that I wouldn't give up on this, so he just said, "Stomach cancer."

"Was he in a lot of pain?"

"Yes." A faraway look came over his face when he answered.

"Uncle Al, what are you thinking about?"

"Chris, I'm thinking about you and what may happen if you continue to have these crazy thoughts about saints and visions."

"Come on, please, tell me what you are thinking."

"I don't remember. It was so long ago." He only said this in hopes that I would stop asking him. But I knew that he remembered everything about my grandfather's death as if it happened only yesterday.

"I think you do remember, and I think it is painful to speak about. No one would blame you, but I need to know Uncle Al. Please, I need to know."

"I just can't Chris. I just can't."

I didn't realize how tough this would be for him, so I said it for him, "He was in the hospital dying, and you were there every day, by his side, every day."

Chief Detective Al Barese lay on the bed and said nothing.

"I know how much you loved Grandpa, and I can't imagine how heartbreaking this must have been for you. You had to see this man, a strong, vital man—one who loved his family, who loved his country, who sacrificed so much to make a better life for you and all his children. You had to watch him die in one of the most painful ways that could be imagined."

A tear slowly came out of the corner of his eye, but he did not cry.

"After a while, the disease became so advanced you couldn't even recognize him. Am I right?"

Uncle Al said to no one, "He coughed up blood. He lost so much weight. He was in so much pain that the doctor had to put him on morphine."

I thought of St. Camillus and the pain he endured, and I thought of Grandpa and his pain. I could see the anguish on Uncle Al's face as he had to relive this event.

"What could you have done to help him? What is it that you could do to help relieve his pain? I know these thoughts must have gone through your mind as you sat at his bedside, totally helpless."

"Why are you doing this to me, Chris? Why?"

I heard his question, but I didn't answer. "Grandma would come to the hospital, too, as did my mom and all his sons and daughters. How awful for you to have to see your family watch him suffer. How awful it must have been for you to feel so powerless as they all prayed for him to die and end the pain."

Uncle Al looked up at me, and for the first time in my life he looked old, but as I continued, he looked away.

"When you and Grandpa were alone, he spoke to you, didn't he?"

"He was so weak, so tired."

"He asked you to help him, didn't he? He asked you to help him die."

Uncle Al immediately looked up at me, astonished.

"Simple. Only turn the morphine drip, and he would have fallen into a coma. He would have died, finally free of the pain that was tormenting him."

"How? How could you know that? No one knows that." Uncle Al practically whispered this.

"But you didn't do it, did you? You couldn't kill your father, even though you wanted him to rest in peace. You didn't kill him because you knew it wasn't your decision to make. It was God's."

Uncle Al continued to stare at me, "He was my dad, and I had to watch him suffer. He asked me for help, and I wouldn't help him. I loved him so much, and I refused him the last thing he asked me to do."

"Grandpa was in so much pain, so incoherent; he couldn't possibly understand what he was asking you to do. He loved you so much, and he would have never wanted you to take on such a burden."

There were tears in my uncle's eyes, and his voice started to crack: "It would have been so easy—just turn the little knob. It would have been so easy."

"It would have been so easy, but it was not the right thing to do. God has plans for all of us, and Grandpa's suffering was part of His plan. I don't profess to know God's will. All I know is that His will be done."

"He lived another 4 days in such pain I can't bear to think of. He died before I had the chance to tell him I was sorry, to tell him I loved him, to tell him what he meant to me, to tell him I couldn't kill him, even though he was in such awful pain."

For a minute or two my uncle wept uncontrollably. He cried a torrent of tears, and his chest heaved with sobs. The pain he had carried over all these years must have been a torture for him, but he kept it to himself, hidden in the back of his mind, so no one but him would ever know.

Uncle Al began to wipe his tears away "How do you know all of this Chris? How could you possibly know what no one else knows?"

"I know because I was told."

"Told? You were told? By who, no one in this world knows about any of this? Who told you about Dad?"

"You're right Unc, no one in this world; it was St. Camillus de Lellis who told me. He told me this, so that you would believe what I've said about my visions and about all the saints who guide me through their visions. He knew of your secret. He knew your inner anguish and the guilt you feel over not being able to help your father."

"What?"

"Yeah Uncle Al, he also told me to tell you that you did the right thing."

"The right thing?"

"Yes, the right thing."

Uncle Al began to weep again covering his face with his hands, and I went to his side, and we embraced.

"I love you."

"I love you, too."

Chapter 19

We both sat in silence, not knowing what to say next but not wanting to be apart from each other. Can anyone imagine how deep this man's pain must be? He has been consumed with a secret buried so deep in his soul that he was never able to forgive himself.

For more than an hour, we said nothing when Uncle Al turned to me, "I believe you, Chris. No one could have known what had happened between me and my father. You must be telling me the truth."

"Thank you, Uncle Al. Your faith, your belief that I am telling the truth means more to me than you will ever know."

"Grandpa, my dad, was a great man. Not the way some measure greatness today, by fame or money, but true greatness that comes from the love, kindness and strength he showed everyone who knew him."

I knew what he was talking about. "Grandpa was always proud of you and our whole family, and he said it to me all the time."

"I will always regret that I never had the chance to let him know how much I love him, how much I miss him."

"St. Camillus told me to make sure you know that you did the right thing."

"Do you think that Dad will forgive me for doing the right thing?"

"He already has."

We both looked at each other, and Uncle Al said, "Thank you for that, Chris. It means so much to me just to be able to tell you and to know that you and your St. Camillus understand."

We talked for what seemed like hours. Uncle Al wanted to unload this burden of guilt he felt all these years, and the time seemed to be right. He spoke of the many things that he remembered of his father, of all the things little and big that built on the love they both felt for each other.

"Chris, can I tell you a little story?"

"Sure!"

"I was about twelve-years-old, and I loved to play baseball. Every chance I got, I would go to the field and play with my buddies. I wasn't that good, but it really didn't matter because I was having fun. Well, there was a YMCA league forming a travel team that was comprised of twelve and thirteen-year-old kids. All my buddies wanted to try out, so we all ran down to the field. The coaches put us through the drills and practice to see how we played and to see if we were good enough to make this elite club."

I just sat there and listened to him speak, and I was glad because I knew he needed to say what was on his mind.

"When my friends and I left the tryouts, we were all sure we had made the team, and I ran home to tell my mom all about it. When I got home, I started rattling off all the excitement of the day, but my mother was cooking. She had her back to me, and all that she would say was, "That's good, Spartaco."

"What I didn't know was the coach had called her earlier and told her that I didn't make the team. All my friends had made the team, except for me, and she didn't have the heart to tell me. When Dad came home my mom told him about the call from the coach. I was in my room oiling my glove when dad came in and sat down next to me."

"Spartaco, I have to talk with you."

"Hey Dad, did you hear about the tryouts for the travel team? I'll bet that they want to put me in right field, but I want to tryout for second base. I think that I can…" but he stopped me.

"Spartaco, I have some bad news."

I became nervous and asked, "What bad news?"

"Dad put his arms around my shoulder and told me that I hadn't made the travel team. I was heartbroken; I didn't know how I was going to face my friends. Back then, I only thought about what that meant to me. I know now that it was the hardest thing for my dad to do because he knew how much I loved to play baseball."

"What happened, then?" I asked.

"Well, Dad decided that he would work with me, so I could become a better player, this from a man who grew up on a farm, became a tailor and never played or even held a baseball. Dad would watch ballgames on TV with me just to understand how the game was played. We practiced daily when he came home from work—fielding, throwing, catching, hitting. He was exhausted, but he made it a point to be sure he was there for me. I guess there are a lot of dads who do this for their sons, but he did it for me, and now that I am an adult, I realize how very special our time together was."

"Wow, I can't ever imagine Grandpa playing ball."

"Oh, he tried and got fairly good at it."

"What about you?" I was hoping for a fairy tale ending.

"Well, I actually became a pretty good ball player, made the travel team after someone dropped out, and I became the permanent right fielder. It was a great feeling and Dad was there, in the stands, at every one of my games. I know it sounds like a *Leave it to Beaver* storyline, but it's the truth. I guess it's nothing really special, but it means everything to me."

"It's a great story about you and Grandpa."

"Yeah, it's a good story. Chris, can I ask you about your saints?"

"Sure you can."

"Why can't I see them?

"I wish I knew. Sometimes it's a great burden to be the only one who can communicate with the saints. Now that you know, however, I can have someone to share these visions with."

"Did they ever tell you why you were chosen?"

"No, they never did, and I've wondered about that for years. It's not like I'm such a holy person, or that I've done anything special. I'm just me. Sometimes I think that I was chosen because I'm nothing special, just a regular guy, flaws and all."

"Did the saints ever tell you how or why they perform their miracles?"

"No, here's what I think: they are moved by the spirit, and this is manifest in their miracles and good works."

"You said that you saw Jesus Christ in one of your visions. Did He say anything to you?"

I thought about this question and how I might answer it so it would have meaning "No, He never spoke to me. In some ways, I am glad He didn't because I wouldn't know what to say. He's my Lord and Savior, what could I possible say to Him?"

"I guess you're better off just speaking to Him in your prayers. This way, you can talk, and He can listen. By the way, do you still say prayers before you go to bed?"

I smiled at Uncle Al. "Yeah, I still do. Imagine a big chooch like me, praying like a little kid."

"I think it's nice; anyway, I've got another question. When do you get to see these saints, their visions? Do all of them speak to you?"

"I can get these visions at anytime, in any place, When I do, I see the saints and speak to them. It's kind of weird. When I have the visions, everything around me just stands still, like time stops for everyone but me. So far, all of them have spoken to me, except for St. Michael. I don't know why he didn't speak, but it doesn't seem to matter. You are his miracle, his gift to me." To be able to talk to Uncle Al, to pour out my innermost thoughts and to have him believe me was what I was missing.

"I know I'll have a million more questions to ask, but right now I'm spent. Know what I mean?"

"Yeah, I know what you mean. I'll be leaving now, but I'll be back tomorrow, and we can continue talking."

"Okay."

"Thanks for believing me."

Uncle Al smiled and said, "You're welcome. See you tomorrow."

Chapter 20

By the time I got home, it was 8:30 p.m., and I was exhausted. The entire event happened in less than one day, but it seemed like it took far longer. I sat down in my chair next to the TV and turned it on. The only thing I was interested in watching was the evening news, so I turned to the local cable news channel. I wanted to see how the whole incident was being reported. The news anchor, a woman with blond hair and a total of 64 teeth, spoke to the camera:

"…MS-13 suffered a major setback in their criminal enterprise with the death of Heriberto Quintana and two of his henchmen. A third man was wounded in the confrontation and is now in police custody. The gang reportedly forced minor girls and boys into prostitution by…"

I assumed that either Manulo or Julio had been killed in the gun battle, along with Heriberto. They must have added Ernesto to the total, and that meant all were accounted for, except for Juliano, but it's unlikely he will ever be found.

The anchor continued, "The police spokesman said that all the young girls and boys are being taken to the hospital where child services will be there to help. They will be reunited with family once the doctors and counselors exam them after their horrific ordeal. In a related event, Chief Detective, Al Barese is recovering from wounds he suffered in the line of duty. Chief Barese—a 36 year police veteran and hero in the Parkway Murders case—confronted the leader of MS-13, Heriberto Quintana. In a fierce gun battle, Chief Barese killed him, but not before Quintana had killed a prostitute caught in the line of fire."

Wow, I thought, they got it right for a change. Note to myself—I have to remember to tell Uncle Al to get a better picture for the news network. The photo was awful. Then again, maybe I'll wait until he feels better, and then I could break his balls for a change.

I got up from the TV and went to the kitchen to get something to eat. I returned to the TV to watch some more news, but before I finished half of the sandwich I made, I fell dead asleep.

When I woke up, I saw sunshine coming through the sliding glass door that led to a deck off my living room. I rubbed my eyes and checked my watch, and I couldn't believe it was past 10 a.m. I had slept on my couch for more than twelve hours, so I guess I needed the rest. I went into the bathroom and looked at my face, cringed and brushed my teeth. After I shaved, I got into the shower, washed all the grime away, and for the next half-hour, I just let the hot water run down my body. I felt like a new man—clean, shaven, with sparkling teeth, and I was ready to tackle another day.

As I picked up my dirty clothes off the floor, a small piece of paper dropped out of my shirt pocket. It was Beth's number, and I made a mental note to myself to call her and plan our first date. I also needed to go to the coin shop and take care of what was needed there. But before I did any of those things, I needed to call Uncle Al.

His phone rang, and he picked up: "Chief Barese, I mean, Hello?"

"Think you're back at work, don't you?"

"Yeah, the phone's been ringing off the hook. Everyone has called to see how I'm doing—from the family, the county executive and the police commissioner to the head cook in the cafeteria. It's really nice, but right now, all I want to do is rest. The phone keeps ringing, and I have to keep saying the same things over and over again."

"Sorry Unc, I didn't mean to bother you, but I wanted to let you know that I can't come by until later. I've got to take care of some business at the shop, but I will be there to see you after 3p.m., okay?"

"Sure, no problem, now what about that hot looking nurse, the one that your mom sent you, you know, Beth Della Russo?"

Like always, I knew he was busting my chops…remember he's that super hero Ball Breaker Man. I said, "Wow, I forgot all about her? What did she look like?"

"Like an angel who speaks Italian. By the way, do you speak to angels, too?"

"No, not yet, but I've got my order in."

"Why don't you give her a call, big shot?" I could see him smiling at the other end of the phone.

I laughed and said, "I'll see you later."

"Okay…I love you."

I usually said it first, but I just answered back, "I love you, too."

After breakfast, I got into the car and drove south down Rt. 110 to my shop. I opened the door to two days of mail lying on the floor. I sat down at my desk and went through the various envelopes; there were some mail orders for coins and other packages. There was really nothing important, so I tossed the junk mail in the trash, which is what I wanted to do with the bills, but I filed them, so I could pay them by the end of the month.

I went to my website and saw that there were quite a few orders for the various coins and medallions I sell, and that made me happy. I'm always happy when I know I can eat and pay the rent. Anyway, I began to process the orders and get them ready for shipping when I thought of Beth. I reached into my pocket and found the paper with her number, but it was too early to call her at home, so I decided I would try the hospital.

The phone rang: "Hello, Huntington Hospital, how may I help you?"

"Good morning, can I speak with Nurse Elizabeth Della Russo; she works on the fourth floor."

"Let me see, ah yes, here is her extension, I'll put you through now. Have a nice day."

"You, too," and my call was put through to the nurses' station.

"Nurse Diane Breuer, how may I help you?"

"Good morning, may I speak with Nurse Della Russo?"

"Whom shall I say is calling?"

"Would you please tell her that Chris Pella is calling?"

"Wait, are you Rambo, I mean Rocky?"

"Huh?"

"Are you Rambo or Rocky?" and Nurse Breuer starts cracking up.

"Did she tell you all about me getting beaten up?" I'm sitting at my desk turning different shades of red.

"One thing you should know, all the female nurses' around the world have a code we live by."

"What's that?" I said.

"Anytime there's story about a new guy, you spill your guts, or you're out of the sisterhood. By the way, Beth was just elected the president of our chapter after the story she told about you." Nurse Breuer laughed out loud, and I think she started to sense I was feeling embarrassed, so she said, "Hang on. She's right here."

"Nurse Elizabeth Della Russo, how may I help you?"

"Thanks for letting the world know about my unfortunate accident with a bad guy's fist."

"Oh, you're welcome; it brought much needed comic relief, at your expense of course, to the very stressful job we nurses do every day."

"Well, glad I could be of assistance."

Now Beth can't hold it in any longer, and she busts out laughing, and I could hear some more laughing in the background as the nurses hold their first annual "Make Chris Pella Feel Like an Idiot Day."

"Sorry, Rocky…it was too good to pass up. How come you called, huh?" Beth knew exactly why I was calling, and I could almost see her smiling on the other end of the phone.

"I wanted to ask you out for Saturday night. What do you say?"

"Wait a minute, buster. Where are you taking me? Remember your promise…"

I stopped her and said, "Yeah I know, the dinner of a lifetime, so I figured that I would leave it up to you. Pick anyplace you want to go, and I'll gladly take you there."

"Well, let me see, there's always Mac's or Prime, but I don't know if I feel like steak. Hmmm, how about Piccolo's, no it's usually too crowded on Saturday nights—I know, Besito! I love Mexican food, and they make the best…"

She's speaking, and I'm enjoying the fact that she picked some of the top places in town so, I say, "You're not scaring me. I just got my allowance, and the money's burning a hole in my pocket."

"Well, in that case, why don't you just make me dinner?"

"What?"

"You heard me. Why don't you just make me dinner at your place?"

By this time, I smell a rat, or an Uncle Rat, "You've been speaking with my uncle, haven't you?"

Now she starts to sound indignant,"Who me? Do you think he would do something so deceitful, so devious as to interfere with what he hopes will be a budding new relationship. I take umbrage at your insinuation that he would act in such an underhanded manner. Of course, he told me! He said you were a great cook, and that you have a condo overlooking the harbor, so what do you say?"

"Beth, I really want to take you someplace nice. I'm not the great cook that I'm sure Al told you I was. Come on. Let's go out, anyplace you want."

Now she is getting peeved at me, so she says, "I don't want to go out to a restaurant; I want you to make me dinner! Si sente che cosa sto dicendo?"

"Si, I hear what you're saying. But remember, if you don't like my cooking, you still have to go out with me again—you can't hold it against me, agreed?"

"Agreed! So I'll get your address from your Uncle. Do you want Al to give me a time, or do you want to tell me when I should get to your home?"

I can't believe that I've got the both of them giving me orders: "No, I'll tell you, how about 6:30 p.m. for drinks and dinner will follow."

"Sounds great, Rocky. Now I have to get back to work. I guess I'll see you later when you visit."

"I count the moments!"

She starts laughing and hangs up, and I lean back in my chair and smile.

Chapter 21

After I hung up the phone, I started to think of two things; first, clean the house, actually my condo looks pretty good—and second, what should I make for dinner? I wanted this to be the best dinner I've ever made. After all, making a good impression on Beth was my goal.

As it was Wednesday, I figured that I had three days to decide, shop, clean and for the bruises to heal.

I spent the rest of the day doing my work and figuring that I would get to the hospital around 5PM and spend the evening with Uncle Al. I entered my sales into the computer, processed and packed up the orders and went to the post office to ship all the items before I headed to the hospital.

While I was in the car, I started to plan my menu. I had all the makings for cocktails—vodka gimlets are my favorite. I needed to look for a good red, maybe Chianti, and a good white wine, definitely Sauvignon Blanc, to serve at dinner and in case Beth wanted either. For dinner, I thought that I'd start with scallops in cognac sauce, then a pasta course of capellini with fresh tomato and basil, and for the main course, a traditional veal osso buco with roasted potatoes (I'm not crazy about rice) and sautéed broccoli rabe. I thought that the menu sounded pretty good, and I planned what I would need to buy at the Italian specialty market where I shop for my special dinners.

All this thinking of food made me hungry, so I stopped into the local deli for a quick roast beef sandwich and iced tea. There is a little area on the side of the deli with tables and seats, so I went and sat down. It is a very peaceful place overlooking Huntington Harbor – I go there often. It was nice being able to just relax and think about all that's happened. When I finished my sandwich, I took one long look at the beautiful harbor and all the boats, and I got back in the car and headed for the hospital.

I parked the car and ran in to see if I could spend some time with Beth and Fred before I went to see Uncle Al. When I got to the nurses' station, Beth wasn't there, but Nurse Breuer was and – my face a dead giveaway – she immediately assumed that I was Rambo or Rocky.

"Hey Rocky! You looking for Beth?"

"Yeah, is she around?"

"Your big date isn't until Saturday, right? So what gives?"

"You're kidding! She told you about our date?"

"Remember the sisterhood! We get all – well, almost all – the details, and we won't take 'no' for an answer."

"Is she around?"

"Sorry, she's gone for the day, but if you have a message – no matter how hot or steamy it is! – you can leave it with me." Nurse Breuer started to crack up.

"No thanks, I'll tell her myself. By the way, how's Fred Klein doing? I'm going stop by to say hello."

"Fred's doing so much better. He's still weak but he's eating, walking around and taking his medication."

"That's great; I'll head over to see him."

"Okay Rocky, see you later."

What could I do? I guess I was stuck with that name, so I just better live with it. I headed down the hall to room 496 and peeked through the door. Through the crack, Fred looked up and gave me a big smile.

"Come in! Come in, Chris. I'm so glad you stopped by."

"How are you doing, Fred?"

"Great! I'm doing great. The doctor and the nurses tell me that I'm getting stronger. Hopefully I'll get out soon."

"That's wonderful news."

"I got some good news about Tina, too. Cathy told me that she's out of the emergency room. They've done all the tests, and it looks like she will be fine, health-wise, but still–I'm very concerned about her mental state."

"I know she'll be fine as long as she has you and your family to lean on. You'll all be in my prayers."

"Thanks, Chris. That means a lot."

"Well, I'm off to see my Uncle Al and get my balls broken."

"Yeah, I stopped by his room and said hello. I thanked him for all he did. He shot the bastard who would have ruined my Tina, and now he got what he deserved. I'm just so sorry Al got shot."

"He's getting great care, and I'm sure he'll be fine. Now, get some rest and I'll stop by tomorrow to see you."

"Thanks, Chris. See you soon."

With that, I left Fred's room and went across the hall to see Uncle Al. When I opened the door, I saw that he was asleep, so I quietly went in and found a chair to sit on until he woke up.

It was then that I had a very troubling vision.

> *He ran into the cave hoping to stay away from the demons that tormented him constantly. But as he welcomed the darkness, he realized that he was not alone. Looking around, the beasts came from behind the rocks, out of holes in the ground; they crawled on the ceiling and descended on him. Fearful and suffering greatly, the outcome seemed preordained. There would be no reprieve as the devils beat him to death.*

I stood there in the darkness with this man and watched him die. It was heartbreaking. Another man, maybe a servant, then came into the cave. He lifted and carried the body outside, mourning his passing.

> *The servant reached down and lifted the lifeless form from the cave floor. Overcome with grief, he laid the body near the entrance to the cave. As the servant mourned, a group of hermits found their way to the place where he lay and they knelt in prayer for this holy man. In the midst of their prayer, his eyes opened – all were astonished that he was alive. Sitting up weakly, unable to stand, he yelled at the men, "Take me back! Take me back immediately! I must face these demons! Take me back now!"*
>
> *Afraid, they did not know what to do, but St. Anthony would have none of it. "Take me back now!"*
>
> *With that, they lifted him and carried him back to the cave. When they let him down, all ran out in terror. St. Anthony screamed, "Come forth! I am not afraid! Come forth and face the might of the God." The demons had transformed into vicious beasts wanting to tear him apart. As the devils approached, a flash of light appeared, so blindingly bright that it filled the cave. The demons became so frightened that they shrieked and ran to the hell from whence they came.*

As St. Anthony the Abbot lay on the floor of the cave, his spirit stepped out of his body and came to my side.

I was astounded. "What was that light?"

"It was the light of heaven and the mercy of God. I was in fear and thought that God had abandoned me, but He did not. He was by my side always."

"Why did you think he abandoned you?"

"He let me suffer, and I could not comprehend why."

"Did you ever find out the truth?"

"I did. God was always beside me. Even in my darkest moments, He was there. I had to prove my faith, show that I had no fear because of my faith – and He would abide my battle with these demons."

"Why are you showing me these things? Your visions – what does it all mean for me?"

"You will be facing your own demons. You will be tormented and you will know true fear. You may believe you are alone in all this but you are not. The Lord is with you, and we are with you, always."

"What will I...." But St. Anthony was swallowed by the light and disappeared, and I was back in the hospital.

Chapter 22

I sat for a few minutes in silence, recalling the vision and wondering what was going to happen now. St. Anthony told me that I would be facing my own demons and I would need to be strong. I remembered the demon Juliano and how powerless I felt when I was tied and held captive. I remembered how St. Mary Magdalene confronted the devil Juliano and how she drove him back to the hell he came from.

What if I was alone, and he appeared? Would I be brave enough to face him? Could I survive such a struggle? I knew the Lord and the saints would be there for me, but I'm no St. Anthony. If I were to die, I guess I would stay dead. With all these thoughts going through my head, Uncle Al woke up.

"Hey Chris. How long have you been here?"

"Oh, I just got here. I've been waiting for you to wake up. Actually, the peace and quiet did me some good." I didn't want to tell him about my latest vision – at least not now. I needed to work it out in my mind.

I asked him, "How are you feeling?"

"Oh, pretty good. I am in a little pain, but I guess it would have been far worse if it wasn't for St. Michael."

"I am so grateful that you're okay."

"I know you are. Hey, did Fred tell you he stopped by? He seemed to be doing fine, and he told me that Tina is recovering nicely. I couldn't be happier for him."

"Yeah, I stopped to see Fred before I came in to see you. He told me."

"By the way, how are you getting along with Beth?"

"What is it with you both? How come you and she are planning our dates?"

"What do you mean?" He said innocently.

"You know what I mean. Getting me to cook her dinner for our first date. Do you know what kind of pressure that is?"

"I have no idea what you're talking about. I would never do such an underhanded thing to the nephew I love most in this world. How can you say such a thing? Who would have told you such a wild story?"

"Beth told me."

"Beth?"

"Listen, she gave you up quicker than Saddam Hussein in that rat hole."

"Oh, well. Guilty as charged."

We were laughing out loud now. Guessing that I would really enjoy cooking for Beth, and that she would love it too, a smile grew over his face.

"Hey, Unc, can I ask you a question?"

"Sure you can."

"You've been in life and death situations, you've confronted the worst of your own fears. What did you do to overcome that fear? How did you find the courage?"

"Chris, the first thing is that you can never overcome that kind of fear. The fear is just there, and you need to face up to it. Take the instance where I came face-to-face with Quintana. He had just killed that poor kid, and then he raised his gun and pointed it at me. I was beyond frightened."

"What did you do?"

"I don't know how to explain it, but I can try to put it into words. In the place you are in, there is only you and your fears. You reach down inside your whole being, and you know there is only one way to survive: to face your fears."

"Is that how you felt when you faced Quintana?"

"Yeah, it was exactly like that. I knew that I could die but I also knew that bastard couldn't live, not after what he has done most of his life. At that point there seemed to be only him and me in the room, and my fears seemed to change into something I could use. I just did what I needed to do. I don't know if that makes any sense to you."

"It does. It really does. Thanks."

"You're welcome. What brought all this on?"

I didn't want to confide in him about Juliano just yet. I knew he was still hurt, and I didn't want to stress him out, so I said, "I don't know, I guess after all that's happened I was doing a little introspection, trying to see what I could have done, what I did wrong. Would I have had your guts?"

"Chris, I hope you never have to go through what you went through again, but I do know one thing: If you had to, you would have the guts to face any fear. No doubt in my mind."

"Wow, coming from the man who shot both the Parkway Murders serial killer and Heriberto Quintana, that is some compliment. All kidding aside, thanks."

"You're welcome. Now, what are you going to make Beth for dinner?"

"What, so you can tell the world? You're the last person I would tell anyway!"

"I'm deeply hurt."

"Good. You deserve it," I said, with a big smile

We sat and talked for a while. I genuinely enjoy these times; it's what I used to do with my mom and dad. We talked a little more about the saints, and I revealed some of my visions. I couldn't tell him about how St. Augustine allowed me to see visions of purgatory. Hell, words would never be adequate. But I did tell him the story of my prom night, and he started laughing so hard that tears came rolling out of his eyes. He could barely contain himself, only taking a breath long enough to say, "Good going Romeo...." Then he convulsed into hysterical laughter.

Rocky, Rambo and now Romeo. Everyone seemed to be enjoying themselves at my expense. Beth, Nurse Breuer and always, Uncle Al, but I didn't care. Just to see him laughing and smiling was a wonderful thing. Finally, he calmed down and said to me, "Chris that is the funniest story I've ever heard. The only sad thing is that I can never tell it to anyone."

"Not unless you want to get locked up."

It was late and I knew that visiting hours had already ended, so I said goodnight to Uncle Al. I promised that I'd be back to see him.

"Chris, before you go, I want you to know that you are brave. Very few people would have done what you did to save Tina. Never doubt your courage, because if you need it, it will be there."

I smiled and said, "I hope you're right."

"I know, I'm right. See you tomorrow. I love you."

"Love you too."

Chapter 23

So in spite of the fact that I have a shop and business to run, I make the time to go shopping. My favorite specialty shop in the village is Grometti's Fine Italian Foods. It's a trip down memory lane, with all the aromas and flavors of Arthur Avenue in the Bronx. I love to look at the homemade pastas and freshly made antipasto platters. Vincent and Angelica Grometti are the owners and managers; they've known me and my family for years.

"Hey, Chris, long time no see. How's your Uncle Al? I heard all about it on the news, and I'm going over to see him later today."

"Thank God, he's fine now, but he could have died. But hey, what are you talking about? I saw you last week when I had to sell a kidney to pay for that marinated flank steak."

"Oh, don't worry about that, you've got another kidney."

"Yeah, and I might have to sell that one to pay for what I have to buy today."

"Oh, a big order!" Vincent turned away from me and yelled out to his wife in the back of the store, "Angelica, you can book that Mediterranean cruise now!" He turned back and asked, "Should I bring in extra help to load the truck or are you gonna eat it here?"

"Wise ass. Just take my order and I'll pick it up on the way home."

"Heh, heh. Okay, what do you want?" I told him my order and that it was an especially important occasion. Everything had to be perfect.

"Special occasion, huh. What's the special occasion?"

"I have a date with the most beautiful girl in the world – except for Angelica of course – and I want to make her the best dinner ever." I told him about the scallop and pasta courses, then said, "I am making veal osso buco for the main course, and I need your best veal shanks, Vincent."

"Hey, maybe I'll come over for dinner, what do you say? Help you out with that girlfriend."

"You can't! I won't do that to Angelica. The minute my girlfriend sees you I know I'll lose her – after all, have you looked in the mirror lately?"

"Ah, you're right. I've been told my looks could sink – I mean, launch – a thousand ships."

"I've got to get back to the shop but I'll stop by after work. Ciao!"

"Grazie e arrivederci!"

I left Grometti's and walked back to the coin shop, spending the rest of the day filling orders, waiting on customers and evaluating a collection that I'd just bought. There was some junk, but there were some treasures. I was excited to sort through them all.

It was getting late and I wanted to say hi to Beth, so I called her at the hospital before I left the shop. The last time I was at the hospital, she had already gone home. I wanted to hear her voice.

"Nurses' station, Beth Della Russo speaking."

"Hi Beth, it's me, Chris. How are you doing?"

"Hey Rocky, where were you yesterday?"

"Oh, I got to the hospital late, and you'd gone home."

"Oh well – maybe the gods are conspiring against us?

"They better not be. At least not until I get to make you dinner."

"I'm glad you're at least buying some of the good stuff from Grometti's."

"How the heck…."

"My family has known Vincent and Angelica for years; they make the best foods. I was there and asked them if they knew you, and I found out they did."

"That son of a – he better not have told you what I'm making." I was getting a little pissed off.

"Don't worry, Rocky; I tried to worm it out of him, but he was tight-lipped and loyal to you. Your secret is safe."

Relieved, I said, "Good. By the way, do you like tripe and lamb brains."

"Don't even try that on me. Ask my grandmother – she'll tell you what I do to people who tell me all those animal parts are delicacies in Italy."

"Okay, okay. I promise not to serve cow guts and sheep brains."

"You better not, if you value your life."

I finally found something that put Beth on the defensive, and I wanted to save that knowledge for a rainy day. We spoke a few minutes more. She told me that she was leaving at 5 p.m. but would see me for our big date tomorrow.

I said, "Okay, see you tomorrow?"

And she said, "See you tomorrow."

It was just a few days after meeting Beth, and I knew I was hooked, including the line and the sinker.

Chapter 24

Things at the shop were slow, so I closed up early and went to Grometti's to pick up the food I'd ordered. The place was crowded, as it usually was on a Friday evening, so I just took a number and waited my turn. When my number came up, Vincent motioned for me to come to the other side of the counter.

"I didn't realize your girlfriend was Beth Della Russo! She is a lovely young lady and comes from a wonderful family. You're one lucky guy!"

"I know I am! Now all I have to do is make sure I don't screw it up."

"Hey, you're good looking and come from a great family, too. Everyone likes you. But there is one problem you got."

"Oh yeah? What's that?"

"You've got no fairy godfather or godmother."

"Well, where do I get them?"

"Right here!" Vincent and Angelica hand me two big boxes of everything I needed for my dinner and much more.

"What's all this?"

"It's a present from your fairy godparents. You take this and make Beth the best meal she ever ate. Don't come back and tell me that you screwed up, you hear?"

I looked at these two beautiful people and gave them a big hug.

"I really can't accept this, but I know you won't let me pay, so all I can say is '*Sono più grato che lei sa, l'amo entrambi.*'"

"Don't worry, we know you're grateful. We love you too."

With that, I hugged them both again and left the store.

I drove home and put all the wonderful food in the refrigerator. The Grometti's also included some of their fabulous miniature pastries for dessert, and I knew that it would really be the dinner of a lifetime that Beth asked for.

I left my condo and jumped in the car to go to the hospital. When I got there I stopped by Fred's room first but he wasn't there so I went to see Uncle Al. He was looking rested. I asked him how he was doing.

"Oh, I'm fine; the doctor is going to take me down to run some more tests, but I think that it's more a precaution than anything serious. I'm not worried. I've got an angel – an archangel watching over me."

I said, "You certainly do. Don't piss him off, though! He can be pretty tough."

Uncle Al just smiled. We spoke some more, and he told me that the Governor's office called – he was fast becoming a celebrity. The representative of the governor had asked about his condition and whether he needed anything. "I told him that I didn't need anything, but my nephew might need a loan to pay for all the food he bought at Grometti's."

"How the hell do you know these things? Did Beth tell you?"

"No, she didn't. By the way, did you know that Vincent and I went to the same high school?"

Now he busts out laughing, and I resign myself to the fact that my life is no longer my own. I might as well get used to it.

"Okay, I give up. By the way, I'm taking a crap at 8 p.m. – tell your girlfriend, okay?"

He laughs even harder, and I join in. When you come to think of it, it's a really small world. Mine was becoming the size of a cozy Volkswagen Bug.

"The Grometti's made me a present of the food I'm making for Beth. They really are the nicest people."

"They certainly are. So you're ready for your big night?"

"Yeah, I'll clean the condo tonight and do what I can to prep for the meal. I'm planning to close the shop at 12 p.m. on Saturday, and then I'll finish everything else. It should be fun. I only hope she likes it."

"She'll love it. I think she also likes you, maybe a lot."

"How do you know these things? I mean…no, I don't know what I mean."

"It's very easy, Chris, I am the Chief Detective for Suffolk County, State of New York, and I have access to the latest technology along with the unrivaled manpower that are represented by the Suffolk County Police Force."

I looked at Al and said, very seriously, "Did she say something to you?"

"Yeah, she said something to me. She likes you, Chris. So don't fuck it up."

"I won't. I better not."

Two orderlies entered the room. They rolled in a gurney and set it next to the bed.

"Ready for your ride, Chief?"

"Yeah, just keep it under the speed limit."

Together they helped Uncle Al lift himself off the bed and onto the gurney. I must have had a worried look on my face because he said to me,

"Don't worry, I'll be fine. Just be sure to enjoy yourselves. Let me know all the sordid details."

With that, the orderlies pushed the cart into the hallway and down to wherever they do the tests. I knew everything was fine, but I was worried, anyway. I went into the hallway and watched as they took Uncle Al to the elevator for his tests.

I wished Beth was here so we could just talk, but she had already gone home. I felt kind of lonely. I did have my date with her, though, and that made me happy. I thought I would head home and get a jump on all the stuff I needed to do before she came.

I was actually beginning to feel like a teenager with a major crush.

Chapter 25

Well, today's the day, I thought to myself. When I got home the night before, I cleaned the condo from top to bottom and began to prepare a few things so that I could be ready to cook them in time for dinner. The food that the Grometti's gave me was perfect. The veal shanks looked especially good, but I knew I needed to allow enough time for the osso buco to cook and for the meat and vegetable juices to thicken.

When I woke, I left home and drove to the shop early, so that I could get as much done as possible. I continued to evaluate the coins I had bought. I was a little more than halfway through when I figured that I'd made back what I paid for the collection, which made me feel good. As I continued to work, the phone rang, "Hello, St. Aloysius of Gonzaga Coins and Currency."

"Hey Romeo, just wanted to call and wish you good luck on your date tonight."

"Thanks, Unc, I'll need it."

"Are you kidding? You are the best cook I know – next to grandma and your mom, of course."

"I doubt it, but thanks for the compliment. I'm just spending a little more time here, then I'm heading back home to make the dinner. I'll be by to see you, but I can't stay long."

"Chris, don't be silly. I'm fine, and you've got to get ready. I'll see you tomorrow. Fred and I are scheduled to play a game of gin rummy and I'll have plenty of company all day with family and visitors. Just have a great time."

"Thanks, Uncle Al, I will." And with that, we hung up.

It was nearly noon when I finished my work, closed up the shop and got into the car. As I put my key in the ignition to start the engine, I received a vision.

As he sat in this prison, he pondered his situation and prayed for guidance in what he must do before he was to be executed. The emperor had decreed that he would be beaten and stoned to death, and the man had accepted his fate.

While he waited for his meal, he continued to pray. A short while passed before the jailer slid the key into the lock and opened the door. A meal of bread and water was put onto the floor of the cell, but the prisoner was more interested in the jailer than in the food.

"What is it that bothers you?"

The jailer looked at the man sitting on the ground. "Why is it that you are interested in my troubles?"

"I am interested in all of God's children and I look to help those that I can help."

"How can you help me, a prisoner condemned to death?"

"My body may be a prisoner and I may soon die, but my spirit, my soul, will remain free and alive in the name of Christ."

"My business is my own."

"I only seek to help, to understand what it is that troubles you. Perhaps I can help."

"How can you help my blind daughter to see? How can you do this?"

With that the holy man knelt in his prison cell and began to pray. He prayed so fervently that the jailer could only stare at the man kneeling on the floor and say nothing at all.

When he was done, the prisoner said, "Go home now, your daughter can see."

As I stood staring at the vision before me, St. Valentine's spirit rose from his body and said, "Even as we await death, we must continue to serve the Lord in whatever he commands. It is His will that the young girl see, and it is through His power that she can."

"I cannot understand how you can be so generous and forgiving knowing that you will be put to death at the hands of people like your jailer."

"It is not for me to judge these people; it is only for God to judge, and He will when the final days are here."

The vision then changed: It was the next day and the jailer returned to the cell. St. Valentine, in the midst of praying, looked up to see his jailer standing before him. The jailer had tears in his eyes.

"Why is it you cry?"

The jailer stood in front of St. Valentine, tears flowing from his eyes and down his cheeks. "My daughter, she...she can see."

The saint smiled at the man. "It is through the power of the Lord, our God, that she has been given this gift."

"How...how did this come to be? How did your God make this happen?" The jailer was totally baffled.

"In Him all things are possible."

St. Valentine rose and stood by the jailer. They looked at each other for a long moment; then the jailer said, "It is beyond my power to help you. If I could, I would free you to go in peace; but I cannot go against the Emperor's command."

"I know my fate, and it is sealed."

"Can I do anything for you?" The jailer was now grief-stricken that he was not able to help.

With that St. Valentine handed his jailer a note. The jailer took the note and read it aloud. "From your Valentine."

"Take this to your daughter, and tell her that I am happy she can see again."

St. Valentine looked at me and smiled. "You have been told that you will need to face the vilest of evil and have the courage to prevail. You should also know that you will find happiness and love and that it will sustain you all your days."

St. Valentine then handed me a note. It was written in Latin and I read it out loud, "Ex tua Valentine." I read it and looked back up. "From your Valentine."

"This is for you to give to anyone you choose. You must choose wisely, for the heart needs true love so that it can keep from being broken. My fellow saints wish this for you, and we will pray you find your happiness, your love."

The bright light encircled St. Valentine. He smiled at me as he disappeared, and I smiled back at him. I was very happy.

Chapter 26

Looking out the window of my car, I saw the traffic on Main Street was getting heavy for lunch hour, so I made my way into traffic and drove home. There, I set about making what I hoped would be Beth's dinner of a lifetime. For those of you who haven't made osso buco, it generally takes about two hours, not counting prep time – I was in good shape for dinner at about 7:30 p.m. I also prepared the scallops, cut the potatoes and made the sauce for the pasta. All that was left was to sauté and boil.

The afternoon went by fast, and at about 5 p.m. I hit the shower. Afterwards, I shaved again – no stubble allowed – and I tried to decide what to wear. I needed to look good and detract from my only somewhat less noticeable bruises. I decided on my blue blazer, tan slacks and a white button-down shirt. I had a great pair of loafers and was considering wearing socks versus not wearing socks – I went with wearing socks. That seemed to complete the traditional preppy kind of look with which I was most comfortable.

I went back to the kitchen to make sure everything was coming along as planned, and it was. I set the table in my dining room, which happened to belong to my mother and father, and used the plates and flatware that they only used on special occasions. Next, I arranged the table with a vase full of summer flowers and long tapering candles in the silver holders, which I also inherited from my parents.

The food smelled wonderful, and everything looked great. I was ready.

Then the phone rang. "Oh no she's breaking our date," I thought, and I answered expecting the worse.

"Hello?"

"Chris, it's me, Beth."

"Hi, Beth, what's up?" I was getting distraught over the prospect of her canceling our date.

"Well, I got caught up doing something with my mother, and I'm running a little late."

I was relieved. "No problem. When do you think you'll get here?"

"I should be there by 7 p.m. Is that okay?"

"Sure! See you then."

"Great. See you then!" She hung up.

Whoa, that was close. I couldn't believe how upset I got over the prospect of Beth cancelling our dinner; I must be in love or at least in like a lot. I would use the extra time to make sure everything was perfect.

There wasn't much left to do so I went onto the deck and just looked out over the water. It was a beautiful summer evening, and I sat there for a while. I was looking forward to just relaxing and talking to Beth, and, as I was thinking it over, the doorbell rang. I ran to answer it. When I opened the door, she was standing there. Her long, brunette hair fell over her shoulders, and she was wearing this striking light purple colored dress.

"Hi, Rocky."

"Hi, Beth. Wow, you look beautiful. Come on in."

"Thanks. You look pretty sharp yourself."

"Thanks, and I'm glad to see you're right on time." It was 7 p.m. exactly, and technically she did call to change the time so....

"Hey, something smells great!"

"It's your dinner of a lifetime cooking in the kitchen. I hope you're hungry." I hoped she was; otherwise I'd have leftovers for a week.

"I'm starving, but didn't you promise we would have cocktails first?"

"I sure did. I have vodka and can make us gimlets, or I have wine – white or red. What is your preference?"

"Vodka gimlet...mmm, I'll have one of those on the rocks, please." I couldn't believe it; she liked my favorite drink.

"Great. I thought that we would sit on the deck and relax before dinner. Why don't you go through the living room out to the deck? I'll be right back with the drinks."

She said, "Okay," and I pointed her in the right direction.

I went to the kitchen, made the drinks and brought them out to the deck. Beth was by the railing looking out over the harbor, admiring the view and commenting on all the boats that were docked or moored. She looked so very pretty standing there in the sun with the water in the background that I was at a loss what I should say next.

"Hey Beth, here's your drink. Would you like to sit down?"

"I would," and we both sat down on the patio furniture that I also inherited from Mom and Dad.

We spent the next hour talking about our lives and families. She told me that she was born in Huntington, and she loved the town. She went to Cold Spring Harbor High School and then onto Molloy College for her nursing degree. She told me that her father owned his own business.

"What kind of business?" I asked.

"He's in construction."

"Wait, hold on – your father owns Della Russo Construction?"

"Yes."

"That's one of the biggest construction companies on Long Island." Oh, my God: It's beautiful, Italian, smart and rich. Mom, what were you thinking? How could I ever hope…?

"It is, and he's a great father, too. He works very hard for us, and I love him very much. I also think my mom is very special, too. She's president of the parish council; she spends so much of her time on charitable work and raising money, but she's always been there for us."

"What is the 'us' in your family?"

"Well, I've got a younger sister, Jamie, and a younger brother, Tim, who can be real pains in the ass. But I love them always." She said this with a laugh in her voice.

"Now it's my turn," she continued. "This is a very nice condo, so selling coins must pay pretty well."

"It's okay, I guess, but I still need to buy my clothes on sale. You see when my mom and dad passed away, they had a really nice three-bedroom home, and they also managed to invest in bonds and save some money. I guess it was for their security in the retirement that they never got to take. Anyway, the home and the money eventually came to me in the will, and I was able to buy this place, open up the shop and put some money in the bank." I hadn't thought about this in a long time, and I said to Beth, "I guess I am blessed in the fact that I had the parents I had and that they gave me everything they could, even in death."

Beth looked at me and said, "Wise beyond your years."

"I'll say it again – if I'm so smart, how come I'm not rich?"

"I think you are a rich man in many ways," Beth said, as she looked into my eyes and maybe even my down to my soul. We sat there and looked at each other for what seemed like an eternity until she said, "Hey Rocky, what about dinner? Didn't I tell you I'm starving?"

"Huh…uh, I mean yeah, no problem it's all done, just a little last minute mixing and heating."

"Need any help?"

"No, I've got it under control. How about another drink?"

"Hey, if I have another one of these, I'll get hammered, and I might have to break our deal."

"Our deal? What deal?"

"No fooling around on the first date, remember?"

"Oh yeah, that silly rule. I completely forgot, and I was hoping you would, too. Anyway, we have wine for dinner, and I promise it is of the pure and chaste variety."

"Okay, as long as it's pure and chaste variety," Beth said with the brightest smile.

I thought dinner would not be long in the making as I sautéed the mushrooms for the scallops, which had been in the oven baking. I added the cognac sauce and baked it in the oven for another five minutes. I would boil the water for the pasta while we ate the scallops and sauté the broccoli rabe while we had the pasta course. Everything was going great, and I was anxious to hear what Beth thought of the dinner.

I went back out to the deck and told Beth that dinner was ready. I took her into the open dining area right next to the kitchen.

"Wow, flowers and candles…I must be pretty special."

I looked over at her and said, "You are."

She seemed to become a little embarrassed and looked away. It was an awkward moment, but I thought that she needed to hear it from me.

She immediately regained her composure and said, "Thanks, but the rule is still in place."

I just said, "Damn it!" We both laughed.

We sat down, and I served the first course and poured a glass of Sauvignon Blanc for both of us. I thought the scallops were a little tough, but the cognac sauce was the perfect complement, and Beth ate them with gusto.

"These are fabulous! How did you ever make these?"

"Oh, they're really not too hard to make. It was my mother's recipe, and we always had them on special occasions. The pasta is almost done, so just give me a minute."

I left the table and went into the kitchen. I was working at the stove, draining the capellini pasta when I felt a pair of arms encircling my waist. I put down the sieve and turned around and was face to face with Beth. We looked into each other's eyes, and it was inevitable, we kissed. It was a long, passionate kiss, and I felt like I had never felt before.

When we stopped she looked up at me and said,

"I don't know what made me do that? We just met, but I feel like I've known you forever." Beth looked puzzled.

"All I know is that I fell for you the first time I saw you."

We kissed again and held each other for a moment when Beth said, "Do you think it might have been the scallops in cognac sauce?" We both cracked up laughing. Beth pulled away and said, "I want to help."

"Okay, take the capellini and put it into the pasta dish and add the tomato and basil sauce to it. I'll sauté the broccoli rabe, and we can eat the pasta while it cooks."

"Okay, Rocky. By the way, I love broccoli rabe," and with that, Beth set about doing what needed to get done. A few minutes later, we were back at the table eating our pasta and enjoying each other's company.

While we ate, I learned that Beth became a nurse because a favorite aunt of hers was one, and her aunt loved what she did. She told me that her family vacationed in Maine every year as she was growing up. It was at a cabin on a small lake near the town of Bridgeton, and they were some of the happiest times of her life. Beth said she learned Italian from her grandmother and loved to speak it when they were together. I smiled at her stories…

It was my turn, and I told her about growing up in the Bronx and how my mother gave me a love of cooking. I told her about my dad and how hard he worked, and that he always regretted never finishing high school. I told her about my great uncle, Zio Francesco, and how I'd watch him play bocce. I told her I loved what I did, and even though I'll never be rich, I cannot imagine doing anything else. She smiled at my stories…

"Hey, I've got to tell you that you are batting a thousand so far. The capellini with tomato and basil was fabulous. I don't know if I can eat another drop."

"Well, you better leave some room for the main course…veal osso buco with roasted potatoes and broccoli rabe. I hope you like it."

"Like it? Osso buco is my favorite dish in the world. You are an evil man, Christopher Pella. Do you know that you have ruined my diet?"

So I countered, "Well, I can always throw it out."

And she counter-countered, "Not if you value your life."

I laughed and went into the kitchen. The osso buco was practically falling off the bone, and the sauce had thickened just a bit, so it was perfect. I thought about this evening for a moment, and I figured out that my mother and some of the saints had to be helping me because I've never cooked so well in my entire life.

I placed the veal on a platter and spooned the sauce over it and put some in a gravy dish. I surrounded the meat with the potatoes and put the broccoli rabe with lemon slices in a serving dish. Everything was done, and it looked perfect—well as perfect as I could make it. I proudly marched into the dining room, and Beth was there with a knife in one hand and a fork in the other, smiling as she anxiously awaited the main course.

I placed it between us and said, "La cena e servita!"

And Beth responded, "Guarda meraviglioso, i miei complimenti al chef."

"Well, the chef accepts your compliments and hopes you enjoy your meal." With that, I set about serving the dish to Beth and myself. I poured us glasses of Chianti, and we began to eat our dinner.

If I do say so myself, the osso buco was fabulous. When Beth took her first bite, her eyes went wide, and she looked up at me with this surprised look on her face: "This is unbelievable!"

I pumped my fist and said, "YES!"

Everything turned out better than I could hope for, and I thought of my mother and how she would so be happy to see us now. After a while,

Beth was completely full, but only half of her meal was eaten. I kidded her and said,

"I'll take that away now."

"Listen buster, if you do anything other than pack this up for me to take home, I'll give you more than a black eye."

"Promise?"

She laughs and says, "Promise."

We cleared the table and loaded up the dishwasher. I put on the espresso and suggested we wait for a while before desert, which Beth agreed to wholeheartedly.

It was dark, but we both wanted to sit out on the deck and enjoy this beautiful summer evening. There was a warm breeze, and the lights from the road across the harbor reflected off the water. Most of the boats were moored, so it was very peaceful, a perfect setting for what was becoming the perfect evening.

"Chris, I'll say it again, that was a fabulous dinner. I know how hard you must have planned and worked for this, and I am so happy you made that for me. Sono una ragazza fortunate."

"I'm the fortunate one. A beautiful woman, a beautiful night, great food and wine — what more can a man ask for?"

Beth looks at me seriously and says, "I told you, no fooling around on the first date."

I just burst out laughing, and she joined in. It was the perfect date.

We sat on the deck for a while in comfortable silence. It's great to be able to sit with someone and just feel that you don't need to say a thing — just being there was enough. After a while, Beth said,

"This is a beautiful spot overlooking the harbor."

"It really is," I answered. "I was lucky to get it, given the location. Some of the furniture you see inside belonged to my parents, and I couldn't give it up, so I brought it here."

"It's nice that you think of your folks the way you do. I feel the same way."

We continued to sit staring at the boats entering the harbor and docking for the night. We made small talk, enjoying each other, the night and companionship. I asked Beth,

"Where do you live?"

"Well, my folks live in Lloyds Neck, but I have a townhouse in Northport in the pits."

"Wow, I've been through there. It's really beautiful, right on the water."

"Yeah, it is great. My family was always into boating, and I have a small boat — a 24-foot Chaparral. I love to go out on the waters off Huntington Harbor and Northport Bay, just cruise and look at the homes along the shoreline. For me, it's very relaxing."

So she's beautiful, smart, rich, Italian *and* she's got a boat. Mom, you're killing me here, "Wow, that sounds great."

"Hey, I've got a great idea. Would you like to go out on my boat one of these days? It really is a lot of fun. We can bring a picnic lunch and cruise the waters. What do you say?"

"Isn't that a coincidence? I've also got a boat."

"Really? What kind?"

"It's a five inch rubber floater, lime green…I use it when I take a bath."

"Very funny, what do you say?"

"Well, okay, but only if you let me bring the gas, my lunches are not nearly as good as my dinners."

"Okay, you've got a deal. You bring the lunch; I'll bring the boat."

We sat for a few more minutes, and I went in to get the coffee. I poured us both a double espresso and put out the platter of the miniature pastries that was another gift from the Grometti's.

"Oh, no!"

"What?" I said.

"Napoleons…my personal favorites of all time. I'm going to kill Vincent when I see him." She looked angry as she reached for the pastry, but her face took on a whole other look when she took her first bite. "This is so delicious, maybe I won't kill Vincent after all."

When we were done with desert, Beth looked at her watch.

"Well, it's way past midnight. I've got to work tomorrow, so I have to get home, but I've had a wonderful time, really."

"So have I, it was the best time I've had on a date, ever. I only say this because I need to put pressure on you for our next date."

I held her hand as we walked to her car. I stood in front of her, pulled her close and held her. She felt soft and warm, and I never wanted this moment to end. I kissed her, and she seemed to melt in my arms. When we stopped to look at each other, it seemed that we both knew we had found something very special.

Chapter 27

It was Sunday, and I got up late, so I went to a late mass. After church, I took a ride to Huntington Hospital to see my uncle and tell him about my evening with Beth and what a great time I had. She was on Sunday duty but not around, so I walked past the nurses' station and into his room. When I opened the door, he immediately asked,

"So how did the big date go, Romeo?

"Uncle Al, she is the most amazing woman I've ever met."

"Wow, sounds pretty special. So how did she like the dinner?"

"I have to tell you this; it was about the best dinner I have ever made. I kept thinking that Mom and the saints were watching over me to make sure I didn't screw it up."

"I can believe that, and whose idea was it to make dinner for your girlfriend?"

"Yours, and you were right. I should only be so lucky if she were my girlfriend. Oh by the way, she has a 24-foot Chaparral, and she loves to go boating."

"Boy, looks like you won the jackpot."

"Yeah right, what does a guy like me have to offer a girl like her? If Mom was involved in this, she overshot the mark."

"Hey jerk, take inventory. You're a good-looking, solid citizen, make a decent living — yeah I know you'll never get rich, but who cares? You're a great cook…all in all, you're not so bad. As a matter of fact, I'd go out with you."

"Wait a second, even I have standards. Oh, by the way, did you know her dad owns Della Russo Construction?"

"Wow, no kidding. Hey, didn't your dad work for Della Russo Construction at some point in time?"

"Holy shit, I totally forgot that. I can't believe what an idiot I am."

As if I wasn't feeling insecure enough, Uncle Al says, "Well, I can believe you're an idiot. Listen pal, let things go the way they want to go, and don't over think this. She likes you, and that's all that matters."

"I guess you're right, but it does give a guy an inferiority complex."

"Are you kidding? You talk to saints. If anything, you are the one who stands head and shoulders above us schlubs."

Uncle Al was looking remarkably good after his ordeal, and I told him so.

He smiled and said, "Well, like I told you, I have a guardian Archangel, and that makes all the difference in the world."

He and I spoke for a while longer, and when I was about to leave, he said things were looking good, and the doctors would let him know in a few days when he might be able to leave.

I had been checking his house every day and picking up his mail, which I had in a plastic bag. I handed it to him, "By the way, I've been to your house, all is well, and here's your mail. I included your checkbook; looks like you've got a lot of bills, too."

"Thanks Chris, I appreciate it. It will give me something to do after I finish cursing."

"Hey, if they let you leave soon, why don't you stay with me for a few weeks until you get back on your feet? I can cook for you and get you what you need, and when you feel better, you can go back home."

"No, I couldn't impose like that."

"Of course you can, you already do, anyways. Come on, I want to make up for almost getting you killed. What do you say big guy?"

"What about your girlfriend? Won't that put a cramp in your style?" Uncle Al has a way of butting into my life.

"No problem. I'll just lock you into your bedroom, and when she comes over, I'll tell her that you're embarrassed about your anatomically correct blowup doll collection. Come on, you know you want to come over. Come on, I'm begging you stay with me."

"You really are a good guy. Sure, I'd love to come and stay with you, and thanks for being a terrific nephew, except for almost getting me killed."

"Great! I'll make sure that everything is set and ready."

We talked a bit more about my date and about the saints. I told him about my vision of St. Valentine and about the note he gave me. It was written on a parchment type of material, and it was written in beautiful script.

"This really happened? Can I see the note?"

"Sure," I pulled it out of my shirt pocket and showed it to Uncle Al, and he marveled at it.

"Ex tua Valentine. Chris, do you know what this is? It's a relic, an actual relic given to you by the saint himself. I am in awe."

"I never thought of it that way, but I guess it is a relic. He wrote it in Latin; I think that's because he knew Beth would love it. I only hope that Beth and I are still together because I want to frame it and to give it to her on Valentine's Day."

Uncle Al smiled at me and said, "I couldn't think of a better gift."

"Neither can I."

Uncle Al and I talked for a while longer. We planned what he would need when he moved into my condo, and I told him I would go to his house and bring back all those things.

"And don't forget my cookies and cream frozen yogurt. I can't wait until they let me eat that stuff again. It's like living with the Taliban here in this hospital."

I said, "Don't worry, if the doctors say you can eat it, I'll be sure to have it for you."

Uncle Al looked a little tired, so we said our goodbyes, but it seemed that he had something else to say to me:

"Chris, you really are a great person. Beth sees that in you, and she knows that you are special. Don't defeat yourself before the contest even begins. You were chosen to be a messenger of God on this earth, and if God saw something special in you, then that's what counts. Capisce?"

"Capisco e ringrazio."

"You're welcome…I love you."

"I love you, too."

Chapter 28

As she became conscious, she felt the cold, damp earth under her body. She tried to move into a sitting position, but with every movement, she became dizzy and disoriented. Where was she? The space about her was dark, and the air was close, and she was at a point nearing hysteria.

"Hello? Hello? Is anybody here?"

No answer, no footfalls, no sound.

"Please, I need help. Somebody, please, help me."

...Still no answer, no footfalls, no sound.

After struggling for a time, she managed to get up into a sitting position; more of her surroundings came into focus. There was cold, hard dirt and small stones on the floor of what seemed to her a prison of sorts. The walls seem to bleed water from the jagged rocks that jutted out from all sides. She thought that she might be in a well...Yes, that's it. She fell into a well but how, when? Nothing seemed broken, but she ached, and she was so tired.

She couldn't stay like this. She had to get up and walk around, even though it was so dark. She had trouble seeing her own hand in front of her face, but she just knew she had to get up. She struggled for what seemed like a very long time...all the while, she thought she would never find the strength. But finally, she did.

Once on her feet, her legs became wobbly, and she had trouble holding herself up. She was only 116 pounds. How could her body feel so heavy? She grabbed at the walls and walked all the way around the enclosure. From what she could tell, it was not so much a well but a cave—no, not really a cave, more like a pit. What was she doing in a pit? How did she get there? She couldn't remember, and that made it all the more frightening.

Wait, she remembered something. Margaritas! That's right, margaritas! But what about them? She loved margaritas, and sometimes she had too many, but after all she was single, 24, pretty, and there was always a guy willing to buy her a margarita or three.

Wait, she remembered something else. Julian! That's right, Julian! But what about Julian? He was so handsome, and he dressed so nicely, very stylish...she loved the look. She was very familiar with his type. After all, she went out with a lot of handsome, stylish men, but Julian was above them all. He liked her; he really liked her.

She walked around her pit once more and thought that this place was shit compared to...what was the name of her favorite hangout place? "Mia's Casa!" That's right, "Mia's Casa!" It all seemed to be coming back now, the margaritas, Julian, Mia's Casa, but where was she? How did she get here, and why was she here? These thoughts ran though her head, but the more she thought of where she was, the more frightened she became. She kept thinking that she needed to keep calm, but that was not easy.

First there was the crunch of gravel—then "Ping," a tiny stone dropped by her feet. She looked up, but it was too dark to see to the top. "Ping," another stone dropped by her feet. She wondered what was happening, and as she looked up, she said, "Hello, is anyone there?" She realized that there really could be someone there, so she screamed.

The screams were welling up from a place of fear so deep she couldn't stop.

When she looked up, a tiny stone came down. This time it hit her in the eye. It hurt, really hurt, so she moved back from the wall and heard a sound that she had never heard before. It was the sound of a million wings flapping and shrill cries. A cawing sound? Cawing birds. What are birds doing here? Maybe they live here?

She tried to understand, but she couldn't think anymore. Her body ached, her head hurt, and she just couldn't think anymore. As she wandered further into the madness of the moment, something brushed her hair, and she screamed. Staring up into the darkness, she couldn't tell what it was, but it had to be one of the birds. "Whoosh"—again the sound by her head, but this time, it seemed to pull on her long, blonde hair. She screamed again and tried to find a corner of the pit where she could hide.

As she ran, she tripped and fell, and one of the birds swooped down and pecked at her knee. She cried in pain but mostly in terror. "Leave me alone!" Another bird came down and clawed at her arms with its talons. As it flew away, she saw the ebony colored feather reflect what little light there was.

"Wait, I know that bird! That's a crow! But why are crows attacking me?" The answer would never come as the flying mass of black crows swooped down

into the pit. They flew, each time closer and closer. But this time when she screamed, no sound could be heard.

First they tore at her clothes, then at her body. Flailing arms, terrorizing screams were her only defenses against the onslaught of the crows. Her extreme pain was changing to numbness.

"What is happening? Why me?"

For a moment, the crows stopped, and there was complete silence. The birds perched throughout the pit, on the rocks and on the ground...waiting all about her in absolute silence. The crows looked at her as she hugged herself. She felt the blood oozing out of the open wounds. Her salty tears flowed and stung the cuts on her face.

She was pretty before, but she knew that she would be pretty no more.

"Hello, Celine."

Who knew her name? Who cared?

"I'm down here," she screamed, but her throat was so raw that it hardly was more than a whisper.

"What are you doing in this dreadful pit?" asked the concerned voice.

"I don't know...I don't remember how I got here. Please, help me! I'm bleeding."

"What happened, Celine?"

"I was attacked. I was attacked! I was attacked by crows! There still here. They're here in the pit, and I'm frightened. Please, help me." His voice was calm, and it seemed to soothe her, and she was finally able to speak without the hysterics.

"Can you help me? I'm hurt, and I need help. Can you help me?"

"Oh, I'm sure I can help."

The crows started to flap their wings, they shrieked a shrill cry, they started to fly—first ripping her arms, then her legs and next, they took out her eyes.

There was the crunch of gravel beneath his shoes as he walked up to the Celine's body. She didn't look at all good, and for this, he was very happy. The crows surrounded him, but he wasn't worried. They always did what they were told.

Julian continued to stare at Celine as if in a trance. He knew that there must be closure, and he knew what he must do. He reached down and lifted her once pretty silk dress. Under her dress, her legs and thighs were smooth and untouched by the crows.

He knew they would be because he told them not to touch her there.

As he lifted her dress, he fondled her mound but not in a way that resembled passion or lust, it was more like an examination. Her panties needed to go, so he ripped them off and threw them aside. Now she lay there dead, naked from the waist down and he smiled.

Slowly, painstakingly, he moved his hand into her vagina. He felt the moisture of her juices. After all, she was only dead a few minutes. Further and further his hand, wrist and lower arm made its way up her canal, and he stopped. There was no strain, no feelings or emotions, no reason on Julian's face or in his mind—he was there for a singular purpose.

He stopped as if he felt something. He did feel something, and he grabbed a hold of it. In a split second, he removed the recently conceived fetus and it died.

Celine didn't know she was pregnant.

Chapter 29

Just ten days after he was shot, Al was released from the hospital. All the doctors and nurses were still in total amazement at his recovery, and he would smile and tell anyone who would listen that it was all because he started drinking beer at twelve-years-old.

He moved into my condo and stayed with me for the next two weeks. It was a great time for both of us. Uncle Al told me family stories that I had never heard, some funny, some sad, but sitting there with him gave us time to bond. During the time he was staying with me, I was also able to make sure that he relaxed and got better. I cooked, so I got to make him all his favorite foods, and I'm sure he gained back all the weight that he lost in the hospital. But the day came when we knew that he was well enough to go home: "Hey Chris, looks like you will be getting your digs back. I'm going to go home tomorrow and back to work next week."

"I figured you'd be leaving when I saw that the silver was missing."

He laughed and said, "Well, the price of silver has never been higher; at least that's what I hear on the radio."

"I really am going to miss you, Uncle Al. Having you here was great, and aside from the fact that you're a slob, I'd do it again in a heartbeat."

"Thanks, I had a wonderful time, too. Now what about the beautiful, smart, rich, boat-owning Italian girl? What was her name? Mildred? Harriet?"

"Beth."

"Yeah, that's right, Beth. How's that going? When are you two getting together again?"

Beth had stopped by the condo a few times to see both me and Uncle Al, but there was no time in our schedules to make another date. Either she or I was working, so we kept trying to find a time that we were both free.

"Well, she came by to visit us, and we talk all the time. But it's been a little low profile over the last couple of weeks on the getting together part, but we have another date all set."

"Really? When?" Now Uncle Al's is curious.

"We're going out this Sunday; we are going boating on the Bay. I've got to admit, though, I'm a little nervous about this 'we come from the two different worlds' thing."

"How many times do I have to tell you this? Just sit back, relax and enjoy her company."

"Yeah, I guess you're right. I look forward to spending the day with her." Beth and I speak all the time, but we hadn't gone out since our first date. I was excited to see her again and to be alone with her.

"I don't blame you. By the way, you remember Dan Orello."

"Yeah, a really nice guy as I recall. What about him?"

"After he gets off the night shift, he's gonna stop by here and drive me home tomorrow, so don't worry about driving me there."

"You sure? It's really not a problem."

"No, I'm sure. Anyway, I want to get a complete update about the department and the case load, so it will be quality time for us."

Uncle Al and I spent the rest of the evening eating, talking and watching TV. As I knew it would be his last day with me, I bought him a half-gallon of cookies and cream frozen yogurt, and he attacked it. When it got late, we said our good nights and went to our bedrooms.

I was trying to fall asleep, but sleep just wouldn't come. I had a vision.

The day was grey and overcast. Mothers, fathers, town elders, clergy were standing on the shores of Lago Delle Grazie, Lake of Thanks—but there was nothing to be thankful for. The bodies of the children lay cold and lifeless on the shores of the lake. The wails of the assembled parents could be heard all the way to Tolentino. How could this have happened? How could their children be dead, drowned? Even though they mourned, they still questioned, pleaded, bring our children back. They asked over and over: Why had God abandoned them?

In the midst of all this sorrow, the people looked to the holy man, the preacher, the worker of miracles for answers to their questions.

It was then that St. Nicholas appeared to the crowd, having heard the cries from his cell in the monastery. Was he not much loved by all in the town; had he not worked with the poorest of his flock? Had he not been the only solace for the thieves and murderers that had been imprisoned or would be put to death by the authorities?

St. Nicholas felt the anguish of his flock, and he wept with them. The villagers implored the holy man to work his miracle for them, for their children.

He wept as he walked over to the bodies of the young children. The men and women of the village surrounded him, but it was only the children that mattered—all else disappeared from his sight. St. Nicholas carried a flower, a beautiful lily in his left hand, and he stopped to pray over these poor souls. He knelt down by the body of a young boy, no more than seven years old. The rest of those present at the lake knelt down as well and prayed with him. The prayer seemed to put St. Nicholas into a trancelike state as he placed the lily on the forehead of the dead young boy.

A few moments passed, then the boy opened his eyes and looked up at the priest kneeling by his side.

The miracle was repeated twice more; each time a young child was resurrected from the dead. The crowd stared in utter astonishment, the children were returned to them, resurrected from the dead in what had to be a divine gift, a miracle, and they had no words—only wonder.

The priest, the wonder-worker, turned to the crowd and said, "Say nothing of this, give thanks to God, not to me. I am only a vessel of clay, a poor sinner." And, with that, St Nicholas of Tolentine made his way back to the monastery.

St. Nicholas stepped out of the scene and looked into my eyes. "I cannot bear to see this suffering, and it is only through the divine mercy of Jesus Christ that I am able to make well their sorrow. These young children will grow to know the Lord, and they will be held close to Him all their days."

"Why am I being shown this? Why am I being shown this miracle?"

St. Nicholas looks up to heaven and then down to me and says, "I am showing this to you so you may know the true power of faith. Faith is what allows miracles to happen; faith and hope are all that is left for the souls in Purgatory."

The vision now changed. I am taken to a hillside outside of Tolentino.

The holy man is kneeling in prayer. He is weak after having fasted for more than four days. There appears beside him an evil figure not of this world whose face is hidden. The demon is tormenting the holy man, and there is no relief from the suffering.

St. Nicholas cannot think. He cannot remember his prayers. The demon is holding a long, wooden stick in his hand, and he is beating the saint who cannot fight back. The devil laughs and continues the fierce blows to the back, to the arms, to the neck and head.

"You are a fool, your miracles are worthless and God does not care that you suffer." The beating continues more brutally than before, and the devil continues to laugh.

"Dear Mother of God, grant me peace, so that I may prepare my soul to appear before the Lord." St. Nicholas, weak and suffering, barely muttered this prayer.

"There is no mercy. There is no reprieve from the pain that I will bring down on you. Your God and your Christ are gone, and you are forgotten." The fiend then brought the long stick down in one massive blow, and St. Nicholas fell unconscious, his body and face swollen and bleeding from the beating he had taken.

The horror of the scene fades into the background, and St. Nicholas stands before me.

"I pleaded with the Blessed Mother for relief from my enemies, and she granted me that wish."

"Why does this demon, this devil, torture you?" I asked not really expecting an answer.

"He is jealous. He seeks the souls of men, but with each miracle performed in the name of Christ, that task becomes harder and harder. He beats me because he knows he cannot defeat the power of Heaven."

With that, the scene comes into full focus, the demon is still beating the unconscious man.

St. Nicholas and I are looking at this, and the devil stops and raises his head. I looked at St. Nicholas, but he doesn't look back. He points to the evil spirit before us. I am transfixed on the figure as he slowly turns to me and my face turns pale, for all I see is Juliano.

The vision of St. Nicholas and Juliano was so disturbing that I had the most fitful sleep. When I woke up the next morning, I felt sick to my stomach, so I ran to the bathroom. The nausea passed. I showered, brushed my teeth and shaved to start another day.

As I passed Uncle Al's bedroom, I saw that his closet was empty and the bed made. I guess it was at that point that I realized he was really gone. I would miss having him around.

When I went to the kitchen, I saw the breakfast table was set, and on top of my plate was a note.

Dear Chris,

Well, these two weeks flew by in a flash, and I am so grateful that you let me stay with you while I was recovering. To tell you the truth, I never really needed to recover, and I think you know why.

I must say, you are the perfect host and a great cook. I went on the scale this morning, and guess what? I am back to being overweight, thanks to you. I must have consumed an extra ten pounds in fat, carbs and calories, so I can honestly say, I forgive you for getting me shot, but not for the heart attack I expect to get in my later years.

I've been thinking about all the stories of your saints and what you have shared with them. What you have experienced is truly amazing, and I can only say that you are blessed. The saints you are privileged to meet and the visions you are privileged to see can only be viewed as the miracle in your life…both as a great gift and a massive burden—one that I know you take very seriously.

I also sense that there is something that is troubling you, and you are very worried over it. I guess you just don't want to speak about it now, but I want you to know that I am here for you whenever you feel like talking.

Well, I hear Dan's car pulling into the driveway, so I'll close this by saying thank you. Know always that I am here for you.

Love,
Uncle Al

PS. I just made the table, not the food. You're much better at cooking than me.

I smiled and put the note down, glad for our time together and glad that he is my uncle. I did wonder how he knew about my worries. I guess, after years of being a cop, you have instincts about these things. I haven't told him about the demons, but because he has a cop's intuition, he knew there was something wrong.

Someday I would be ready to share that side of the story, but not now.

Chapter 30

Sunday was finally here, and the weather was picture-perfect. Bright sunshine, clear blue skies and warm breezes made this a beautiful summer day on Long Island.

I had gone to Grometti's the day before and bought all the items that I wanted to make for lunch. I made sandwiches with fresh baked semolina bread, prosciutto sliced paper-thin, fresh mozzarella, roasted red peppers and romaine lettuce with a special oil and vinegar dressing. I also made a wonderful arugula salad with cherry tomatoes, sliced onions and more of the special dressing.

I packed the cooler with a bottle of delicious Cabernet Franc, along with a few of bottles of Peroni Nastro Azzurro, and Italian brewed pale lager, and a dozen bottles of water. For dessert, I made a fresh fruit salad with seasonal melons—cantaloupe, honeydew, watermelon—and I mixed in some red and white grapes. I snuck in some napoleons, so Beth could curse at me while she ate them. I was all set…

Beth lives in a gated community in Northport, which is part of the township of Huntington and just a short ride from where I live. I packed up the car and headed towards her townhouse on the water. As I turned down the hill leading to her place, I got a glimpse of Northport Bay and all the pleasure crafts that were enjoying the spectacular day. The sun glistened on the water like sparkling diamonds, and the salt air was fresh and fragrant.

I pulled up to the gate and punched in her number. "Hello?"

"Hi Beth, it's Chris."

"What do you want?" She said in a perfectly serious tone.

"Uh, I thought we had a date today."

"Wait, let me check my calendar. Hmm, I don't seem to have a Chris written in for today, but I do have a Rocky."

"Oh, sorry—hi, Beth! It's me, Rocky."

"That's better. Come on in; I'm number 72, Northport Bay Court."

A buzzer sounded, and the gate opened to let me in. I drove down the private road into a beautiful residential complex of townhouses all along the water. There are attractive plantings of trees and flowers, lovely ponds with fountains and expansive manicured lawns. I passed the clubhouse with its pool and tennis courts, even a small playground. All in all, it seemed like a fabulous place to live.

I pulled into a parking space reserved for guests, walked up to her door and rang the bell. Beth opened the door, and for a minute I was speechless. She looked simply stunning. She was in white shorts that seemed to add about twelve inches to her already long and flawlessly shaped legs. She was wearing a light blue blouse that clung to her body and emphasized the contour of her waist and breasts. To complete the look she wore elegant leather sandals, jewelry and some wonderful perfume.

"Wow, you look gorgeous, if you don't mind me saying so."

She blushed a little, but bounced back and said, "I don't, but thanks. Want to come in and see my place?"

"Sure, I've always wanted to know how the other half lives," I said as I walked into the foyer.

Her house was about what you'd expect. There are vaulted ceilings, hardwood floors, a kitchen with cherry cabinets and terra cotta tiles, a huge master bedroom and bath, two spare bedrooms with two more baths and a family room with the latest in audio and video. There is a living room and dining room decorated in a combination of modern and antique furnishings. Light floods into all the rooms through large windows and sliding doors that look out onto a lagoon that leads to the bay. There is a large deck that's off the main floor and a patio on the ground level.

From the deck of her townhouse, you can see the private marina at the end of the lagoon.

"That's where I keep my boat, the 'Fun-A-Bout.'"

"Your boat is called 'Fun-A-Bout'?"

"Yeah, I don't get much time off, so it's a thinly veiled reference to my favorite leisure time activity—having fun."

Beth had prepared coffee and some bagels, and we relaxed on the deck and talked about the beautiful day and her beautiful home.

"I know I'm a lucky girl, and, looking around here, you'd probably think that I was given everything on a silver platter. But that's not the way it happened. My dad and mom always made me realize the value of accomplishing something on my own. I think that's why I work as hard as I can—because I don't want people to only consider that I'm a member of the lucky sperm club. I really want people to know I did a lot of it on my own, of course with some help from my family." She was very serious when she spoke, and I knew it was something that was very important to her.

"I know what you mean. If it weren't for my family I couldn't do what I do—but I also know that they cannot make me succeed. I need to do it on my own to truly know I've made it." Now I was being serious.

We sat in silence for a few minutes. I was feeling a bit uncomfortable with the somber tone that the conversation had taken, so I said to Beth, "Did you know that my father worked for your father?"

"You're kidding! Really? I have to tell my dad. Your father's name is Anthony, right?"

"Yeah, it is. I looked up some of his old records, and it seems that he was a foreman on a number of your dad's sites. It's amazing how small our world has become."

Beth looked at me and said, "I think that's why I feel like I've known you forever."

"Hey, what do you say we walk down to the marina? You can show me the Queen Elizabeth, a.k.a. 'Fun-A-Bout.'"

"Sounds great, but we have to do one thing before we leave."

"What's that?" I said.

Beth got up from her chair and walked over to me. She put out her hand, and I took it and got up from my chair. She looked beautiful as she put her arms around my neck and looked me in the eye. We embraced as our lips met in a long and passionate kiss.

When it ended, she looked at me and said, "I wanted you to hold me and I didn't want to wait any more."

"I'm glad you're the impatient type."

Beth smiled and allowed me to continue to hold her in my arms. The day, the place, the time all seemed to be ideal and I thought that I'd never felt like this before. We kissed again, and Beth said, "Okay, too much fun; let's go boating."

This was one funny girl. I said, "Okay, but you drive."

I grabbed the cooler from my car, got my sunglasses and we started walking toward the marina. There are paths through the complex, and I got to see the clubhouse and some of the other townhouses. When we got to the gate of the marina, I was able to view the panorama of the bay with all the pleasure crafts. As I looked over the water, I saw a small island in the center of the bay that I had forgotten about.

"Hey, Beth, what's the name of that island in the middle of the bay?"

"Oh, that's Pit Island. It was named that because this entire area used to be a sand pit. Over the years the sand was mined and used to help build I-95. When it was all mined out, some enterprising developer built these townhouses. Dug out the lagoon, and the rest is history."

"That's some story and some great place to live," I said, just admiring the incredible view.

We walked down the dock until we reached the slip space, where I dropped the cooler down and helped remove the canvas.

"What a great-looking boat. How long have you had it?"

"I bought it used, and I've had it for four years. I just love it. It's not too big and not too small, and it's great for the bay. Sometimes I go water-skiing with friends, and sometimes we just chill, but we have fun all the time. Hence the name 'Fun-A-Bout.'"

"That works for me."

Beth started the engine and expertly maneuvered the boat out of the slip and down the lagoon to the bay. Her plan was to cruise along the perimeter of the bay, so we could look at the beautiful waterfront homes. There were a number of other crafts on the water, but there was plenty of open water—so we motored at a low speed to give us time to enjoy the day.

"Aren't those places along the water wonderful? I just love to cruise around Asheroken, Eaton's Neck, Centerport and Lloyd's Neck. I enjoy looking at the homes," Beth said to me as she seemed to totally relax and put herself in the moment.

"This is truly a beautiful place and I can see why you love it," I said.

So she said to me, "Hey Rocky, what's in the cooler?" See what I mean? Totally at ease.

"Remember? I promised to bring the gas. Well, Vincent and Angelica made sure that I wouldn't disappoint you. There are my special prosciutto sandwiches on semolina bread, a nice crisp salad and some red wine and Italian beer. I hope you like it."

"Sounds wonderful! Why don't we finish the tour and then we can anchor near Pit Island and have our lunch?"

"That works for me."

The sun and the warm breezes felt good as we continued motoring around the bay. It was a very relaxing time. Beth and I didn't need to speak; we just felt comfortable in each other's company. It had gotten close to 1 p.m. when we decided it would be a good time to anchor and stop for lunch. Beth spotted a place near Pit Island where she could anchor the boat so we would be out of the way of any traffic.

We took out the deck table, set it up in the hole in the floor (provided for just that purpose), and I took our lunch out of the cooler. I placed a sandwich on Beth's plate along with tossed salad and the dressing and handed it to her along with a cold Peroni.

Beth's reaction to her first bite was to say, "Mmm, this is delicious. You have to tell me how you made the dressing."

"It's really simple—white vinegar, canola oil, spices. I'll write it down for you when we get back."

"Great."

The day was like a dream, calm waters and a beautiful woman. I felt lucky just to be there. Beth and I talked through the entire lunch about many things, great and small, all the while feeling more and more comfortable with each other.

My gaze fell on Pit Island, and I asked Beth, "Have you ever been to Pit Island?"

"No, the water is very shallow, and there are large, jagged rocks just under the surface. Trying to get a boat close enough is a blueprint for distaste—or at least a $5,000 fix-the-hull bill."

"Who owns it?" I couldn't imagine why but I was becoming more curious about this place.

"I don't know. I guess it belongs to the county, but since no one ever goes there it just stays the same. Why are you so interested?"

"I don't know, maybe pirate treasure. Do you know what pieces of eight and gold doubloons are going for?"

"No. What are they going for?"

"Well, depending on the age, the denomination and the metal content of the coin, the value could range from…"

"I was just making small talk and trying to be polite—don't try to make me one of your coin collector buddies." Beth said this with such a beautiful smile that I didn't care that she wasn't interested in coins or collecting.

"Okay, you got me at my boring best. I promise never to bring up how I make a living and one of the things that make me happiest. Who cares if you don't care? I can take it. I remember when I was a little boy…"

As I was speaking, Beth got off the seat and sat right next to me. She put her arms around my shoulder and looked me straight in the eye. "Do you want to discuss some old metal coins, or do you want to kiss me?"

It was a question that needed no answer. I reached over and held her tight in my arms, and I kissed her with a passion that was returned in kind. My feelings for Beth were becoming so strong that I had to stop in the middle of the kiss and just look at her.

"Beth Della Russo, you are beautiful, and I can't believe that I am here with you."

"I think you're beautiful, too, or should I say handsome? I love being here with you, too. It's just so weird how I feel about you; I know I've said it before, but it's like I've known you forever."

While we were speaking, the air suddenly turned cold. When I looked up, a large, grey cloud blocked the sun, and it became darker. The wind had picked up, and when I looked over the hull of the boat to Pit Island, I saw strong gusts actually bending the trees near their breaking point.

"I've never seen anything like it before. The only place that is dark is right over the island," Beth said, with great bewilderment in her voice. "Just look at the trees bend in the wind, you don't see that anywhere else. What could be going on?"

"I don't know, but do you think it's safe out here?" I said, worried that something might happen to Beth.

"Maybe you're right. Why don't we head back to the marina, and we can sit on my deck and enjoy that so-called fabulous Cabernet Franc?" She said this in a lighthearted way, but I could sense she was worried.

"What do you mean 'so-called fabulous Cabernet Franc'? Just wait until we get back. You'll taste for yourself."

I told Beth that I would hoist the anchor and secure all the other gear on the deck, and she could start the engine. She turned the key, but the engine wouldn't turnover.

"That's funny. It always starts on the first try. I wonder what's wrong." She tried to start it again, but the wind was picking up; we realized then that the boat was being carried toward Pit Island and the jagged rocks that surrounded it. Beth yelled to me to lift the anchor, so I ran to where it was to be stowed and tried to open the hatch.

I struggled to lift the hatch and to stow the anchor, but the hatch wouldn't budge. The anchor was too heavy to lift by hand. Beth was still trying to start the engine, but the anchor seemed to be dragging along the bottom. The boat kept drifting closer and closer to the rocks. I called out to Beth, "Beth, where is the engine compartment?"

She told me that it was under a hatch near the stern of the boat. I hoped and prayed that it was not stuck like the anchor hatch; but once I got over there and lifted it, it opened fine. I looked down into the engine and smelled gas—maybe there was a leak. In a few seconds I saw the problem. A fuel fitting had come loose from the tank, and gas was spilling into the engine compartment.

"Beth, don't prime the engine anymore; the fuel fitting came loose, and I need to hook it back on."

"Okay, but hurry, please. We are getting too close to the rocks."

The waves on the bay had gotten very choppy, and the boat was rolling back and forth. I knew Beth was frightened and so was I, but I needed to get this done. I reached into the engine compartment and grabbed the fitting and reattached it to the tank. I also found the coupling that had kept the fitting in place, and I reattached that.

"Try starting the engine now." The first attempt was no good; neither was the second attempt.

"Try giving it a little more gas," I said.

The anchor became useless as it dragged along the bottom of the bay toward Pit Island. As the situation became more desperate, the moment froze in time. I had a vision.

Appearing on the water on the port side was a saint clothed in the brown habit of a nun and surrounded by a halo of golden light. Her hands were folded in prayer, and there was a fresh, bleeding wound on her forehead. The scene suddenly changed, and I was in a medieval church.

> *At the altar stood the groom. By the look of his robes he was a wealthy man and not used to be kept waiting. The priest walked to the middle of the altar and faced the crowds that had gathered. The bride approached from the rear of the church. She was a child no more than twelve years old, and she was to be married.*

I stood on the side of the altar when the scene again changed, and I was in the home of the now-adult woman.

> *Her tears would not stop as the men carried the body of her husband into the home. Rita had built a life together with Paolo, and, through the prayers, patience and kindness of his wife, Paolo Mancini had become a better person. But now he was dead. He was killed by Guido Chiqui who had sworn vengeance for some real or imagined insult.*
>
> *Her sons, Giovanni Antonio and Paulo Maria, stood silent as they stared at the body of their father. La Vendetta had taken his life, but vengeance would be theirs. Their uncle had been poisoning the minds of his nephews demanding vengeance for his brother's death. "You cannot let this go unanswered. Your father lies in the cold earth because of Guido Chiqui, and for this he must die. Do you hear me? Die!" With this Giovanni and Paolo Maria swore revenge.*
>
> *Rita knew this would be their response, so she stood before her two sons. "Do not listen to your father's brother, who would have you commit an act of murder. You must not seek revenge. It is a mortal sin, and you will be punished, condemned to spend eternity in hell. You must know that it is only God who can deliver the justice you seek. I have forgiven Guido Chiqui, and you must too."*

The scene changes yet again, and now it is Rita who is standing alongside the graves of her sons.

St. Rita of Cascia steps out of the scene and turns to me.

"I mourned the loss of my sons, but I thank the Lord that they did not seek revenge. They did not die in sin."

I asked her, "How did your sons die?"

She answered, "They died of the bloody flux."

St. Rita, the patron saint who helps those in very anxious situations, had lived through such things that no parent should have to.

I realized why she was sent to us, and I begged her, "I don't know what to do. Beth and I are in great trouble. Can you please find a way to help us?"

St. Rita looked me in the eye and said, "I know you are in a desperate circumstance, and I am here to show you the way."

St. Rita reached into her cloak and took out a perfectly formed red rose. She handed the rose to me and said, "The power of God is infinite as is His mercy. Place this red rose on the waters and all will be calm."

St. Rita of Cascia, a woman whose life, devotion and piety are glorified still today, slowly vanished. I was back in the moment. The storm kept raging as the boat was carried closer and closer towards Pit Island and the surrounding rocks.

I screamed above the wind, "Beth, can you start the engine?" Just as she was trying to answer, an enormous swell came over the side of the boat and lifted Beth right off her feet. She screamed, and the rose dropped from my hand as I leapt to save her from being washed overboard. At the exact moment she was about to go overboard, I jumped to her side of the craft, managed to grab her arm and bring her to the relative safety of the deck before she was washed over the side and drowned.

As she was coughing up water, Beth said, "My God, you saved my life."

I saw the rose floating in a puddle on the deck so to distract Beth I told her, "Try to get the boat started." She turned away from me, and I lunged for the rose. I grabbed it then threw it off the side, onto the waves that were threatening to swamp the boat.

In an instant the waters calmed, and the dark grey cloud literally melted away. Beth turned the key, and the engine started on the first try.

She looked at me in stark disbelief. "What—what happened? How in the world…?"

Beth seemed to be in shock, so I had her sit down. I was able to get the hatch open to lift and stow the anchor. Then I took hold of the steering wheel and guided the Fun-A-Bout away from Pit Island and the rocks that would have wrecked the boat and possibly killed us both.

As I steered the boat and set a course back to the marina I looked back at Pit Island. All seemed to be just like it was before. The trip back took about fifteen minutes. By the time we got to the slip space, Beth was feeling much better.

"Hey Chris, you've done enough good deeds for one day. Let me dock her—this can get tricky."

"Wait? Who's this Chris guy? I thought I was Rocky—or at least Rambo?"

"Believe me, you're both right now," Beth said as she expertly brought the boat into the slip space and we tied up the Fun-A-Bout.

We got off the boat and just stood there, dripping wet. For a moment we tried to gather our thoughts to come up with the words to say to each other. When I finally spoke, all I could think to say was, "Some fun, huh!" I burst out laughing. Beth joined in, and soon we were in hysterics. After a few minutes, we calm down.

"Why don't we go back and have some of that fabulous Cabernet Franc?" Beth said.

"Oh sure, you practically drown, and all of a sudden my so-called fabulous Cabernet Franc becomes my fabulous Cabernet Franc."

"Well, after the kind of day we've had, I think that as long as I get to drink a glass of Cabernet Fran—or or any wine for that matter—it's always fabulous." Beth just looked at me and smiled.

I looked back and said, "How true."

I took her in my arms and just held her, and she held me back.

Chapter 31

She embraced her mother and father, holding them tightly, for the journey to Proceno would be long. She may not see them for many months.

She is leaving her beloved Montepulciano, her beloved Franciscans. Even though Agnes was born into wealth, she had been happiest in the convent with these wonderful nuns and their simple ways of life and devotion to prayer. Agnes was only fifteen, yet she had been enjoying complete peace. Now she must leave for Proceno in the county of Orivieto, to found a new convent for the Dominican Order. The journey was very tiring, but Agnes would use this time to explore the secrets of God, the Father in prayer.

It is late winter in the year 1283 when Agnes arrives at the large stone building that serves as the convent. At the entrance to the convent there is a group of priests assembled anxiously awaiting her arrival.

"Good priests, I am honored that you would be here to greet me on my arrival." Agnes was truly surprised by this, uncomfortable with what she felt was more importance than she deserved.

The leader of the delegation said, "Good sister, we bring blessings, greetings and a message from His Holiness Pope Nicholas the IV."

"The Holy Father has a message for me?" Agnes was incredulous. What could the Pope possibly want of me?

"You are being called to serve your God and your church in a way that you may not have imagined."

"In what way does His Holiness ask me to serve?"

"You are to become the abbess of the monastery in Proceno," the priest said to all present.

"I? An abbess? Surely His Holiness knows that I am only fifteen years old. I am not worthy to serve in such a position." The shock of such a request was apparent on the young girl's face.

"The pontiff has asked me to make it known that you are to receive special permission and dispensation to perform your duties as an abbess at so young

an age. You are to build your community with all due haste to begin serving the Lord and His faithful."

What was she to do? She had come to know joy and peace through prayer, and now this would become harder and harder for her. Agnes did not know what to do, how to respond to such a request. At fifteen, she was not worthy. It would be better for the nuns, the community and the church if she refused. But how could she refuse the Pope? It all seemed preordained, and, with that, Agnes reluctantly accepted appointment as the abbess of the monastery at Proceno.

Seven days passed. All were gathered at the church to witness her election as abbess. There were the group of priests and nuns of her order present and, with them, the entire townsfolk of Proceno. Young Agnes, wearing the robes of an abbess, stood in the center of the altar awaiting her appointment, humbled by the blessings she would receive from the bishop.

Once she was consecrated, Agnes rose from her kneeling position, faced the assembled crowd and said, "Let us pray to our Lord to grant me the holiness and wisdom I will need to succeed in this mission in His name." A worshipful stillness fell over the church as the entire congregation bowed their heads in prayer.

It was then that the church lit up as hundreds of small white crosses appeared miraculously overhead. These crosses, light as feathers, began to fall on the priests, nuns and all the townspeople assembled in the church. They looked around, above and at each other in wonder. Agnes knew it was a sacred sign, for she had seen other signs in her young life.

Someone in the crowd shouted, "It is a miracle! God has pronounced his blessings on the new abbess." The crosses rained down on all, and all knew it was a signal from heaven, a celebration of Agnes' consecration.

The consecration of a young woman, born of divine lights and ready to serve the Lord in ways she has yet to fully understand.

Chapter 32

My relationship with Beth was going great, we saw each other as often as her schedule allowed, and it was apparent that we genuinely liked each other. Maybe we were even falling in love, and that made me very happy and nervous at the same time. My business was also going well, especially with what I was doing on the digital side of things, and I was looking at other opportunities to expand. All in all, life was good and getting better!

Uncle Al and I still met on a regular basis, so I asked him to meet me for dinner. It had been a few months since the episode with Tina, so he was in great shape, and I was looking forward to seeing him and having one of our leisurely, fun times together.

My favorite neighborhood restaurant is a place called Sal D's. Frank and Sal make great Italian food, and their chicken scarpariello, on the bone of course, is the best you will ever taste. It's one of those places where you always feel relaxed, and it's where I go to enjoy great food, conversation and a little too much wine. I told Frank that Uncle Al and I would be there at 7 p.m., and as always, he made us feel like family.

First, I need to explain this outward show of affection that you notice throughout this book—it's mostly an Italian thing. We like to hug and kiss each other, men and women alike, and I really don't know why. All I know is that I've done it since I was about one hour old.

I immediately saw Frank and, because he's Italian, he gave me a hug and a hardy handshake. "You know you're my best customer, so where have you been? I expect you to eat here at least three times a week."

"Three times a week, huh? How about you pay my credit card bill, and I'll eat for free?" He kids me, so I kid him right back.

"Okay, no problem, just be sure you send the bill to me, and when I get around to it, I'll send them a check. After all, what are friends for?"

"Right, and I'll have my perfect credit score ruined by your sloppy bookkeeping. I'm gonna continue to eat here at least twice a week, and nothing you or anyone else says will stop me," I said indignantly.

Frank quickly responded, "Okay, Okay, no problem. Wait. 'At least twice a week?' Does this mean you might eat here three times a week?"

I responded, "Well, yes, I might."

"Then I'll see to it that you get my special first class treatment! After all, I've got three kids to send to college," Frank said, with a big grin on his face.

"Hey, you're beginning to sound like Vincent Grometti. He expects me to pay for his Mediterranean cruise, and now you expect me to pay for your kids' college? What the hell is going on here?"

We both laughed, and he took me to my table.

I got to the restaurant about fifteen minutes early and had a chance to get seated when Uncle Al walked in. I was in a good mood, and when I saw him come in, I waved and pulled out his seat. As he came close, though, I looked at his face, and I all I could see was a tired, troubled man, and I knew that he needed time to relax a bit before we could open up to each other.

We embraced, sat down and ordered a bottle of my favorite Chianti. We also ordered dinner: I ordered chicken scarpariello, and Uncle Al ordered their amazing pork chops with vinegar peppers.

"Hey, Chris, how're you doing?"

"Good, Uncle Al, really good."

"How's the shop?"

"Oh, fine. Business seems to be getting better, and I get to hear jokes from the old guys who like to come in to get away from their wives. Their wives actually make them do chores around the house. Imagine that. They expect these guys to work!" I thought that he would smile at my poor attempt at humor, but Uncle Al was uncharacteristically quiet.

"Hey Unc, there's a naked woman behind you with a toll-free number on her chest and a sign that says, 'I want Al.'"

"Uh, sorry what did you say?"

"What's up? You look like something's really bothering you. Are you feeling okay?" Given what he had been through and the stress of his job, I became a little worried.

Since I told him of my visions, Uncle Al and I would discuss police work. He usually never gave me all of the intimate details of the cases he was working on, but he often needed to unload on someone outside the department, and I was his favorite sounding board. For Al, it was a way to think through the crime and organize his thoughts.

Before he spoke, he heaved a very heavy sigh and looked me in the eye. "We found another body, same mutilation, same m.o., same wounds, same sex. We'll need to wait to see the coroner's report, but I know that she was pregnant just like the other two."

Uncle Al had mentioned only one such crime in the past, but the brutality of it was so shocking that my heart sank, and all I could do was ask, "When did this happen?"

"The body was found yesterday, and the coroner guesses that the victim was dead for a few days, but he's not sure. I'm waiting for the results of the autopsy." He looked at me with genuine sadness in his eyes and, I could tell, in his heart.

The wine came to the table, personally served by Frank, who made some small talk combined with his usual good nature. When he saw that we seemed to be preoccupied, however, he told us to enjoy the wine and the meal would come soon.

As if talking to himself, he pondered a question, "Why are these women being killed in a particularly ugly way?"

"What do you think, Unc?"

Al looks around to be sure no one is listening to our conversion. "This is just between us, so what I am telling you doesn't leave this table, right?"

"Right," I said.

"We don't know much, but it looks like we have a serial killer on our hands—three pregnant women, three bodies brutally mutilated in the same way. We have no motives, the killer has left no actionable clues as far as we have determined, at this time. Plus, I'm afraid that if the media starts digging into this, it will cause panic and make our work even tougher."

"Whoa, I am so sorry. I don't even know what to say."

"All three women we found were in some kind of deep hole: one in a deep gully, one in a deep, dry well and the last one was found at the bottom of a pit. Toxicology screenings showed that the women were drugged. But the weirdest thing of all was that crows had ripped apart their bodies and gouged out the eyes on each of the murder victims."

"Crows?"

"Can you believe it? Crows!"

"Did the attack happen after the women were killed?" I couldn't imagine crows attacking someone.

"According to the coroner, the first two women were alive when they were attacked by the crows. I don't know for sure yet, but I'd bet money that the third victim was also alive." Uncle Al said this with a very heavy heart.

"Do you think the killer trained these crows, trained them to kill? It seems impossible to me."

I would never betray a trust. When Uncle Al unloaded the horrors of these murders, all I could do was remain seated in stunned silence. What kind of person could do something like this? And crows…why crows? How could this happen? It seemed to me that it was an act of pure evil, and I thought of my saints and the type of evil they had confronted through the centuries. I also thought of Juliano, and that frightened me.

Uncle Al was thoroughly perplexed. The victims were all attacked and killed by crows, but he didn't know how or why. If there was someone behind the killings, he had no clues to follow up.

He looked around to see if anyone was listening: "Chris, I know that I shouldn't ask you, but can you ask for help? You know from your … compatriots." Uncle Al sometimes had problems calling the saints, saints. It wasn't because he didn't believe, but if he acknowledged that I was talking to saints, he was sure both our sanities could come into question.

"Unc, it really doesn't work like that. I get the visions when they come, and they can come at any time. I have no control over them."

"I wouldn't ask, Chris, but I am very troubled that this will happen again soon. If you could see the bodies and speak with the families of these murdered women . . . I mean, we can't let this happen again."

"I know, but I don't have a way to summon my saints. They come to me when they want to come, and they can visit at anytime. It's their option, not mine."

The waiter, a good guy named Rich, came to our table and placed the food in front of us and refilled our wine glasses. Rich asked if we needed anything else. We didn't, and he left.

"I guess you're right, but I feel so powerless. These women are being murdered, and there are no clues, no evidence, nothing I can follow up on. It's like there is an evil spirit that just comes and goes as it pleases."

My face must have turned ghostly pale because Uncle Al seemed to snap out of his funk, and he said, "Chris, my lord, you just turned white as a sheet. Are you okay?"

"Uncle Al, I have to tell you something, but I don't know if you'll believe me. You've taken my word about my visions, but there is something else I need to tell you. It's something I couldn't say to you before because I needed you to believe me about the saints first."

Uncle Al looked at me bewildered and said, "What do you need to tell me that made you turn so pale?"

"You even hinted at it in your letter when you left my home to get back to your house."

"I knew it. Chris, tell me, I am always here to listen and help if I can."

"I know you are Unc. I've told you I've seen the holiest of visions, but you should know I've also seen the purest of evil. I've seen the devil himself."

"What?"

I know that Uncle Al was taken aback by what I had said, but I continued, "I've seen Satan himself. Well, at least I think he's *the* Satan or at least one of hell's legion. He is a demon so vile, so vicious that…"

I stopped to gather my thoughts and continued, "Let me put it this way, he was there in the house when I was looking for Tina. He was in control of the men that were getting kids hooked on drugs. It was he who wanted me to rape Tina."

"Chris, I understand this was the worst of men. A vile human being, but…"

"No, Uncle Al, he wasn't human. He was a demon sent from hell to corrupt, to create havoc, even to kill. He knew about me, and he knew about my visions—no one knew these things, not even you at the time."

"Chris, I can see why you would think this, but how can you be so sure?"

I then began telling my story of St. Mary Magdalene and of how we were transported to the crypt after the Resurrection. I told Al that the demon became frantic at merely being in the place where Christ's body was interred. I told Al about how the demon transformed into such a hideous figure that I couldn't even look at his face.

"His first name is Juliano, but I don't know his last name or even if he has a last name. I guess when you're from hell, it doesn't matter what your real name is." I looked down at my plate of food and realized that I hadn't eaten a bite.

I looked across at Al's plate, and it also hadn't been touched. I looked back up at my uncle and said, "I've thought about this a lot. It seems to me that you can't have the consummate good without having the consummate evil. Kind of like the flip sides of a coin."

Uncle Al looked at me with those penetrating eyes and said, "Chris, I believe you. I guess if you can talk to saints, it's not out of the realm of possibility that you can speak with demons or to Satan himself."

I thought about this and said, "This is different. He can be seen by anyone, and he can speak with anyone, whereas the saints only seem to speak with me."

"You say it was at the drug house where you first saw this Juliano character. What did he look like? How old was he? How did he dress? You say his name was Juliano—did he speak with an accent?" Uncle Al, being a cop, always asked such questions. The questions kept coming, and I tried to answer.

"He was a very handsome man, elegant and polished looking. You know the type. He looked about my age, maybe a little older or even a little younger. I don't know for sure. He was dressed very well in expensive suits, the kind I can't afford, even on sale."

"Okay, anything else?"

"Well, he didn't speak with an accent, but he did speak in that very refined manner, kind of like an English gentleman, but without the British accent. Know what I mean?"

"Yeah, I do." I could tell that he was thinking like a cop who was in the midst of an investigation.

"You know Uncle Al, when you said that you thought it was some evil spirit doing these horrendous murders, I immediately thought of Juliano."

"Why? Do you think he committed these murders?"

"Oh, I didn't mean to say he was the killer. It's just that these murders were so vile, so evil, that I could see it might be the work of the devil."

At that moment Rich came back to the table and looked down and saw our two plates were still full of food.

"Is there anything wrong with your dinner, gentlemen?" Rich was clearly upset we hadn't devoured out meals.

"No Rich, everything is fine, but when Al and I get to talking, we sometimes lose track of time. Do you think you can take these back to Frank and ask him reheat them for us?"

Rich smiled and said, "Sure, no problem." With that, he took the plates and went back to the kitchen. As Rich walked away, Al was watching him to be sure he was out of earshot. When he knew we couldn't be overheard, he said to me,

"It's probably, at best, a long shot, but I'm going to run that name through our criminal data base to see what comes up."

I was glad that Al was trying to do something, even though I suspected it would be futile. I said, "I expect you're right and nothing will come up, but it seems like it's worth a try."

"Hey Chris, getting back to what we were talking about, can you please ask your friends to help us out here? I hate putting you on the spot, but it seems that's all I have left. These poor women are being killed—no, not killed. They are being mutilated beyond recognition, no forensic evidence, no leads, no nothing, and we are powerless to do anything about it."

He was dead serious, but I didn't have the heart to tell him again that I couldn't control when or where the saints would appear. I told him that I would try, but not to hold out much hope if I didn't get the kind of help he was looking for.

We continued to discuss this when Rich came back to the table with our food. He placed the plates in front of us and said, "Frank told me to tell you that you better finish this before it gets cold again, or he's coming out to kick your asses. I think he meant that in the nicest possible way."

I looked up at Rich and then over to Uncle Al, and we both crack up. Al said, "Sure, I'll bet he feels real brave with a ladle in his hand."

Well, it turned out that we were both very hungry, so we dug into our meals with genuine gusto. My chicken was excellent, as usual, and it was served with linguine in the same sauce as the scarpariello. Al's pork chops were tremendous with just the right amount of heat from the cherry peppers, and he also had pasta on the side in a garlic lover's marinara.

For five minutes, we ate like condemned men eating our last meal, and the next time we came up for air, Al says,

"I can't get over how much I love this food. How's yours?"

"Great, this is my favorite dish, but I have to say the pork chops are my second favorite."

We continued eating and talking about different things…anything but the murders. Uncle Al had met a new woman who he seemed to like very much. He said her name is Eileen Silverman, and she's a schoolteacher.

"Yeah, she teaches eleventh grade math at Huntington High School and is a widow. Her husband died five years ago in an automobile accident, and she is just starting to get back to having a social life. I think she's very pretty. She has a wonderful smile and great sense of humor."

I was curious, "How did you meet her?"

"You're not going to believe this, but I actually met her at a supermarket. Can you believe that? Right next to the barbecued chicken! She lives alone, and she was buying dinner for the evening, just like me. We talked, and I guess we just needed some company, so I asked her if she would like to have dinner. I took her to the Golden Dolphin diner."

"You're kidding, my uncle the pickup artist, meeting strange women in the supermarket." I pretended I was making fun of him, but I was really very happy. He is such a great guy, and it would be a good thing for him to meet someone, and she sounded like a good woman.

I was curious, "Does she have any children?"

"She has a daughter and a son, but they are both out of the house and living on their own. Her daughter works as a pediatric nurse practitioner, and her son is software design engineer."

"Wow, they sound really smart. Have you met them yet?"

"Nah, it's really too soon."

"What did you tell her about yourself?"

"Well, I told her I was a cop, and I think that's the only reason she agreed to go out with me to the diner. That was our first date, but I asked her out for dinner next Saturday and she agreed. I am looking forward to it. Speaking of dates, how's Beth?"

"Well, if it got any better, I'd think I died and went to heaven. She's a great person in so many ways, and she doesn't take any shit from me."

Al smiled and said, "That's good, keeps you on your toes. Are you two getting serious?"

"Yeah, well I'm getting serious, and I guess she feels the same way. But I think that I could never offer her the kind of life that she now has."

"Cut the bullshit. If you love each other, all that other stuff will work itself out. Oh, by the way, you aren't exactly destitute."

"Well, I may not be destitute, but you should see her parents' home in Lloyd Harbor. They've got more bathrooms than I've got cans of San Marzano tomatoes, and I've got a lot of cans—by the way, they're on sale, the 28 oz cans are only $1.99 with a minimum $25.00 purchase, so I stocked up…"

"Shut up and listen to me, Julia Childs. Does she keep bringing up her money to you? Does she flaunt her family's wealth in front of you? Does she expect you to buy her expensive dinners, or expensive anything, for that matter? Does she look down on what you do or how you live? If you answered yes to any of these questions, you're right; she's a shallow, self-absorbed, money-hungry bitch. If the answer is no, then you need to give this whole two different worlds thing a rest." I guess my uncle was right, but I still couldn't get it out of my mind, and I thought that this was the reason that I hadn't let the relationship get really serious.

Uncle Al saw that I was quietly thinking about what he said, so he turned the conversation back to the demon Juliano.

"This guy, or should I say devil, Juliano, did he tell you anything else that could be used to get insights into the situation?"

"Not really, but his right-hand guy, Heriberto…you know, the guy who shot you."

"Yeah, I seem to remember something about being shot."

"Well, Heriberto ranted about bringing the forces of hell down on me. I took it as tirade against the world, but now it seems that it could mean he knew the true nature of Juliano. I don't know. It's just so weird that I don't know what to think."

"Anything else?"

"Juliano told me that I had never had to face the ultimate evil, and that he would show me its true meaning. After that episode, I was sent a few visions, and the message in each one was that I would face the vilest of evils—I need to be strong in my faith and have courage against what I would be facing."

"Is that the reason you questioned me about facing your fears?"

"Yeah, and I keep questioning whether I would be brave when the time came to man up. It's easy to hope that I would be brave, but in facing that kind of horror, I don't know if I can."

"Chris, you can never know how you would react to the kind terror you may have to confront, but you should know that you are not alone. You were chosen by God for a reason, and that reason will become apparent to you at the time of your greatest horror, a time when all you hold dearest is questioned."

When all I hold dearest is questioned…Uncle Al's words rang like a warning bell in my head, and it made my very frightened.

Chapter 33

I'm usually not the depressed type, but when I got home after my dinner with Uncle Al, I was really down.

I was exhausted, but all I could do was pace up and down the floor in my condo trying to think things through. I thought of the horror that awaited me and the evil I would confront. I thought about my own faith and my own dread as I kept asking myself, would I have the courage to face it on my own? Fear is such a crippling illness; yes, it is an illness, I thought. I only wished that I would have the ability to cure myself when the time came.

I wanted to call Beth just to hear her voice, but it was late, and I knew she had an early shift at the hospital. Even though I was wide-awake, I went to bed and turned on the TV and switched to the news channel, knowing that I would get bored and fall asleep. But exactly the opposite happened as I heard the anchor:

"We have breaking story! It has just been reported to the News Center that the horribly disfigured body of woman has been found. When examining the victim and the crimes scene, the investigators determined that that the young woman, possibly in her twenty's, may have been pregnant."

When I heard this, all I thought of Uncle Al and the uproar that the leak of this murder would cause.

"Our sources also tell us that the woman—whose name will not be released until her family has been notified—was so badly mutilated that she was unrecognizable and that forensics would need to use fingerprints and dental records to identify her."

I thought of my dinner with Al and how he wanted to keep this under wraps until they had solid information on the killer. How could the details of the story get out? Who could possibly have told the media? I was still listening when I nearly fell off the bed:

"Sources also said that this was not the only incident where a young woman was killed. It seems that there were two prior murders committed in the same brutal way, and the police have been keeping this under wraps. Speculation is that there is a serial killer on the loose, and the police department is trying to determine who it could be. We will continue to bring you updates on this breaking news story as we get them..."

I had to speak to Uncle Al, so I lowered the volume on my set and picked up the phone to make the call.

"Hello," a disheartened voice answered the phone.

"Hi Uncle Al, I guess you turned on the news."

"I did. Chris, this is the thing I was worried about most, and it's happened, blasted over the news so every nut in the world will try to claim responsibility. I am at my wit's end. What do I do now?" Uncle Al was not talking to me; he was just talking.

"Can you guess who might have told this to the press?"

"I can't imagine that anyone on my team, or in the whole department for that matter, would ever leak this out. I'm calling a meeting first thing in the morning, and I'll try to get to the bottom of this, but I'd stake my life that it wasn't one of my team."

I stayed silent because I didn't know what to say to him.

"Chris, you still there?"

"Yeah, I am. I just don't know what to say to you. I wish I could help. I really do."

"Chris, you can help by getting your saints involved. Ask them to help you like they did with Tina. Please, we have to catch this scumbag, so he can't harm anyone, anymore."

The last thing my uncle wanted to hear was all the reasons why I couldn't summon the saints to help, but he needed to have some hope, so I said, "I will try. I really will. I promise." There was little more I could do, but I wanted to give him some solace.

"Thanks, Chris. Listen, I have another call coming in, so I have to get off, but please, call me if you have any visions, and let me know what they are."

"I will, Uncle Al. I promise I'll call if I have any visions, any at all. Just take care of yourself. I love you."

"I will, and I love you, too."

He hung up the phone. I sat on the bed, more depressed than before. I kept thinking of the words "when all you hold dearest is questioned." My family, my friends and Beth are all I hold dear. I couldn't let go of the feeling that they were in danger and that Juliano could somehow be involved.

Thoughts kept swirling around in my head. I said my prayers like I always do, and then I looked at the ceiling until sleep finally took over, and I was out for the night.

The next day I awoke still troubled, but it was a sunny day in early autumn, and my mood seemed to change. I started to make breakfast but stopped, and instead, I picked up the phone and called Beth.

"Hi Beth, it's Chris, how are you?"

"Hi, I'm great. Had a few emergencies earlier, but things are down to a dull roar. How come you're calling? Is everything okay?

"Everything is fine, I just wanted to speak with you and tell you that I miss you."

The line went quiet for a moment until Beth said, "I'm glad you did, and I miss you, too."

"Actually, Beth, I lied. Something is wrong…very wrong."

"What! What's wrong? Are you okay? Tell me, Chris, what's wrong?"

I didn't want her to worry, and maybe I shouldn't have said anything, but I guess it's too late now.

"I had dinner with Uncle Al last night and…"

But Beth interrupted, "Is he alright? Oh my God, he didn't get hurt on the job, did he? Chris, please tell me what happened."

"No, Beth, Uncle Al is fine. Well, he's in good health, anyway. He is in the midst of an investigation, and it's tearing him apart."

"Can you tell me about it?"

"I guess I can. It's been all over cable news and online. I haven't seen the papers this morning, but I'll bet it's in there, too."

"Oh my God. I just picked up the paper, Chris, and it's on the front page. They say it could be a serial killer. Those poor women, Chris."

"I know it's truly a horror story, and it's been eating Al alive."

"Does he have any leads or suspects?"

I made a promise to Uncle Al that I would never talk about any of the things that we discussed related to an ongoing investigation, but so much had already been leaked to the press that I knew I would still be able to keep the promise.

"Listen Beth, do you think we can meet for lunch? I'd really like to see you, and we can talk. I'll tell you what I know, which is just about the same stuff that's in the news."

"Sure, I have lunch scheduled at noon. Does that work for you?"

"That's great, Beth. I'll meet you in the hospital cafeteria at noon."

"See you then." She hung up the phone.

Chapter 34

The mood at the Suffolk County Police Headquarters was grave as the team of detectives gathered in Chief Barese's office. The Chief was visibly upset as he faced the group:

"This is a bad situation that has just gotten much worse. Since the story came out, we've had over fifty calls from the usual group of nut jobs, all confessing to be the serial killer. We need to check them all out, but you know as well as I that they're dead ends. What it will do is cut the manpower we have down, and that's going to make our job much harder. I feel bad having to ask this, but I need to know, did any of you mention this case to anyone, anyone at all? Family, friends, anyone?"

Dan Orello was the first to answer, "Chief, you've known us all for years. We've been through a lot together, and I can say this on my life; no one in this room told anyone about these murders."

"I know. I know, Dan. I'm sorry for even asking the question; it's just that this is tying me up in knots. These innocent women, innocent pregnant women, have been killed in such a vicious manner, and I feel powerless in trying to find the killer, or killers."

Det. Christina Shannon spoke next, "I was thinking about these women, too. They are all young women, and all were pregnant, but I can see this causing fear and panic among all women of any age. What makes me most disheartened is that we can't even get a solid lead, and that scares me."

"Me, too. When I saw those photos of the women and the fetuses on the ground, my heart broke. What kind of person, or persons, would do such a depraved and evil thing? Using crows to rip apart flesh like that and some maniac ripping the fetus from the womb like that…" Det. Avery Michaels couldn't find the words, so she went quiet.

The group sat silent for a few minutes, and then it was Det. Christian Oliver who spoke:

"Chief, I don't know about the rest of you, but I'm not used to feeling powerless. We have to do something. We have to have some kind of plan to catch this bastard and stop these killings. No matter how remote, I think we need to follow up on anything that could be connected to the case—anything."

"I agree, but there are no—wait, I want you to check out this name, Juliano. It is probably nothing and will lead to nowhere, but let's try anyway."

Det. Shannon asked, "Who is this guy, Juliano? Does he have a last name? Do you think he has any connection to this case?"

Uncle Al was beginning to have second thoughts about sending his team on a wild goose chase, but it seemed to awaken the team from their very somber mood.

"I really can't say who he is or if he has a connection to the case. I don't have a last name, but he's supposedly very good looking, well dressed, with posh manners. I'd like to know if he is in the data base, or if he, or a person like him, has been connected to any other crimes, including murder."

"Okay, Chief. Anything else that you think we could work on?" Dan was always looking to explore all the angles, all the possibilities.

"Not right now, but I would like to know who leaked this thing to the press, so keep your eyes and ears open for anyone who could be the guilty party. Got it?"

They all responded, "Got it."

The detectives were walking toward the door when the Uncle Al said, "Wait a minute. There is one more thing. I want to you interview all those young girls and boys that were being pimped out of that drug house on the South Shore. Ask them if they ever heard of this Juliano. You might also want to talk to that scumbag we caught at the house; he might know Juliano."

Det. Michaels asked, "Do you think this guy may have been involved in both incidents?"

"I spoke with my nephew Chris the other night, and he seemed to remember overhearing some of the kids saying that name. He didn't say anything about it because he was worried about me, and he thought it was just another john. I really don't know if he has anything to do with this, Avery. It's just a hunch. But I've learned to play hunches, so let me know what you find."

"We will, Chief." They left the office.

Chief Al Barese suddenly felt better—not because he felt any closer to catching the killer. He just felt better because he and his team were doing something—no matter how far off-track it might be.

They were doing something, and sometimes something is better than nothing.

Chapter 35

I felt a little better after speaking with Beth, but I was still very troubled. Once I ate breakfast, I went to the shop to catch up on the mail and the orders that had piled up over the last few days. I was doing my work, but my thoughts always went back to the evil that I could be facing. I also kept thinking about Uncle Al and his problems, and I wanted justice for the murdered women. Justice would let them rest in peace, and their families could find closure.

It was then that the shop disappeared. I was in a tower high above the city of London.

The executioner was waiting for the man he must behead. The King had commanded his execution, and it would be carried out. How could someone so high, so respected have fallen to so low a state? He had lost everything, his position, his estate and his prestige, and now he would lose his life. He could have obeyed his sovereign lord and compromised his beliefs to a small degree. What harm could it have done? He was a wise and learned man, and he could have found the words to help conciliate his faith and his king—he would be restored to his former position.

How could he be so foolish? How could he sacrifice his own life? After all, he had a family.

The blade was honed—very sharp indeed. It would be a clean cut at the neck, momentary pain, and it would be over. A man who had the ear of the king, who was revered for his brilliance and integrity, was now the subject of scorn and ridicule.

Why had it come to this?

The executioner looked up as the door to the top of the tower opened. In walked a man whose grace, dignity and strength were more apparent than ever before. As he walked into the room and smiled at the men who were there, he turned to the executioner and said, "Be swift with the axe. I have not a moment to waste."

He continued to smile as he remembered what he had written as a margin note in his Book of Hours: "Give me your grace, good Lord, to set the world at naught . . . to have my mind well united to You; to not depend on the changing opinions of others . . . so that I may think joyfully of the things of God and tenderly implore His help. So that I may lean on God's strength and make an effort to love Him . . . So as to thank Him ceaselessly for his benefits; so as to redeem the time I have wasted . . ."

As he readied himself, he made the sign of the cross and walked towards his executioner. His hands were not bound as he laid his own head on the wooden block. When the axe fell, the head of St. Thomas More came to rest in the basket below.

I watched in silent sorrow for the man before the saint appeared in front of me. I looked at him, and he seemed to know what I needed to ask:

"Why was this done? Where is the justice? You lost everything—why aren't you angry?"

St. Thomas More looked at me with a penetrating stare. "Have you learned so little from my brothers and sisters? I did what I must do. You must first learn to love the Lord and never compromise the truth. If I would have compromised my faith and all that is sacred, it would mean that I had no faith at all."

I was trying to find words to reply, but they weren't coming. I just looked at him dejectedly.

St. Thomas More continued, "You asked, 'Where is the justice?' At the end of days the answer will be: in the Lord's hands. But until then, it is for man to dispense their forms of justice, and how justice is dispensed will determine man's fate."

"Will there be justice for the murdered women?"

"That is for you to decide." St. Thomas said this as the vision changed; I was transported to a place I didn't know. It was dark, spacious, and the walls were dripping wet, water seeping through crevices in the rocks surrounding me.

I didn't know where I was or why I was there, but I began to hear the sound of traffic noise, cars and trucks. Judging from the noise, I was near a highway or some major road. Then I heard bulldozers along with the rattle of jackhammers. I tried to look up, but all I could see was blackness.

I had started to walk around this dark space when I saw some movement on the ground in a far corner. I couldn't make out who or what it was, so I slowly walked in the direction of the movement. As I did, I heard what sounded like the flapping of wings, the flapping of many wings. I turned away from the moving thing on the ground then looked up again. This time there was more than darkness. On the ledges above were tiny shining eyes staring down at the same movement that I had been walking towards. In an instant something crossed my field of vision and went straight through me. At first I didn't comprehend, but then I realized I was not actually in this place, I was only seeing what was happening.

As I turned my gaze to the huddled mass on the floor, I began to realize that it was a person. The person seemed to be struggling to get up. As I moved closer, I saw it was a woman who looked to be in her twenties, and she did not seem well.

"Are you okay?" I said before remembering that she couldn't hear me.

When she got to her feet, she looked around, not comprehending her situation or even where she was.

In a low, muttering voice, she said to no one, "Oh, my head. What happened?"

She was off-balance but, leaning on the wall, she started to walk and to explore the cave.

"Where the hell am I?" Her voice was getting stronger.

As panic began to set in, she shouted as loud as she could, "Hello? Hello? Can anybody hear me?" There was only silence in response.

Then she yelled "Ouch, what the..." and looked up.

As she did, a large black bird dropped from the ledge above and jabbed its beak into the frightened woman. She screamed. Her screams didn't stop.

I recognized then what was happening, but it was too late for the woman.

Thousands of crows swooped down in a torrent of shrieking black menace. They tore at her body, ripped at her arms, and then they took out her eyes.

I shouted at the dreadfulness of it all, and in a moment, I was gone from the scene. I found myself surrounded by darkness again; then, a light grew, and St. Thomas again appeared before me.

"How could you allow this to happen? That poor girl, how could you allow this to happen?" I said this to him, finding myself near hysteria.

"It is not for us to be in command of evil in whatever form it takes. It is the essence of evil that has allowed this to happen. Do you not remember St. Agatha, St. Rita, St. Fabius? Why did God allow their suffering, their martyrdom? Free will... It allows for good, and it allows for evil."

"Why was I shown this horror?"

St. Thomas More stood before me in the bright glow of his heavenly halo and said, "To deliver justice." With those final words, he disappeared.

The next moment, I was back in the shop and still in a state of shock. When I realized that the vision was over, I grabbed the phone, quickly dialed and was put through to Uncle Al's office.

"Chief Al Barese here."

"Uncle Al, there was another murder."

"What!"

"There was another murder, Uncle Al, and I was there. I witnessed this poor woman being torn apart."

"Wait, Chris, slow down a little. Tell me what happened."

"I was in the shop thinking about all that you are dealing with, and I had another vision."

"You did? Who was the saint in your vision?"

I caught my breath and said, "St. Thomas More."

"St. Thomas More? You mean the lawyer, the philosopher? That St. Thomas More?"

"Yes. I witnessed his execution in the Tower of London," I said, trying to catch my breath.

"Calm down, Chris—what did he say to you?"

"Well, I asked him about the women who were murdered. I asked about justice for their deaths, and he said that it was for me to decide whether they got it."

"What did he mean by that, Chris? He can't possibly expect you to bring this lunatic demon to justice."

I didn't know how to respond to this because I didn't know what was expected of me. Sts. Cosmas and Damian had asked me for my purpose in life and what was expected of me. I thought that I knew the answer, but now I was questioning it all.

Uncle Al heard my silence and said, "You said there was another murder; tell me what you saw."

"I was in a cave or pit or whatever. I saw the helpless woman being torn apart by crows. Thousands of crows, Uncle Al, and it seemed that they knew what they were doing. They knew she was helpless, and they were there to tear her apart."

"Chris, listen to me. Do you have any idea where this cave or pit was, any idea whatsoever?"

I thought about my time in the cave and remembered the sounds that I had heard. I told him that I seemed to be in a place near a highway or some large main road, and there were the sounds of cars speeding by.

"Anything else?" Uncle Al was getting anxious.

"I also heard the sounds of some construction going on. You know—bulldozers, jackhammers, that type of stuff. That's really all I was aware of."

"What about the cave or pit—was it small? Large? What else can you tell me, Chris?"

"I really couldn't say if it was large or small. It was very dark, and the woman was huddled on one of the sides of the cave. Uncle Al, if you could have seen how they attacked her, how they…" I trailed off as I thought of the terror she must have felt.

"Okay, Chris, it's okay. Did St. Thomas tell you anything else about the murdered women, anything that could be useful?

"No, nothing."

"Okay, Chris. Can you come down to the office? I want to go over all this, and I think that it would be better to do it with you in person."

Uncle Al usually has good instincts, but I know that he was totally puzzled by all of this. If he thought that it would be better for me to go, then I would go. "Sure, I'll get over as soon as I can."

"Thanks Chris, see you in a little while." And he hung up the phone.

As I began to put things away at the shop, I remembered that I had told Beth I would meet her for lunch. I called the hospital.

The phone rang, and she answered, "Nurses' station, Beth Della Russo speaking."

"Hi Beth, it's me, Chris."

"Oh hi, how are you doing? How's Al?"

"Well, I just got off the phone with him, and he'd like me to come to his office. I think he needs to bounce things off someone outside the department, and he asked me to stop by."

"You know, Chris, I can't stop thinking about those poor women. I read the paper and heard some of the reports on the radio and TV, and it sounds so senselessly violent. It's hard to imagine who might have done this."

"I know, Beth; I feel the same way," I said, knowing that there was another dead woman ripped apart by crows and someone or something so evil that it defies description. After a short lull in the conversation, I said, "Listen, Beth, I know I promised you lunch, but Al sounded really down. I think he'd like me there now. I need to break our lunch date."

"Sure, no problem." Beth sighed and said, "Well, I guess I'll see you sometime." She sounded as disappointed as I was.

"Hey, wait a minute Beth, how about dinner tonight? I'd really like to see you, and we can have more time together. Are you free?"

"I was hoping you'd ask. Sure, I'm free. What time do you want to meet and where?"

"Can I give you a call later at home? I don't know how long I'll be with Al, but as soon as I know, I will give you the time. How about Santa Rosa Café?"

"Sounds good, see you then." She stopped for a second and then she said, "I miss you and can't wait to see you."

"Me too, I...I'll see you later." I wanted to say, "I love you," but the words just didn't come out.

Chapter 36

It was forty minutes before I arrived at the Suffolk County Police Headquarters. I went to the front desk to ask for Chief Detective Al Barese, but he was just coming down the hallway and rounding the corner when he saw me.

"Hey Chris, thanks for coming. Let's go to my office."

He walked me down the hallway to his office. Before he opened the door, he said,

"Listen Chris, I am going to come up with something that explains the whole Juliano thing, so just go along. Okay?"

"Sure Uncle Al, whatever you say."

When he opened the door there was his team sitting on chairs surrounding a small conference table in his office.

"Chris, I'd like you to meet my team. I think you know Det. Orello."

"Sure, hi Dan, good to see you again."

"Same here, Chris, good to see you, too."

Next he introduced me to the two women on the team: "This is Detective Michaels, and this is Detective Shannon."

"Wow Chief, you didn't tell us he was so cute!" They both said this just before they started to laugh.

"Okay you two, cut it out." Their laugh turned into a smile as my face turned red.

"And this is Detective Oliver. Now you've been introduced to the group, I want to tell you what we've been talking about." Uncle Al said this as I sat down in one of the chairs around the table.

"Chris, my team knows that you were responsible for rescuing Tina Staley and exposing those pieces of shit that ran that prostitution ring. I've also told them about our conversations and some of the things you remembered after you were questioned."

I became nervous. I couldn't imagine that he said anything about my visions, but what else do these people know? So I held my breath and waited for him to continue. Then my uncle looks me straight in the eye, as if to say, just keep your mouth shut.

"I also told them about the name you overheard from a kid that was in the house. Juliano. You said that you thought it was just the name of some john, but we have been doing some digging around in our database, and we've come up with a few things."

I immediately sat up straight in my seat and asked, "Things, what things?"

"Well, I'll let each one of my team members tell you what they've found, starting with Detective Michaels."

"Thanks, Chief. Well, we came up with some interesting things. First, we got a hit on a guy with the name Juliano who was somehow connected with a string of suicides last year in California. There was no real connection between the victims, but they all committed suicide in the same way; they slit their own throats. In one of the suicide notes, the young woman mentioned the name Juliano, and it seems he was of the same general description that Chris gave the chief. We checked to see if the Orange County police had any leads, but it seems that this Juliano just vanished."

The group sat there in silence as Det. Michaels continued, "Next, we got another hit on the database, not on the name Juliano, but on a Julian—again, no last name but the same general description. This time it was a series of brutal murders committed by the serial killer, Sam Stellment. Sam pretty much didn't care who he killed, so we have men, women and child victims, and in each case, he cut out their hearts while they were still alive. He was judged to be criminally insane, and he is now locked up in some Illinois institution and should be there for life. Stellment told investigators that he did it because he was asked to by Julian."

You could almost feel the tension in the room mount as she continued: "The last incident of a crime connected with the name Juliano was, and here's the interesting part, the deaths of eight young prostitutes from the Atlanta area in a crack house. It seems that this Juliano was involved in some way with a drug ring that pimped out these kids by getting them hooked. Sound familiar?"

We all started to look at each other as she continued, "What happened was that one of the fathers of some poor kid that was dragged into this mess came looking for her. Well, he found her alright, but when he confronted the scumbags that were operating out of the house, they captured him and tied him up. Sound familiar, Chris? Before they killed him, they went around to all the kids that were in the house and murdered them. They did this because they thought that the police were onto them, and they wanted to get rid of all the potential witnesses. The plan was then to leave town and get as far away as possible. Now here's the weird part…"

Did she say, "Weird part?" I was thinking how could this get any weirder?

"The killers now come to get the father, but he has managed to get free of the ropes that he was bound with and gets hold of a baseball bat. When the killers get to the room, the father smashes the bat into the face of one of the guys, immediately jamming his nose through his brain. When the other guys see this, they grab for their knives and guns. But Dad is ready, and he gets another one in the balls, I mean testicles, and he is out for the count. Gunshots are fired, but everyone is scrambling for cover. The next thing, batman takes aim at one of the two men left standing, and he clips him on the side of his head, crushing his skull. I mean brains and all are on the floor. So the last guy sees this, and he takes the gun and starts to fire widely, but the dad is one step ahead, and he clobbers the last one but not before he gets shot dead himself."

I couldn't believe this story, so I said, "How the hell did they get all the details of this horror show?"

"Glad you asked. When the police arrive, they see the carnage, and they are tearing the place for any survivors, and who do they find? The guy who got busted in the balls—I mean testicles…"

Uncle Al interrupts, "It's okay. You can say balls."

Det. Avery Michaels smiles and says, "…In the balls, and he is scared shitless, so he starts to spill his guts. He is telling the cops everything about the killings, everything about the dad with the bat, and that's when he says that his gang is headed by…want to guess?"

Uncle Al is getting a little peeved, "Just tell us."

"Juliano."

I am sitting there in stunned silence. I can't imagine having to deal with what these police deal with everyday, but as I heard of the bloodshed and the butchery, I have to be glad it's not me who's on the frontlines of this.

Uncle Al asked her, "Avery, do you have anything else?"

"No, Chief. If he is involved in other mass killings, he hid them pretty well."

"Thanks. Det. Shannon, it's your turn."

"Well, Chief, Det. Orello and I interviewed the kids from the drug house. Most were still in pretty bad shape given the trauma and the drugs, but I did get some interesting information from some of them." Det. Christina Shannon then took a very dramatic pause before she continued, but maybe it wasn't such a good idea because Uncle Al was getting impatient,

"Well, are you going to tell us or what?" Everyone could see the chief was getting peeved.

"Sorry, Chief. Of the twelve young women and young men we interviewed, there were three who acknowledge that they had seen Juliano. There may have been more who knew, but some were either so scared or screwed up that we felt their information could be suspect. The first kid we interviewed was Destiny Pride—that's her real name. She's a local kid who is only fifteen but has been on the streets for more than a year. She told us that Heriberto raped her every week, and she was forced to have sex with the others in the gang. We asked her if she ever heard of the name Juliano, and she became very nervous."

I asked, "Why did she become nervous?"

"Well, as she explained it, Juliano was a very, very creepy character. So creepy that hardly anyone would even look him in the eye. She said he talked funny like, and I quote, 'Some of those news guys on TV.' She also said every time he was around, something bad would happen. I asked her to tell me what happened that was bad, and she said that one of the girls accidentally spilled soda on his fancy shoes, and she disappeared. Another time, one of the boys was fooling around with a cigarette lighter he found. He said it belonged to Juliano, and the next day he was dead. There were other incidents, but she said that all the girls were so frightened of him, and that they just kept quiet."

As the picture of Juliano emerged, I could see that all the detectives were conjuring up descriptions like "psychopath" or "sociopath" or some other psychological term to describe a serial killer of historic proportions. I knew differently, and I think Uncle Al thought the same as I.

"The next young girl we interviewed was Aisha Thompson. She was from out of town and taken to this drug house by members of MS-13 who supplied a lot of these kids from all over. She is only sixteen, but she has been a prostitute for almost three years. She says that her parents were both drug addicts, and she grew up on the streets. Aisha met Juliano at the house, and she thought that he was nice at first. He gave her candy and cigarettes, and she liked that he was so good-looking and had such fancy clothes. She said that one night he came into her room and lay down beside her in the bed. She thought that he wanted to have sex, but he just laid there. She turned over to try to touch him, and when she did, her hand got burned. I saw the scars."

Det. Oliver asked, "What happened to Juliano after the kid got her hand burned?"

"She said that as she was crying from the pain, he got up out of bed and walked to a dark corner of her room and disappeared. She might have been high or in shock at the time, so we need to presume that he just walked out of her room."

Uncle Al looked very tired at this point and asked, "Anything else, Christina?"

"No, Chief. But I'd love to get my hands on this Juliano or Julian. These are just kids."

"I know you would, so would we all. Anyway, your turn Christian."

"Well, gang, it seems to me that I won the lottery when I got to interview Manulo. He is a low level hood who took his orders from Ernesto Vasquez, a higher-level hood who reported to Heriberto Quintana, the top-level hood at LI chapter of MS-13. I spent more than two hours questioning this bastard to see what he knew about Juliano, and I've got to tell you, this guy is six fries short of a happy meal. It was beyond strange that Manulo wouldn't even say the name, Juliano. All he did was refer to him as el Diablo, the devil, for the uninitiated."

When Det. Oliver said this, Uncle Al and I just looked at each other.

He continued, "Anyway, Manulo tells me that Juliano would come by the house every few days, and when he did, something terrible would happen—pretty much what Christina heard from the kids."

"Did he let you know some of the 'terrible' things that happened?" I was getting very nervous hearing all these horrific things, but it was kind of like a train wreck; you didn't want to look, but you couldn't turn away.

"It seems that this guy Juliano didn't only target kids for torture or death, he reserved some of that for the crew. A little story...there was this soldier in the gang, a low level thug who was used as kind of an enforcer. His name was Oscar Rivera, and he was about a tough as they come and about as insane as you can be without getting locked up. Heriberto used him to keep the girls and boys in line, to keep the neighborhood in line and to take care of problems when they came up. In his case, a problem meant to kill someone who needed killing. As Manulo tells it, one day Rivera comes into the house, and he seems high on something. He starts to beat up one of the hookers, practically kills her, for no reason. Quintana tries to stops him, but even he was scared of Rivera, especially a high "I don't give a shit" Rivera. When it's over, Oscar collapses into a stupor, and Manulo and Julio drag him into a bedroom to sleep it off."

You could feel the tension as we all sat listening to this, trying to guess what's going to happen.

"As I later learned, it seems that Rivera had a penchant for beating up people of all sizes and shapes. It had been costing the drug enterprise undue loss of revenues and an undue amount of scrutiny by the authorities, so to speak. Well, as luck would have it, in walks Juliano who sees the hooker and questions Manulo about what happened. Manulo tells him the whole story, and when he was done, Juliano asks him where Oscar was. Manulo points to the door, and Juliano thanks him and goes into the room. Well, a few minutes go by, and Manulo can't fight his curiosity, so he goes to the door and tries to listen in, but he can't hear a thing. So next, he figures he'd open the door a crack to peek in. As he does, the door swings wide open, and Manulo is face to face with Juliano. Juliano grabs Manulo by the throat, lifts him two feet in the air, you heard right, and with one hand throws him across the room. This must be one strong dude if you can believe Manulo. Anyway, Manulo lands on his ass, and when he looks up, he sees Oscar Rivera hanging in midair, nothing holding him up, just his body floating in midair, and he's literally cut down the middle like a pig in a slaughterhouse. Now get this, while Rivera is hanging in midair, he starts to cry and tries to speak to Manulo, but his jaw is cut in half, so he can't. Juliano now walks over to Manulo, and while he is standing over him, the body of Rivera spontaneously combusts—it turns into a ball of fire."

Det. Oliver stops for a moment to look around the room, trying to gauge everyone's reaction to what they are being told. He sees that each person is somewhere between incredulousness and disbelief, so he continues,

"Manulo freaked out and started screaming, but Juliano simply turns to him and says, in Spanish mind you, 'Si alguna vez respiras una palabra de esto a nadie, podrá disfrutar de la misma suerte que tu amigo Oscar. ¿Entiendes lo que estoy diciendo?' Manulo refused to say it to me in English, but I got it translated, and he said, "If you ever breathe a word of this to anyone, you will enjoy the same fate as your friend Oscar. Do you understand what I am saying?"

Virtually at the same time, Avery and Christina say, "Holy shit!"

"Holy shit is right. Manulo said that he covered his eyes, and when he opened them again, Juliano was gone. There was no trace of Oscar anywhere in the room, not an ash."

Chief Al Barese said, "You don't believe any of this bullshit, do you?"

"Well, Chief, I don't say I do, and I don't say I don't, but all I know is that Manulo believes it."

There was a collective sigh around the room as each of the detectives tried to comprehend all that was told to them about Juliano. At last, Dan broke the silence: "I don't know about anyone else here, but I think we must immediately suspect—because we are dealing with mentally unstable individuals, drug addicts and a career criminal—that is beyond redemption. We have to assume that most of it, or at least some of it, is bullshit."

"Maybe. But one thing they all have in common is Juliano or Julian, and that's a fact."

Dan rubs his neck and admits, "You right about that, but what do we do now?"

Det. Oliver said, "It should be brought to everyone's attention that there is already an APB out for Juliano in relation to the mass suicide in L.A. Plus, we'll add the incidents at the drug house to the list. I think we should leave Manulo's account off for now. What do you say, Chief?"

Uncle Al looked back at his team and said, "I think that's a good idea. We need to get as many eyes on this as possible. I think we can all see that this guy, Juliano or Julian or whatever the fuck his name is, has been involved in some very grisly events. I also think, and I may be way off base here, but I also think that Julian or Juliano could be a person of interest in the murders of the women that are currently under investigation."

Det. Shannon was the first to answer: "You could be right. It seems like a possibility, and quite frankly, it's the only lead we've got."

As the entire group was discussing the possible options, the door to Al's office opens and in walks a uniformed police officer.

"Sorry to interrupt Chief, but I've got some bad news. They found the body of a woman, pretty much in the same condition as the others."

Uncle Al looked miserable as he asked, "Where did they find her?"

"They found her in a large pit in the path of some road construction off Exit 61 on the LIE. The road workers were doing a survey when they came upon the hole, the men climbed down to investigate, and that's when they found the body."

Det. Orello lamented, "Well, that just adds more fuel to a very hot fire under our asses to get this solved." He turned to the uniformed officer and asked,"Was there anything else that was found?"

"Well, the investigators are still combing the scene for clues, but there was a footprint of a man's shoe found near the body. We should be able to get a plaster form of it, and we will try to determine the size and brand."

Uncle Al interrupts the officer, saying, "Listen…" the chief now squints to read the name on the badge, "Listen, Officer James. I want you to tell the police at the crime scene that they are to close it off. No one enters unless I approve it. Do you understand?"

"Yes, Chief."

"Thanks. You can leave."

"Yes, Chief." The police officer turned and left the room.

The entire team seemed to fall into a depressed state when they heard another knock on the door.

Another young police officer entered the room and asked to speak to Detective Oliver. Christian identified himself and asked the uniformed cop what he wanted. "Well, Detective, I was told that you interrogated a prisoner Manulo Estaquino yesterday, and I thought you should know."

This couldn't be good news, but we all held our breaths: "Know what?" said Det. Oliver.

"Manulo Estaquino was found dead in his cell. He hung himself in an apparent suicide."

Chapter 37

We all sat there, shell shocked after hearing the news about the poor, mutilated woman. The team was doubly depressed because Manulo was dead, and he could have given a detailed description of Juliano. I felt guilty that I couldn't admit to having seen him. In the end though, it all seemed useless to me anyway. This was a demon who could transform into anything or anyone he wanted, so what was the point? The police were chasing a phantom, a soulless, heartless beast from the depths of hell. There was little they could do about stopping this.

Chief Barese was the first to break the silence: "Dan and Avery, I want you to go to the scene of the latest murder, and be sure that nothing gets left out or missed. Report back to me as soon as you can, got it?"

"Yeah Chief, we got it." And they both left the room.

"Christian, go down to the prison cell and see what you can find…a note scribbled on the wall, some kind of clue, anything."

"Will do, Chief," and he left the room.

"Christina, update that APB on Julian to include the things we discussed, except about Oscar Rivera, and be sure it goes out immediately."

"I'm on it, Chief," and she left the room. Now it was just Uncle Al and me alone to go over what we knew and what we could do.

"You know that the APB will be useless; Juliano or Julian is a demon and can change to whatever he wants to be. That poor kid Aisha and creep Manulo were telling the truth about what they saw. You know that, don't you?"

Uncle Al sighed and said, "I know. I know." He sunk into a deeper state of melancholy.

"Unc, you've got to figure that he could have been involved, but how can we possibly stop him?"

"Listen Chris, this is why I am asking for help from the saints. I figure the best way to fight hell is to get help from heaven. You've got to reach out to them again. Beg them. Plead with them for any way to stop this evil." Uncle Al said this with such a heavy heart that I had to get up and put my arm around his shoulder.

"You know I will try, and if the saints appear, I will ask them to help. I promise. But, did you forget what I was told?"

"No, I didn't, Chris. But this whole "delivering justice" is way out of line. You are not equipped to battle drug dealers, let alone a demon from hell. St. Thomas More told you that justice for these women was up to you, but how are you supposed to deliver this justice? Huh, how? Are you going to fight him with fists or guns or knives? Here's a thought; maybe you can put him under citizen's arrest and prosecute him under the U.S. Justice System like they want to do with those terrorists. Chris, the last thing you should do is to try and help by putting yourself in the middle of this mess."

Now Uncle Al was animated, and he wanted to make sure that I got the message.

I wanted him to know that I wasn't looking to be a hero, so I said to him, "I know, and believe me, the last thing I want to do is to put myself in the middle of all this, but if it is meant to be...my fate or destiny or whatever, then how can I control what happens?"

"You can control it by calling me and letting us handle it. I love you, you are my sister's only son, and I promised her that I would take care of you. I take my promises very seriously."

"I know you do, and I love you for all you have done for me." I said this to him because I think he needed to hear it, and I also wanted to get off this subject. As we continued to talk, my uncle kept reminding me that I could get killed trying to stop this evil, and that I had a responsibility to let law enforcement handle bringing justice to the victims."

I asked him in all seriousness, "How can you, the police, bring a demon to justice?"

He thought for a while and said, "Maybe you just confront this demon with goodness—maybe that trumps evil? I don't know, but I know that this has to stop, and it will if I have anything to say about it."

You may have gathered while reading this book that Uncle Al is a man of principle, and when he says something, he truly means it.

"Maybe you're right. Maybe we can use good to trump evil." I looked at my uncle, hoping for another miracle in our lives. I also thought of St. Mary Magdalene, how this devil became furious when confronted with the goodness of prayer.

As we continued to talk, the phone rang, and Uncle Al picked it up: "Chief Barese here."

"Hi Dan, what's up?" He listened to Det. Orello and then said, "Hold on a second." He cupped his hand over the receiver and said, "Listen Chris, this is going to take a while, so if you want to leave, go ahead. I'll call you later, and let you know what's happening. In the meantime, please, don't take any chances. If something comes up, just call and let me handle it. Okay?"

"Sure, Uncle Al. I'll speak to you later. Thanks, and I love you."

He smiled back at me and said, "I love you, too."

I walked out of his office and down the hallway to my car. It was about 5:30 p.m., and I thought of Beth. We had planned to have dinner, and I was looking forward to seeing her again. Her shift ended at 3 p.m., so I called her at home, but no one answered. I got in my car and started to drive home.

About halfway to Huntington, my cell phone rang, and I was able to connect through my car's Bluetooth wireless.

"Hello"

"Hi Chris, it's me."

"Hi Beth, I just tried to call you, but no one answered."

"Sorry, I was on the other line, and I couldn't get off in time to answer your call. How's your Uncle?" She seemed genuinely concerned.

"He's okay, but this case is really a mess, and it's so strange that it defies all logic. I know I promised to tell you what I know, but some of what I've been told is so tragic and horrific that I can't even bring myself to repeat it."

"Chris, I understand. Believe me, I do. I just want to be able to see you. We can talk or not talk about it. It's up to you."

"Thanks for understanding, Beth. I was calling because I wanted to know if we are still on for dinner."

"We sure are."

"I can meet you at Santa Rosa's Café at about 6:30, if that works for you? We can relax a bit; I think I could use a gimlet."

"That would be great…I could use a gimlet, too."

"Terrific. See you then."

"Actually, Chris, I'll need to be a little late. I have the guy coming over to look at my boat. He's going to service it and wrap it for winter storage. Can we meet a little later, say 7:30?"

"No problem. That works for me. See you then."

"Chris, before you hang up, I want to tell you something."

Beth sounded like she had something important to say, so I asked, "What is it? Are you okay?"

The voice on the other end of the phone went quiet, and I asked, "Beth are you still there? Hello?"

"Hi Chris, I'm still here…I just wanted to tell you something, but it can wait until we meet for dinner."

"Is everything okay, Beth? Are you sure you don't want to tell me now?" I started to get a little concerned.

All of a sudden, she seemed to perk up and said, "Don't worry, Rocky; everything is fine. I'll see you at Santa Rosa's Café at 7:30."

"Great, I'll see you then."

I got to the condo thirty minutes later, and it gave me enough time to shower, shave and relax a bit before I would meet Beth. The days were already getting shorter, and by six, it was nearly dark. I was troubled by what I had heard in Uncle Al's office, and I resolved not to speak to her about any of it. At the same time, I was very glad that I would see her at dinner. My feelings for her were already very strong, but I questioned why I couldn't tell her that I loved her.

Before I got into the shower, I called the café and made a reservation. I showered, and it felt good letting the hot water run over my body. It relaxed and reinvigorated my whole being. I put on some khaki pants, a long sleeve polo shirt and a leather coat that I had bought at an end of the season sale last year.

The drive to Santa Rosa's Café was only fifteen minutes, and I got there early. I was seated at a table, and the waitress brought me water and tortilla chips and salsa to munch on while I waited. I thought about ordering a gimlet before Beth arrived, but I decided I would wait, so I ordered an ice tea instead.

I gobbled down the chips and salsa. It was late, and I was getting hungry. When I looked at my watch, I saw the time was 7:24, and Beth would be arriving soon. I kept thinking about what she wanted to tell me. We hadn't been intimate yet, and it really didn't seem to bother either of us, but I am sure it was something we both had thought about. Maybe she wanted to become lovers? Maybe she wanted to take our relationship to another level? Maybe she wanted to tell me that she loved me?

I thought about all the possibilities, and then I thought about what my answer would be and why I couldn't bring myself to tell her what I knew I felt in my heart—a simple, uncomplicated "I love you."

Chapter 38

The night wind turned the temperatures lower as the cold air passed over the grounds surrounding the townhouses.

Beth was waiting. She was anxious. There were so many things that needed to be said, but that would have to wait. She looked out over the bay at the lights on the other side and to the left and to the right and always the darkness in the middle.

The cheeriness of the fire burning in her fireplace should have warmed more than the body; it should have warmed the spirit. The flames threw off little warmth, but it didn't seem to matter. Was it this feeling of expectation? Was it her own imagination?

What was this yearning, this feeling, this passion she felt?

The doorbell rang as she expected. She wanted to answer, but there was something that first held her back. The excitement started to mount as the doorbell rang again. This time she could not resist. She had been waiting for this time to be here.

"Who's there?" but it seemed she already knew.

"Mr. Apollyon," he answered

"Mr. Apollyon?" she questioned, but she opened the door to let him in anyway.

"My word, don't you look lovely this evening. I hope I haven't intruded on your plans."

"Thank you, won't you come in, Mr. Apollyon?" She smiled and liked this man.

"Thank you, and please, call me Julian."

Chapter 39

I looked at my watch again, checked it against the time on my smart phone, and they both read the same, 7:56 p.m. It was not like Beth to be late. I thought about her lateness and rationalized that it was taking more time than expected for the man readying her boat for winter storage. I would give it until 8:00, and then I'd call to see how things were going.

I had already ordered a vodka gimlet on the rocks because I needed some fortification for a conversation that may never happen or happen only in my mind. It was now 7:58, and the door to the restaurant opened, but it wasn't Beth. I continued to wait until my self-imposed deadline came around.

At 7:59, I said what the heck, and I called her home phone, but it answered with a prerecorded message: "Hi, this is Beth, and I'm not available, but just leave a message after the tone, and I will call you back as soon as I can. Have a wonderful day…" Nice message, I thought. So after the first beep, I said, "Hi Beth, it's me, Chris. I'm at Santa Rosa's, and I was wondering where you were…" but before I could complete my message, a voice came on the phone:

"Hello, Christopher. It has been a while since we last spoke. I hope you are doing well. It is I, Julian, or Juliano, if you prefer."

My mind froze, and I found myself unable to speak.

"Christopher, are you still there? It is rather rude for you to not acknowledge my greeting; after all, it is only common courtesy. Christopher, I know you are there."

"I'm here." It was all I was able to say.

"Ah, that's much better. Are you enjoying your drink? I hope you are because I expect that you will need to buttress yourself for what I fear will be a very long evening."

"Where is Beth? What the hell are you doing at her house?" I found myself yelling into the phone, and the patrons of the restaurant began to look over at my table.

"Beth is quite a woman, isn't she? I find her most charming, an eager ingénue—more than a nurse, don't you think? As luck would have it, she will be playing the role of a lifetime, and I expect to be her costar. I imagine we will become quite close, and it is rather exciting for me—quite exciting!"

"Listen, you piece of shit from hell, if you harm even one hair on her head, I'll…" but Julian didn't let me finish.

"What will you do Christopher? Your saints will abandon you. Did you know that? They will set you aside like so many old magazines."

"You lie. They are more powerful than you can ever imagine."

Julian chuckled a bit: "You mean that pathetic attempt to intimidate me at the cave? Mary Magdalene was a whore in life, and she will always be a whore. Anthony, that pathetic abbot—who brought back to life those children I had taken—felt my wrath. Do you think that they, or any of them, can ever defeat me or my minions?"

"What about St. Michael the Archangel. I seem to remember that he kicked your ass and sent you to the depths of hell. What about him?" I felt the need to defend the saints.

"Ah, Christopher, I have learned so much more since then, and I've had far more practice than you could ever imagine. Mankind, the weaknesses, the lusts, the excesses, the sins. Men, now let's be sure to have gender equality in this equation, and women are fodder for my cannon. They are easy prey because the freedom of evil is easier to accept than the constraints of good. I do hope I am using the proper grammar and context." Julian laughed out loud over the phone.

I became frightened for Beth, fearful for the women he would continue to murder and, for the first time, doubtful about my saints. I was overwhelmed and totally helplessness. What I should do?

"Oh Christopher, I do hope you are still there. We should try to meet as soon as possible. I recall that you and I have discussed having ultimate evil confront consummate good, and unfortunately, it appears that you are the only advocate for the good side of things. This will be a daunting task for someone, how shall I put it, of your limited ability. What say you?"

I didn't know how to respond.

"Christopher, Oh Christopher! Do I detect some reticence on your part? Time marches on, and you will need to confront your own fears, your own weaknesses and yes, your own faith."

My only response was to say, "Where?"

"Oh, come now, Christopher, take a guess."

"Fuck you. I don't feel like playing your games. Where?"

"My, my, aren't we a bit testy. Pit Island. I believe you know where it is. You and Beth had that wonderful day on the water, remember? You may want to bring something warm and dry. It can get a little wet at times, which I'm sure you can attest to."

The realization hit me as I said in stunned amazement, "It was you who caused that storm, and it was you who almost got us killed."

"Of course, it was me. I love it when you struggle, but alas, I let you live to fight another day."

"Wait, scumbag. Have you forgotten about St. Rita? It was her intervention, her miracle that saved us. Your power may be great, but her power comes from God."

"Believe what you will Christopher, but I fear that when you most need God, He will be as absent as He was when those women died. Comprendere?" He said this mocking the Italian that Beth and I liked to speak.

Julian continued toying with me, and I knew it, but I needed to buy some time to try and figure out what I could do.

"I want to speak with Beth," I demanded.

"I'm afraid that's impossible."

"Why? Where is she? I want to speak with her now." I was starting to realize that I had no power at all, and Julian was looking to make Beth his next victim.

"I'm afraid she's in an area with very poor cellular reception. Pit Island has little in the way of cutting edge technologies, amenities or guest services, so to speak, but I assure you that she will be in fine spirits the next time you see her." I knew Julian was enjoying every minute of this conversation.

While I was speaking, I put $25 on the table and left the restaurant. "I won't come until I speak with Beth." I said this, all the while knowing that I would go no matter what.

"Oh, you'll come, Christopher. You'll come. There are two irresistible reasons: one is Beth, and the other is to face your fears. This conversation has become too sophistic, and I am going to end our discussion now."

"Don't you hang..." but Julian, the demon sent from hell, hung up the phone before I could finish.

I rushed out the door and stood on the sidewalk outside the restaurant thinking about my next move. I ran to my car and headed for Beth's townhouse, trying not to think the worst but knowing the worst could happen. It was close to 9 p.m. when I reached the gates leading to the complex, and then I realized that I had no code to open them. Just as I was prepared to dial her phone, the gates opened.

"Son of a bitch..." I knew it had to be Julian, so I went through the gate.

My mind was going in all directions while trying to contemplate what I would do next. I remembered that I didn't call Uncle Al. I grabbed my phone and dialed his office. When the desk sergeant answered, he told me that the chief was out,so I hung up and dialed his mobile phone.

"Hi Chris, what's up?"

"Uncle Al, He's got Beth. Julian has Beth."

"What! How do you know?"

"I called Beth's home when she was late for our date, and while I was waiting at the restaurant, I tried to phone but he..." and then the line went dead. I tried to call him back, but the connection was completely gone. I drove my car down the road that winds through the complex until I reached her townhouse.

I jumped out of the car and ran towards the entrance. The front door was slightly open, and all the lights were on. I pushed it wider to get a better view, but there was no one I could see on the first level. I slowly walked into the kitchen from the foyer and then into the great room, but there was still no one there. The remnants of logs were still smoldering in the fireplace, but they didn't throw off any heat. I started to search for Beth, going from room to room, but no one was home.

As I went back down to the first floor, I remembered that I hadn't looked in the garage. The garage was off the kitchen, and as I went to the door, I became more cautious. I slowly opened it to avoid any surprises. When I turned on the lights and looked inside, all I saw was

Beth's car on one side and her bike, water skis and some storage boxes piled on the other. I decided to walk into the space to look around. As soon as I did, I saw the note tacked to the garage door. The note was written on a material that I had never seen before, and it felt very strange when I picked it up. As I stood there, I read the note aloud to myself:

> My Dear Boy,
>
> I am thrilled that you could make it. As you can see, we are gone and await your arrival. Beth is in good health and good spirits, and I know that she is anxious to see you, too.
>
> Pit Island will be a bit difficult to get to and since we are already using the Fun-A-Bout (don't you just love the name), I have taken the liberty of reserving a watercraft for your convenience. You will find the conveyance tied to a cleat in Beth's slip space.
>
> By the way, your uncle will be of no use to you. I hope that my discussions with the media didn't cause too many problems? At any rate, I'm afraid you are all alone in this quest of good versus evil, and I assure you that evil will win. Oh, Christopher, I think it's only fair to warn you that if you have any reservations about coming to our little soirée I will have no alternative but to assure that Beth enjoys the same fate as Celine and the rest.
>
> At any rate, we eagerly await your arrival.
>
> Bon Voyage!

When I finished reading the letter, it went up in flames, and as it dropped to the floor, it totally disappeared, ashes and all.

I ran to my car and drove to the marina. The marina was lit with a few lights, and I was able to see a small inflatable in Beth's slip space. The boat had a 15 hp outboard motor and was tied to the cleat, as I was told. Before I left, I tried to call Uncle Al again, but the line was still dead.

There was little else I could do but take the boat to Pit Island. I got onboard, untied the rope, and I pulled the cord for the outboard motor, starting it up immediately. I guided the boat out of the space and headed toward the darkness that was in the middle of the Bay.

Chapter 40

"Chris! Damn it! Chris! Answer me! Damn it!"

Chief Detective Al Barese was practically screaming into his phone, but there was no answer on the other end. What little he heard on the call made him very afraid. They were still at the crime scene, and he turned to Det. Dan Orello,

"Something's very wrong, Dan."

"What? What is it, Chief?" Now Dan was getting concerned.

"I just got a call from Chris. He said something about his girlfriend Beth being held by Julian."

"What? You're serious?"

"I am serious. I told Chris that if there was even a sign of any trouble, he needed to call me. But before I could get any details, the line went dead." Al Barese seemed more frightened than Dan had ever seen before.

"Chief, calm down. Did he say where he was?"

"No, not exactly, but he said he called Beth's home and that's when the line went dead. You got to figure that's where he's headed."

"Right Chief, I'm going to call the local precinct and ask them to send some officers to her house. Do you have the number?"

"No, but she lives in Northport, those townhouses by the water—have them look up her number. The name's Beth, no Elizabeth Della Russo, brunette, very pretty. I think she's 29 years old, 5'6" or 7", 115 to 120 lbs. She's a nurse, and she works at Huntington Hospital. She drives a 2010 Ford Escape, and she owns a boat called the "Fun-A-Bout" that she keeps at the marina in her complex. Dan, she's Chris' girlfriend, but she was also my nurse when I was in the hospital, and I want to get this scumbag before he does anything to her. Got it?"

"Got it, Chief. We're just about done here, and Avery can tie up any loose ends. Do you want to go over to Northport to see if we can find anything?" Dan was becoming as anxious as Al, and he wanted to be there when they got Julian.

"Are you kidding? Let's get moving now!" Chief Barese and Det. Dan Orello climbed the ladder that led out of the pit, and they ran to the Chief's car. With sirens blaring, they sped off west on the LIE towards Northport.

Chapter 41

The cold wind made the bay waters choppy as the small boat pushed through the waves. The distant darkness that was Pit Island now loomed larger as I got closer. I was only focused on getting to the island, but I had no idea about what I would do when I got there.

When I was about halfway to the island, it started to rain a cold and constant downpour. I thought to myself, "It just figures..." but then I thought that this must be Julian's way of welcoming me to my nightmare, his hell.

I was less than fifty yards from what appeared to be the shoreline when I heard a creaking sound and saw a boat jutting out of the water. I tried to make out what it was, but I fear it could only be the wreckage of the Fun-A-Bout. With the bow of the boat sticking out of the water, I couldn't be positive; however, in my mind, I knew it couldn't be anything else. It was impossible to get there any faster than my small inflatable could take me, but I was trying to close my eyes to the possibility that something may have happened to Beth.

I cautiously maneuvered my craft toward the wreck since I was aware of the rocks that were very close to the surface of the water. The boat had a very low draft, so I was able to move closer without having the deck of the inflatable ripped apart by the rocks below. When I was about thirty feet away, I saw a huge hole in the hull of the sunken boat, and it appeared to be abandoned. Still, I needed to see for myself, so I reduced the speed of the outboard to a crawl.

A few minutes later, I was close enough to know that it was Beth's boat by its color and markings. I managed to grab a line and toss it over one of the railings on what had been the Fun-A-Bout. I anchored my small craft, so I could pull closer to the wreck to see if there were any clues as to where Beth might be. That's when I saw the message. The message was burned into the side of the boat and it read, "Abandon all hope, ye who enter here. Love, Julian!" When I finished reading, the message exploded into flames and evaporated into thin air.

The shallow water and rocks below made it impossible to motor on any further, but I was close enough to the shore that I was able to paddle in a bit and jump out. I was in about three feet of water and was able to grab a line and drag the inflatable onto Pit Island.

The rain came down harder now, and the wind picked up. I was soaking wet and the cold wind penetrated my clothes and stung my skin. I looked around to get my bearings and try to see where I might find some kind of shelter from the wind and rain. When Beth and I were out on the boat, I seemed to remember that the island appeared to be about seventy yards long and about forty yards wide. There were large boulders and some trees but not much else. There was no light from the moon, so I was unable to see ahead. I stumbled and slipped over a large rock as I tried to get up the embankment.

Step by step, I tried to walk when I could and crawl when I had to. There was no path and there was no sign of where Julian was holding Beth captive. As I was moving towards what I thought was the center of the island, I stopped to rest by a huge boulder, and that's when I saw something that looked like it was chiseled into the side of the stone. I looked closer and saw what it read: "Christopher, you're getting cold," and as soon as I read the chiseled message, the entire writing burst into flames and vanished.

I expected this of Julian, playing games and taunting me. I looked around hoping to see something that would point the way, but there was only rain and wind. I started to head back in the direction that I came when I fell over a tree stump. As I grabbed onto a low hanging branch I saw something carved into the tree: "You're getting warm, good lad!" and as usual, the carved message burst into flames and disappeared.

I lifted myself up off the ground and looked around again. I continued to walk in the same general direction that I had been going when I came upon what looked like a piece of material torn off of a woman's yellow slick raincoat. I picked it up off the ground and looked at another message written, in magic marker, on the back: "Oh Christopher, you are getting hot!" I threw the torn piece of coat to the side, but before it hit the ground it burst into flames, no remnants, no ashes, no message.

I was sick and tired of these games, and I became more determined than ever to find Beth, to confront this demon from hell, to just get this over. While I was struggling to keep my footing, I reexamined my own doubts about the saints. I needed to try and understand that after all I had been shown, after all the saints have taught me, how can they desert me now? I asked that question of myself over and over, and the answer always came back the same, they won't desert me, not in my hour of greatest need.

The wind and rain were now so strong that they nearly lifted me off the ground. I had managed to walk another thirty feet when I saw what appeared to be a sign. The rain was coming down too hard for me to read it from where I was, so I pushed against the wind to get a closer look. When I was next to the sign, I grabbed a hold of the side of it to help keep my balance:

> **Warning Trespassers**
> Oh, not you Christopher.
> Well, I must say I am proud of you.
> You are sizzling hot,
> Welcome!

I immediately backed away from the sign and looked around to see if Julian was there. My mind was running wild as I didn't know what to expect next. He is a demon and has command over forces that I could never understand, let alone defend against.

In my panicked state, I tried to take a step backwards, but at that exact moment the ground beneath me seemed to give way, and I fell into an abyss. I tumbled down the side of the hole and crashed onto the ground below. I banged my head during the fall, and I was fading in and out of consciousness when I heard, "Welcome, Christopher! Welcome! We are so happy to see you, dear boy! You are a sight for soar eyes! Welcome!"

Chapter 42

Uncle Al was at the wheel of his car careening down the expressway, with the sirens blasting, at over 95 miles per hour. The cars in the center lane shifted to the left or right to give his police car the right of way.

Dan's hands gripped the dashboard, and he said, "Chief, you got to slow it down. You can get us killed, and that won't help Chris or Beth."

Dan was right, so he slowed down to a moderate 80 miles per hour. It was at least ten minutes before he said his first words: "Dan, this has to end. No woman is safe while this bastard is out there, and I intend to see that he is brought to justice." Uncle Al suspected what Chris knew to be true—Julian was a demon, and there was little chance he would be brought to justice. What was important was to see that Chris and Beth were safe. They had to be safe.

"It seems that he's made his first mistake."

The chief looked over at his partner and asked, "What's that, Dan?"

"I know this guy is like a ghost, Chief, but this is our first solid lead ever. As a matter of fact, Chris is the first person who's not an addict or thug or serial killer that has even spoken to the man."

"I guess you're right, but we still need to get him, or I'm afraid that Chris and Beth could be his next victims."

The detectives continued west on the LIE until Uncle Al got off exit 53 and headed for the Sunken Meadow Parkway. It was after 11 p.m., and there was little traffic on the road as it wound toward the last exit for Route 25A.

As the car sped west on the road towards Northport, a voice came through the two-way car radio: "Unit 9 to Unit 1, come in, Unit 1."

Uncle Al answered, "This is Unit 1, Chief Barese here."

"Chief, this is Officer Jim McGowan out of Northport PD. We are at the home of Ms. Della Russo."

"Well, what did you find?"

"When we arrived, the front door was open and the lights on. My partner and I did a thorough search of the residence, and there was no one there."

Det. Orello jumped into the discussion: "This is Detective Orello, was there any sign of a struggle, anything out of place that you could tell?"

"Nothing that we can see. Everything seemed to be in place. Ms. Della Russo's car was still in the garage, and we were just about to go to the marina to see if her boat was still in its slip."

Uncle Al says to the officer, "We are on our way and will meet you at the marina. What's the number of the slip space?"

"It's number eight, Chief."

"Okay, see you in about five minutes."

Chapter 43

My entire body ached after the fall. I had the wind knocked out of me when I fell, and I couldn't get enough breath to speak. I checked my arms and legs and nothing seemed to be broken, but when I tried to get up off the ground, I only fell back down. When I finally could focus, I saw that I was in a huge underground cavern. In the main area, there were many dark corners, and where it was more open, there were a number of large rocks and boulders scattered about. I lay on the ground dazed and confused, but slowly my mind became a bit clearer.

When I was able to get up into a sitting position, the figure of Julian appeared.

He was standing above me looking down, and he said, "I do love dramatic entrances, don't you? I believe they set the tone for all that is to come. Don't you agree?"

I thought I could speak, but I didn't want to give him the satisfaction.

"Come now, Christopher, you can at least be civil."

I finally found my voice, "Fuck you, you piece of shit!"

"Christopher, there is no need for such profanity. After all, I am among the Sainted, aren't I?" He seemed to sneer at the word "sainted."

I then screamed at him, "You are not anything like the Sainted, you are a murdering piece of shit from the depths of hell!"

"Now, now, what did I say? Let's be civil. What say you? You are most welcome. I would have had something specially prepared for you, but as you can see, there is little in the way of cheer in this place." Then he looked at me with mock distress, and in a condescending way he said, "Oh my, Christopher, now I can see why you are so testy. You are soaking wet and still a little foggy. Here, let me help you." With that my clothes became completely dry, my mind was clear, and the pain was gone.

I lifted myself off the floor and bewildered I asked, "What the hell? What did you do?"

"Christopher, *I* could see you were in very sorry shape, and as *you* can see, I am in perfect shape. We cannot have these kinds of imbalances: dry versus wet, up versus down, cold versus hot, love versus hate and of course, good versus evil. As it is ordained, I intend to assure that evil has equal billing with good—maybe even have the starring role. What say you?" Julian offered this with the utmost sincerity. Of course he expected no answer, but he asked again, "What say you, Christopher?"

"I say go fuck yourself. Where's Beth?"

"Oh, she's in make-up right now. Beth will be appearing for the first and, most likely, last time in the starring role of this passion play. Isn't that exciting! And the best part, I am her leading man! Imagine that, a leading man in a passion play. Mom would be so proud!"

"Fuck you, let's cut this bullshit and get it over with." I was very angry and had little else to lose.

Julian smiled, "Oh my, you are in a hurry to die and endure everlasting torment, aren't you? Well, I will be sure to accommodate that, but there is so much more to see before the conclusion of this drama of good versus evil."

"I don't want to see anything you have to show me."

"Oh, Christopher…"

I interrupted him: "Stop calling me Christopher, fuck face."

Julian looked at me, and his face turned into that of the demon that I saw in Christ's tomb. He grew to twice his size, and his eyes turned flaming red, and he spoke in a hideous shriek,"I will call you whatever I choose!"

When I saw his true nature, I was frightened and began to step back away from this beast. Then in a flash, he was back to being Julian, and he spoke,"Dear boy, you do not want to make me angry. I do dreadful things when I'm angry, so please, forgive my momentary lapse. Now that it's settled, I will continue to call you Christopher, is that acceptable?"

I just looked at him and said nothing.

"Good. Isn't that nice—friendly enemies, you and I!"

"I will never be a friend to a murderous fiend like you."

"That is probably true; however, I do have a special evening planned for you, and there will be guests and all. I am so very excited."

"Where's Beth?"

"All in good time, Christopher, all in good time."

Then, in a split second, the floor of the pit changes to what looks like the set of a late night TV talk show. The sound of a drum roll can be heard along with wild screams and applause as Julian appears in a tuxedo with an eerie red spotlight light that surrounds him. He looked at me like I was the audience, and I heard an announcer that sounded exactly like that guy who announces the wrestling matches at the arena: "Ladies and gentlemen, welcome! Welcome to the premier of "What the Hell!" We have a fabulous line up for you tonight, but before we begin, let's give a rousing welcome to the one, the only, JULIAN!!!"

The invisible crowd was in frenzy, yelling and hooting, screaming and laughing at what they hoped would be a show of shows. Julian relished in the applause, and he kept saying, "Thank you! Thank you!" while pretending he is calming down the crowd.

Finally, Julian hushes the audience until all you could hear was a low murmur. He then looks me straight in the eye, and with hellish delight, he started to speak in a slow, deliberate way until he reached a nerve-shattering crescendo:

"Christopher, and all our visitors in the studio tonight, I have a special treat. Dead from the depths of Hell, our first guests have been waiting in the wings and are ready for their time in the spotlight! Ladies and Gentlemen, please put your hands together for a trio that has helped give evil more meaning than before. Ladies and Gentlemen, I give you

ERNESTO VASQUEZ, MANULO ESTAQUINO and JULIO ALMENDE!"

This invisible audience goes absolutely wild. There is cheering, yelling, whistling, screaming with peals of laughter and thunderous applause.

Julian seemed to be in his glory, basking in the out-of-control reaction of his minions. I was frightened by what would come next. It didn't take long for me to find out.

From the large boulder to left of the set where Julian was sitting appeared something out of a nightmare. The three men, or rather remnants of men, were attached to each other in such a way that they looked like they were playing some perverted game of Twister. Their bodies were covered with gaping wounds and cysts, oozing blood and puss. They were screaming for mercy, screaming for forgiveness, screaming for release from their torment.

Julian turns to them, "I know you three have so much to say, but we have a special surprise for you, our guests!" A hush comes over the audience as they wait to hear what his special surprise is.

"For all of you in the studio tonight, I want you to give a warm, or should I say hot, welcome to the merciless angel and the all fire demon, Aftemelouchos or as you may know him, TEMELUCHUS!"

I slowly turn toward the boulder where I first saw the three spirits of the evil men from the drug house. As I did, I saw the figure of Temeluchus, a demon of enormous proportions, appear from behind the rock. The demon carried in one hand a fork of fire and in the other, he carries an iron rod with three hooks. Ernesto, Manulo and Julio are now staring at Temeluchus in abject fear, and he is staring back.

The audience goes completely wild. They sound like they are out of control, and Julian senses that this is the moment he must act. His minions are waiting for what is to come, and he will not disappoint them.

"Ladies and gentlemen, would you like to hear from our three guests?" Immediately, there was a roar from the unseen crowd,"YES!"

Ernesto screams, "Forgive me, please, forgive me. It was all Heriberto's fault! You must forgive…" and then Julio jumps in:

"I am innocent! I didn't do nothing! I was just there; please, I didn't…" and now Manulo joins in, "You must believe me. I was only following orders from Heriberto. I am not guilty of nothing. You must believe me."

Now all three tortured souls are screaming over each other so much that you couldn't understand what they said, but you knew what they wanted.

Temeluchus stood in front of the trio, glaring down at them as they scream for forgiveness. We hear a bellow from the demon that seems to come from the depth of his being.

"BE QUIET. YOU HAVE DAMNED YOUR SOULS!"

The three cowered as the demon stared down at them with blazing eyes. They would not speak at first, but Julio summoned up enough courage to make an appeal for him and the group. He looked up at Temeluchus: "Please, please have mercy on us. We have done many evil things, but we now know that we have sinned against God. Please, forgive us. We did not…"

Temeluchus roars, and all goes quiet.

"He who has not had mercy, neither will God have mercy on him. I am His chief of torment. Let that soul be delivered into my hands, and he must be taken down into hell. Let me take him into the lower prison, and let him be cast into torments and be left there until the great day of judgment."

It seems that Ernesto, Manulo and Julio came to a new realization of the horror that they will face for eternity. They continued to beg for mercy as they to tried to explain their vile and evil crimes against so many. All the while, they are crying, cursing and screaming, and it is a pitiful sight that the audience is taking delight in their suffering.

The three continued, "Please, you must listen; you must forgive us. We will repent. We will atone …"

But Temeluchus would hear no more from any of these damned souls, and he screamed,"Your pleas for forgiveness come too late. You are condemned to suffer an eternity of torment, and I am here to make it so!"

With that, Temeluchus took his fork of fire, and in three short strokes opens the entrails of each of the men. Their guts spill onto the floor of the cavern. They frantically try to pick up their guts and stuff them back into their bodies, but it is a lost cause. Now the three turn back, cowering at the giant demon in their midst.

Temeluchus took his iron rod and with one mammoth stroke he jams the hooks into the heads of Ernesto, Manulo and Julio. The demon lifts the men off the floor of the cave, shrieks a savage cry and in a burst of fire, they all disappear.

It is a mind-numbing and horrific scene, and I felt like I was going into shock. The sheer magnitude of what I had witnessed left me with feelings of fear and dread and beyond that—a creeping sense of hopelessness.

There was complete silence until Julian spoke, "Ah, Christopher! Wasn't that magnificent? Ladies and gentlemen, wasn't Temeluchus wonderful!" A thunderous roar of approval came from the imaginary crowd.

Julian continued, "And what about the trio of evil? Weren't they fabulous? What say you all?!"

Another gigantic roar of approval from the shadowy minions...

Arms held high in the air, Julian is now acknowledging the screaming, whistling and deafening applause. He is reveling in it all.

I sense what is happening as Julian allows this horror to continue. He wants to terrorize me, and he's enjoying the prospect of my denying the Sainted—denying my faith before I die because I will have "abandoned all hope"...as God will have abandoned me.

I might not be in hell, but I was as close as you can get, and I'm thinking now would be a good time for a sign, another vision, but I am alone. Julian gets up from his chair on the talk show set and walks closer to the audience and me. There is a low murmur from the crowd as the devil looks around at his undetectable adoring fans:

"Thank you, thank you all so very much! Drum roll, please! Ladies and gentleman, our next guest needs no introduction. He grew up on the streets, became an entrepreneur at an early age, and he's enjoyed success in the drug and child prostitution arena." The crowd noise now is starting to increase, and the air seems thick with anticipation.

Julian is now becoming even more animated. "Few people know this, but I, your ever dutiful host, have worked with this man, but let's not wait another moment!" The crowd clapped in unison, and they are starting to chant, "HERIBERTO . . . HERIBERTO . . . HERIBERTO!"

Julian shouts above the crowd, "Now for the first time on any stage anywhere in this or any plane, heavenly, earthly or otherwise . . . HERIBERTO QUINTANA and his sidekick GLASYA-LABOLAS!"

All of a sudden, there is a massive burst of applause and cheers from the phantom audience. I am frantically looking around trying to see where he will appear, when out from behind a rock next to the stage came what I feared was Heriberto Quintana, but he wasn't alone.

Quintana floats onto Julian's set three feet off the ground. On his back and shoulders is a hideous demon with a long knife, and with it, he is peeling the skin off of Heriberto's body. The evil spirit appears in the shape of a dog but with the wings of the mythological Griffin and hands, instead of paws, for slicing flesh with his knife.

Heriberto eyes are pleading with me as he tries to scream, but he can't—he has no mouth. The fiend, Glasya-Labolas, is slicing large chunks of skin off his back, sides, stomach and even his face. Once the demon cuts off skin, more grows back immediately, and all the while Heriberto looks at me in wide-eyed terror.

"Come Heriberto, come! Sit down. I am sure there are so many things that the audience would love to know about you. Before the show, we asked these lovely people in our studio to write down questions, and I'll bet they can't wait to hear the answers." Julian seemed to be taking special delight in the horror of this situation.

With that, Heriberto floated over to the set where Juliano sat. There is a chair, but Heriberto does not sit down; he merely floats above it. Glasya-Labolas, however, does sit down, and he continues to cut the skin—this time down Heriberto's legs.

Julian has a group of index cards in his hand, and he started to read from them: "Heriberto, the first question is from Milt Lessenton from the Halls of Montezuma who asks, 'Why the hell are you are in Hell?'" Julian looks questioningly at the card, and he turns to his guest and asks again, "That's a good question, why the hell are you are in hell?"

Heriberto was in unbearable pain as he looked at Julian and tried to bellow, but there were only his screams of silence. Julian looked back at the audience and said, "I think that our guest is a bit shy, but I have inside information, and I will share it with you. Heriberto is here because he was very naughty—very, very naughty. He saw to it that some people did not get to see their next birthday. But I have special treat, if anyone in the audience can guess how many people Heriberto has murdered, he or she will win this brand new Veg-O-Matic! It slices, it dices, it crinkle cuts and juliennes—it washes easily with plain soap and water, and you can take it with you when you travel!"

The invisible audience went crazy yelling numbers: 7, 56, 2, 12, 8, 63 and all the while, Julian in enjoying this immensely. Then the voices go still, and Julian speaks, "Are those all the answers? Any more? Well, ladies and gentlemen, I am sorry to say you are all wrong." There were groans from the unseen fiends, but Julian continued, "Heriberto Quintana has killed an incredible eleven people; yes, you heard right—eleven people, and, as if that were not enough, he ordered the murder of seven more! I also have it on good authority that it was Glasya-Labolas who was Heriberto's inspiration!" And the groans change to wild cheers as I sit in terror while this travesty continued.

The unseen audience finally quiets down, and Julian continues, "The next question is Hermione Loglin of Dodsonville, Iran who asks, 'What does Glasya-Labolas do with all the skin he's peeling off Heriberto?' That's a very good question, Hermione." Julian then turns to Glasya-Labolas and asks,"What do you do with all that skin?"

Glasya-Labolas shoots a quick look at Julian but does not answer. He is far too busy peeling the tattoos off of Quintana and waiting for them to grow back, so he can do it again.

"Well, it seems that I will have to intercede again. I happen to know, from the same good authority, that his skin is used for any number of things. As a matter of fact, I use it for my personal stationary." And he looks at me with blazing eyes and a revolting smile.

"Stationary?" I say to myself. The garage, the note—oh, my God; it was the note from Julian on Quintana's skin that I picked up and read. I looked back up at Julian while I unconsciously wiped my hands to rid them of the filth. He sees this and knows that I know, and he smiles.

Glasya-Labolas was getting angry. The devil starts to shriek and rant at Heriberto. Heriberto's terror only grows, but he cannot move. He is powerless to act. Glasya-Labolas then stops ranting and howling and raises his blade, but this time, he doesn't bother to peel the skin on Heriberto; he just drives the long knife into Heriberto's body.

Again and again, the demon thrusts the blade into Quintana and with each thrust, Heriberto writhed in all-embracing agony, but he couldn't die: he could only feel unbearable pain. He cannot scream. He has no mouth, and the whole time the audience is silent, and Julian is grinning with utter delight.

At once, Glasya-Labolas stops driving his knife into Heriberto. In an instant, the beast swings the long knife and cuts the head off of him, and it falls on the floor. I turn away in revulsion, but something made me look back, and when I did, I saw Heriberto's head on the floor—eyes wide open with the same terror and pleading eyes as before.

The demon fiend picked up the head in one hand and placed it back on Quintana's body. An almost imperceptible smile comes across Glasya-Labolas as he stares at the object of his torment, and with one deafening howl, the both of them burst into flames and are gone.

At first there was deathly silence, and then, almost at once, the entire phantom crowd roared with riotous approval.

Now Julian is back in his best host mode, and he makes his way to the stage. "Ladies and gentlemen, was that not the most amazing feet of hellishness you've ever seen?"

Again, another riotous roar of approval.

I closed my eyes and tried to escape from this horror, if for only a moment. I used this time to say a silent prayer, a prayer I hope will be answered by the sainted.

The peace was very short lived as Julian says in a singsong voice, "Christopher, oh Christopher."

"What the fuck do you want?" I was angry and afraid at the same time, but that was the only thing I could say.

"I hope you are enjoying our show. I must admit it was a bit impromptu, given Manulo's recent, shall we say, departure. No time for rehearsal, no time for practicing our lines, but it was spectacular in spite of it all, don't you think?"

"Fuck you…"

"No, Christopher, it is you who will be, as you put it, fucked. Your prayer will go unanswered. God and your precious Sainted have all abandoned you, and you will have to face evil all by your lonesome."

I stood there dispirited. I have seen the true nature of hell, the true nature of malevolence, and for the first time, I saw the possibility of evil triumphing over good. I fell on my knees in despair waiting for some sign but recognizing that it may not come, and I would need to face this on my own.

"Ah, I see you are finally coming to terms with the inevitable. But don't fret. You still have time to come around. Our show is only starting, and there is so much more to see."

Julian looked up at his unseen minions and spreading his arms wide, he says in a loud voice, "My dear friends, are you ready for more?"

The crowd responds in an earsplitting unison, "YES!"

"Are you ready for more surprises, more intrigue and more evil?" and The crowd responds with another resounding "YES!"

"Well, get ready for our next guest!" Julian continues to revel in the adoration of the crowd. There is a broad, openmouthed smile on his face as he is encouraging the riotous applause.

"Ladies and gentlemen, please welcome someone who needs no introduction! The gracious, accomplished and beautiful woman who has stolen the heart of our honored visitor, Christopher Pella!"

I immediately looked up in a complete and utter state of panic.

"BETH DELLA RUSSO!"

Chapter 44

The rain came down hard, and the wind continued to be strong as the chief's car speeds through the opened gate toward the marina at the end of the complex's main road.

In the distance, Dan and Al could see the lights from the patrol cars that were already at the scene. He turned into the same area where the other cars were parked and pulled into an open space near the marina entrance. Both men scanned the area until Uncle Al spots his nephew's car.

"Dan, that's Chris' car by the gate." Dan looks over and says, "Let me go take a look to see if he left any clues behind."

While Chief Detective Barese is concentrating on the area surrounding the marina, he's approached by one of the uniformed officers: "Hi, Chief. I'm Officer Jim McGowan; we spoke over the two-way a few minutes ago."

"Yeah, what have you got to tell me?" Chief Barese is all business now.

"Well, we did another thorough search of the townhouse, the parking lot and marina—all came up empty. It's dark, and we may have missed some things, so we'll be sure to cordon off the area and come back in the morning for another search."

"Right, what else?"

"We went down to the marina to slip space eight, and it was empty. We looked at all the other crafts in the rest of the slips, but there was no boat with the name Fun-A-Bout, so we came back to the lot, and we're waiting for your orders."

"Okay, I want one of you to go back to the house and make sure that it's secure. Monitor any activity—calls, neighbors, anything, and get back to me immediately. Got it?"

"Got it, Chief. Oh, by the way, there was something strange."

"Well, you gonna keep me guessing? What was it?"

"Well, Chief, when I was down at the slip space, I seem to have heard the sound of an outboard engine somewhere out on the bay. It seemed strange given this weather. I couldn't see what type of boat it was or where it was going, but it sounded like it was headed for Pit Island, but I can't be sure."

"Thanks Officer McGowan. Just want you to know that one of the missing people is my nephew, Chris Pella, and I'm worried. I didn't mean to snap at you, and thanks for your good work."

"No problem, Chief. I'll head back to the townhouse and keep my eye out for anything that looks strange."

Al smiled at the cop and said, "Everything looks strange tonight. Stay safe."

"I will." And with that, Officer McGowan left.

Al looked around and saw Dan still by Chris's car, and he walked over. "Dan, find anything?"

"No, there's nothing here. Let's go down to the marina and check out the slip space."

"We can, but I don't think it will do us much good. The uniforms were down there and did a search of all the slips, and they said there was no sign of the Fun-A-Bout. Officer McGowan did say something that could be useful, though. He said that while he was down on the dock, he heard the sound of an outboard engine. He couldn't tell what kind of boat, but he thought it could be headed for Pit Island."

"You're kidding, a boat out in this weather? Seems strange, don't it?" Dan turned toward the bay, but all there was was darkness.

"Yeah, it is strange. That's why I think we need to check it out. Call the Harbor Patrol, and tell them to get out here pronto. We'll meet them down on the dock."

"Will do." Dan ran towards the chief's car to make the call.

Uncle Al turned to the darkness and tried to make out any form, but it was useless. He fears for Chris, he fears for Beth, and he fears that more people will die tonight.

Chapter 45

My heart was pounding so hard that it felt like it would burst through my chest. I am looking in every direction waiting to see Beth. I didn't have to wait long. From the opposite end of where the others made their entrance came Beth.

She looked beautiful, as she seemed to glide across the hard earth floor. Beth wore a loose fitting, long flowing and dazzling white gown that went up to her neck. She was radiant with her long hair falling across her shoulders.

I was still on my knees as I watched Beth walk towards me. She stopped in front of me, bent over, put her hand on my cheek and smiled. I didn't know how to respond, but I asked her, "Beth, are you alright? My God, what happened? What did Julian do to you? Beth, please, say something."

Beth didn't answer me; she just continued to smile. She then looked over her shoulder at Julian and turned toward the stage and began to walk to him. I screamed, "Beth stay away from him. He is evil come to life! He's killed all those women, and he will kill you. He must have you under some kind of spell, Beth. Stop, before he kills you!" I was becoming hysterical. She was about halfway to the stage when Beth turned back to face me. Her smile was even brighter, and she said,

"Don't be so sure." She turned back and walked to Julian.

I was able to calm down a bit, but I was more confused than ever. Why was Beth acting like this? Julian must have some kind of demonic hold over her. In my mind, I am searching for some idea, some way to get us out of this horror show. If there was ever a time for my saints to appear, it's now, but it's still clear that I am alone.

On my knees, I put my hands together and begin to pray, "Oh Lord of all, I pray that You and all Your Sainted will hear me. I pray that you will show mercy on us, and lead us from this darkness into Your light."

When I looked up, I saw Julian and Beth on the stage. They were standing next to each other, and they were both smiling,

Julian spoke, "Christopher, what must I do to convince you that there is no relief for you from your precious Sainted, and dear boy, there is no mercy of God? To quote an old phrase, 'God is dead,' especially for you."

"Julian, let me speak to him." She looks at me with loving eyes and longing in her heart. "Rocky, I have learned so much since I have been here. You need to understand that all you believe in, all you have hoped and prayed for is gone. It was never there. God and the Sainted have turned away from you; they have turned away from all of us long ago."

She knew about the Sainted. She knows my secret, and Julian has told her. I look up in shock, and I am speechless. How can this be? How can Beth be saying these things? But she will not stop.

"Yes, Julian has told me about your visions, but you need to understand that it has all been a hoax, a game that God plays with Julian. It's all a sham to get you to believe. But what are you to believe? In them? These Sainted are charlatans; when you need them, they are gone. They toy with us, lead us on, they show us the light of God, and when we are in the hour of our greatest need, then they turn on the darkness."

Julian stood to the side of Beth and was content to let her do the talking. Beth did not appear to be under any kind of spell. She seemed lucid and in complete control. I tried to understand what was happening, to find the logic to explain it all, but my mind was spinning from the realization that everything I felt for and about Beth was false.

"How can you say these things, Beth?"

"I can say these things because I now know the truth. I know what you call evil is the only truth. If it was not for evil, there would be no God. The truth behind what Julian represents cannot be denied. Men and women are inherently evil. They look to commit sin, and they have an insatiable appetite for what they consider bad. But is it really bad? Isn't it more the freedom of choice? Oh, I know people do bad things, and they get punished. Remember Heriberto?"

"You can't possibly believe that, Beth? You can't possible buy into what this beast represents? This twisted logic that says if you like it, it's fine. You are too smart for that." I said this, but there was no conviction in my voice and none in my heart.

"What is the nature of evil, Rocky? Is it Heriberto killing someone, or is it Julian punishing him? Come on, Rocky. What is true evil? I think you know the answer, and it's not what you have been taught all these years. That has been the lie, the fable created by monks and priests and rabbis to keep us all in fear and under their control." Beth was confident, even cocky, in her twisted logic, and I was beyond knowing what to do.

"It seems to me that both Heriberto and Julian are guilty. Both are meant to be condemned to eternal damnation. What I have seen today just makes it clearer what the monks, rabbis and priests have taught. There is evil, and there is punishment, and there are rewards reserved for those who love God and..."

Julian now interrupts, "Oh Christopher, don't be so naïve. There is no reward because there is no mercy of God—only incentives, shall we say, for His select few. Ah, but there is punishment because there is me!"

"What about those poor women you killed? What punishment did they deserve? What was the purpose of their deaths?" I found myself screaming at Julian who just stood there and smiled.

"Well, to tell you the truth, the reasons can be found in the age-old battle between heaven and hell. Christopher, it is God who commands that souls be the sole arbiter of who wins and who loses in this eternal conflict. It is God who made me seek the souls of men, and women of course, because the one who gets the greatest number wins! Unfortunately, and I admit it, I am not infallible. When you make an omelet, you need to break some eggs, don't you agree?"

"Are you kidding? You killed those women and their babies because of some kind of game you are playing?" I was incredulous.

"Ah Christopher, the babies, yes, the babies—two souls for the price of one. Alas, when I'm angry, I do dreadful things. You must admit, though, God also allows dreadful things to happen; does He not?" Julian is baiting the exchange, and he smiles as he waits for my reaction.

I was speechless.

Julian sensed that I had no response, so he said, "Death is inevitable. If God did not want us to die, He would have made us eternal, but alas, He does not care, and He is content to allow evil to flourish under the guise of free will. A little secret, Christopher—there is no free will. Mankind has evolved, and now there is only good and evil, and over the ages, more and more have turned away from God towards me. Quite frankly, God is getting worried. It seems preordained that one of us will triumph, and guess who that one is?" Julian stood there while he let his words sink in.

Beth reached out and put her hand on Julian's shoulder. "Julian, may I speak to Chris?"

"Of course you can, my dear, but I fear you will need to do a lot to convince this young man of his misplaced faith in a misplaced faith. Very droll, if I do say so myself." Julian continued to smile.

Beth comes and stands in front of me, takes my hand, and I rise to my feet. "Chris, do you remember the last time we spoke?"

"Yes, I remember."

"Do you remember that I wanted to tell you something?"

"Yes."

"Do you want to know what I was going to tell you?" There was a genuine desire in her voice and fire in her eyes.

"I don't really care," I lied.

"I was going to tell you that I wanted you and me to become what I've wanted for so long. I wanted you and me to become lovers. I wanted to tell you that I love you and that you are all I've ever wanted."

I stood there thunderstruck, but before I could find the words to respond, Beth let her gown drop to the floor, and she stood before me completely naked. She looked flawless, the most beautifully perfect woman I have ever seen, and I felt the fear and hatred in me turn to excitement as I gazed at her magnificent naked body.

"Chris, am I all you have imagined? I am here for you. I am yours for eternity." Beth reached over and put her arms around my shoulder. Making love to Beth was something I had only thought of, but now I was holding her in my arms. She was all I've ever imagined, and she looked at me longingly, lovingly. As she came close, I felt her body press against mine, and the warmth of her touch was like an elixir that made my desire for her stronger than ever before.

"Chris, touch me. Please, kiss me. Make me feel you inside me." And with that, our lips met, and I was transported to a place of unimaginable pleasures.

Chapter 46

Al and Dan walked down to the dock and waited for the Harbor Patrol to arrive. They had gone to the car for rain gear, but it was little help as the rain continued to come down heavy, and the wind was blowing fiercely.

"How long did they say it would take for them to get here?" Chief Barese was getting both nervous and wet.

Dan responded, "Not long. The harbormaster was at home in bed when they called, but he lives right near the harbor. He said that he and his crew would be here in about twenty minutes." Al seemed to be grateful for the news and thankful that help would be here soon.

At the far end of the dock is a small cabin with an ice machine and a place to stow gear for the boaters who leased the slip space. The two men went to the cabin and stood there looking out the window over the dark waters. Al tried to focus, but his thoughts were on Chris and Beth and what terror they may be confronting.

Waiting is always the worst part of a cop's job, and both Dan and Al had done their share of waiting. They had run out of coffee, and they had run out of things to say, so they just stood there, in silence, waiting for the boat to arrive. They didn't have long to wait, for in the distance appeared lights from a fast moving boat that was headed right for the marina.

"Dan, why don't you call Officer McGowan, and let him know that we're going with the Harbor Patrol to check and see if we can find Chris and Beth and to see if we can find her boat. He should also keep us posted if anything happens on his end."

"Will do," and Dan made the call.

Once they saw the Harbor Patrol boat getting close to the marina, Al and Dan left the cover of the shed and went down to meet the boat as it arrived. When Al saw the craft, he sighed. It was mostly an open deck with a small protected area that could barely shelter a dog from getting wet, but it did have two powerful 250 hp Mercury engines, so at least they can get wet fast.

One of the crew jumped onto the dock as the boat pulled in, and he tied the lines to keep the craft as stable as the strong wind would allow. The harbormaster was the first to introduce himself, yelling above the howling wind, "Hi, I'm Ron Cunningham, Harbormaster."

Al introduced himself, "Hi, I'm Chief Al Barese, and this is Detective Dan Orello."

"Pleased to meet you both, can you give us some details about this search we are going on?"

"Well, there are two missing persons; one is my nephew, Chris Pella, and the other is his girlfriend, Beth Della Russo and…"

But Ron Cunningham interrupted, "Is she any relation to Paul Della Russo who owns the construction company?"

"Yeah, that's his daughter."

"Well, he and his family have been great supporters of what we do. You know boating safety and training, fundraising and all—whatever you need, we'll be sure to get it for you."

"Thanks, Ron. But you should know that they may have been kidnapped. Have you been following the story about a serial killer mutilating women?"

"Yeah, I have."

"Well, we have it on good authority that this serial killer may have identified Beth as his next victim, and Chris is out there trying to find her right now."

"Enough said. Let's get onboard. By the way, where are we headed?"

Al and Dan said, at the same time, "Pit Island."

"Wait a minute, did you say Pit Island?"

Again Al and Dan said, at the same time, "Yeah."

The harbormaster looked really worried: "Do you guys know anything about Pit Island? Because if you did, you'd know what a dangerous place that is, especially if you're on a boat."

"Listen, Ron, we don't care. Just get us close enough, and we'll take that inflatable you have on the rear of your boat and motor in ourselves. Just stay close enough in case we get into trouble."

"Chief, I really don't think this is a good idea. Maybe we should get the Coast Guard to help us out."

"By the time the Coast Guard is able to get here, both Beth and Chris could be dead, and the killer could get away. Just take us to Pit Island, and in the meantime, you can call the Coast Guard if you want. Okay?"

"Okay, Chief, but I still don't think this is a good idea." With that, Ron Cunningham and his crew began to prepare to get underway.

Al and Dan got onboard and tried to get out of the way so the men could do their jobs. The crew had some extra rain gear onboard, and Al and Dan each grabbed one and put it on. It seemed to help a bit, but the men were reconciled to the fact that they were getting soaked, whether they liked it or not.

The engines came to life, and the boat eased its way out of the slip space and into the darkness of the bay toward Pit Island.

Chapter 47

I never imagined I could feel like this. The cave evaporated and became a place where light met liquid and melted into one another. There were soft sounds but unlike any I had heard before. We were alone, floating in the liquid light.

Beth held me in her arms, and I felt the passion she wanted me to feel. Her lips were soft and moist and she put all inhibitions aside as she pressed her supple body against mine.

Slowly her hand found the buttons on my jacket. She stopped kissing me and looked into my eyes, and as she did, my coat slipped off into nothingness. I took her in my arms again, and I held her tightly with my hands exploring all of her curves, all of her.

Beth slipped her hand under my shirt, and she ran her long nails lightly across my chest. I felt myself quiver as my body tightened at the delight of her touch. She stopped kissing me, but as she gazed into my eyes, she tore open my shirt and began to caress my nipples with her tongue. I have never felt anything like this, ever. All I could think was that I want to possess her, to make love to her, to make her mine.

I stopped her and began to kiss her lips while working my way to her neck, shoulders and her breasts. I gently touched her perfectly formed, rounded breasts and began to suck on her nipples. I was in a rapturous state, experiencing a sensation that I had never felt before.

Beth was breathing heavy as she moved her body back and forth against me, and all I wanted to do was be inside her, feel her juices and watch her as she had an orgasm. "Chris!" she said panting, "Chris, put your cock inside me! I want to feel you inside me! Please!" Beth was pleading and groping for the belt on my pants with one hand and stoking me with the other.

My feelings were so intense that I wanted them to last forever, but there was so much I needed to say: "Beth, I love you, but I have to know."

Beth stopped kissing me and looked up as she answered, "I love you, too! I love you so much."

"Where are we Beth? Why are we here? I need to understand."

She smiled and said, "We are in the perfect state of bliss. We are here because we love each other, and we will be together forever."

I'm trying to allow the passion subside because I need to comprehend, to hear Beth tell me what this was all about. "Julian, what has he to do with all this? You can't possibly believe all of what you said."

"Julian does not matter. Chris, all I believe in is you and me. We need each other, and we need to be together, in love forever. That is all that matters; that's all there is." She whispered this to me as we were wrapped in each other's arms. Our desires continued to mount as we embraced and explored one another's bodies.

I didn't want to, but I pulled back for a moment, "No, Beth. That can't possibly be all there is. What about growing old—children, family, friends, home? What about helping people and providing comfort to those in need? There is so much more to life."

She takes a step back, and I get to see her in all her stunning nakedness, and she says, "Chris, I am your family, now…I am your best friend. How about helping me and giving me comfort? Chris, my love, I am your life."

Beth's words snapped me back to reality. I didn't want to face it. I was trying to find a way to let her know how I felt. I did love her, but my entire life couldn't be a mistake. There had to be more. "Beth, life cannot only be about the two of us; it has to include so many others. It has to include God, His Son, the forces of Heaven and the Sainted. I have seen miracles; I have seen the joys and heartache of loving beyond oneself."

Beth looks at me; she looks at my face, searching to see some sign that I'm questioning my beliefs. I look back at her as she practically begs me to listen. "Chris, what you have seen was false. It is God and His Sainted playing games with your soul. God would do anything to get His own way—including coercion, lying, temptations and even miracles to get what He wants. Chris, God is not here for you. He is not here for me. God has abandoned us, given up on us, and He will ultimately concede in the game He plays with Julian. That is the future of humanity, and that is why there is only us."

"Beth, that's just not true, and you know it. God has never abandoned any of us. He is always there to give us His blessings and mercy. What He doesn't do is tell us what to do; we have to figure that out for ourselves. That is our decision—that is free will."

Beth raised her voice, "Chris, there is no free will. There is only what we want in life; there are only our desires because, in the end, there is only us."

I am now staring at her. The passion I felt before vanished, and I am looking at someone I thought I knew, but now I recognize that I knew nothing about her at all.

Beth steps back. She is now fully clothed with her gown having mysteriously reappeared. She is no longer the loving beauty that she was moments ago. Her eyes now tell the story of the hate she feels for me and that becomes more apparent with every passing moment.

The blissful state that we were in begins to transform. As her hatred grows so does the darkness, and when I try to reach out to Beth, there is an explosive force that sends me reeling backwards. When I come to my senses, I am back on the floor of the pit looking up at a smiling Julian and an angry Beth.

Chapter 48

When the patrol had come close to Pit Island, the harbormaster switched on a bright spotlight secured to the bow of the boat. Ron Cunningham had slowed the boat down considerably, as he was familiar with the currents and the dangers that hide just beneath the surface of the bay waters.

When they had gotten about seventy yards from the shore of the island, the harbormaster cut his engines and gave the order to anchor the craft.

Turning to Al and Dan, Ron says, "This is about as close as we should go. It's dark, and with this rain and wind, we could find ourselves in serious trouble."

Al says, "We understand. Dan and I will use the inflatable to get to the shore and start our search. You can call the Coast Guard whenever you want. As a matter of fact, I think it is a good idea just in case..." Chief Barese's voice trailed off. Everyone knew that he was confronting the possibility that Beth and Chris could be dead and the Coast Guard would need to look for their bodies.

"Okay, we will." The harbormaster turned to one of the crew and told him to give us one of the two-way radios. "Here, take this with you. This way, we can keep in contact. When the Coast Guard arrives, they will have the ability to get to you and help with your search."

Al replies, "Thanks for all your help. By the way, how big is Pit Island?"

Ron thought and said, "Roughly 80 yards long and about 50 yards wide. It's not very big, but in this weather, it'll seem a lot larger."

"Thanks, Ron."

Dan is all set and says, "Ready to go, Chief?"

"Ready as I'll ever be." And with that, they boarded the inflatable that had already been lowered into the water. The small outboard motor started after three tries, the lines were untied and thrown to Dan, and the tiny boat slowly made its way towards Pit Island. The short journey was treacherous as the boat was buffeted by the strong wind and rain along with swells of two feet or more.

The light from the patrol boat helped at first, but the further away they got, the dimmer the light, and after a while, it was no help at all. While Dan navigated the small craft, Al seemed to spot something, "I think I see the hull of a boat jutting out of the water, near rocks along the shoreline—over there, see? Can you try and get closer?"

With that, Dan slowly maneuvered the boat until they were practically next to the sunken craft. The men tried to see if they could find the name of the boat, but there was none they could see. They were able to see a registration number along the side near the bow, and Al used the two-way to call and ask if the harbormaster could help.

"Ron, this is Chief Barese. Can you hear me? Over."

"Yes, Chief. I hear you. Over."

"We found a partially sunken craft but can't identify her. We found a registration number; can you get us any information? Over."

"What's the number? Over." Al read him the numbers, and Ron said it would take a few minutes, but he would get right back to him as soon as possible.

The rain and wind continue to pound both Al and Dan. At this point, they were close enough to Pit Island that they both decided that waiting was not an option. They were about ten feet from shore, and Al was the first to jump in. He was about waist deep in water, but he was able to get a foothold. He struggled his way onto shore with Dan who was immediately behind him. When they both were able to get beyond the rocks along the shore, they saw the small inflatable.

Al yells to Dan, "This looks like it might be the boat that Chris took to Pit Island."

"I think you're right," Dan yelled above the wind, "We should check our weapons. This could get ugly!"

Al knew that given the nature of the evil that Chris and Beth were confronting, a gun, no matter how large a caliber, would be of little use. Still he couldn't disclose this to Dan, so he just said, "Okay, I'll check mine."

After the weapons were checked, they tried to get a fix on where they would begin the search. They would walk toward the center and head for the east end of the island and work their way across. It was a very small area to cover, but with the rain and wind, it would take far longer.

As they made their way inland, Dan noticed that there was something sticking out of the ground. He couldn't make it out, so he tapped the chief on his shoulder, "Take a look over there. What do you think it is?"

"I don't know." Al was trying to see what it was, but the rain obscured it. "Let's walk over and see."

As they got closer, they could make out that it was a sign. Al read the words aloud: "Warning Trespassers"

Chapter 49

I shook off my disorientation and got up off the floor. The stage was gone, the audience quiet, and Julian and Beth are just watching me, waiting to hear what I would say. They both realized that I was able to fight off the temptation and with it my doubts about God, Jesus and the Sainted.

Julian spoke first: "Ah, Christopher, how sad. Look at what you have given up, the pleasures of the flesh, of eternal joy, of life without end. Now you will be relegated to being another witless soul who will spend eternity knowing that God and the Sainted were not there for you. Much to your regret, I'm sure, you will now come to realize that I am the only one left standing."

"You can do with me what you want, but I will never deny my faith."

"How noble of you, Christopher. I am very impressed. You think that your pitiful death will have some meaning in the vastness of heaven and hell. Let me assure you that your death will have no significance whatsoever because no one cares."

As Julian's words began to sink in, I heard noises that seemed to be coming from all the dark corners of the pit. They were sounds that I had never heard before, which sent chills through my being down to my soul. The terror of my situation became all too clear as I looked into the dark corners of this forsaken hole in the ground and saw hundreds of eyes shining bright.

Up to this point, Beth had remained quiet, but she left Julian's side to stand in front of me.

"Why? What could you possibly gain? I was willing to give you all that I am, my all, my whole being. Why did you reject me?" Her voice cracked, and I saw a tear in her eye.

"Beth, it does not have to be like this. Don't let Julian's lies dictate how you will spend eternity. We can be together always, even in death. We can live in the light and in the mercy of God."

Beth's look hardened, and she turned away from me and back to Julian.

"He sees nothing." Beth's gown falls to the floor, and she is standing naked in front of Julian. He smiles as he looks at her nude form and reaches for her. She goes to him willingly, and they embrace as I watch in total disbelief.

"Beth, no, don't do this. He is a demon. He will..." but I stopped in mid-sentence as the hideous shrieks and snarls from the corner of the cave grew louder. I looked around, and at first I could see nothing, but then I did. From every dark hollow, the legions came out from hiding. Demons as dreadful as Temeluchus and Glasya-Labolas but in such numbers that I stood there in abject terror.

Julian smiled, "Ah Christopher, I have asked my minions to entertain you while Beth and I enjoy some pleasures of the carnal variety. Every now and then, I enjoy diversion of this type. It helps to keep me grounded."

I am only two feet from the wall behind me, but I back up anyway. The demon creatures are coming at me from all sides, and I am in a hopeless circumstance facing my own death. I screamed at Julian and Beth,

"I am not afraid. I am not alone."

"Oh, dear boy, I'm afraid you are alone." As Julian said this, I heard another noise and looked up. It was the flapping wings of thousands of crows circling above my head.

Chapter 50

"It's just a warning sign."

"I know, but maybe Chris came past this way looking for Beth. If she was with Julian and..." but he was cut off by the voice on his two-way radio.

"This is Ron Cunningham. Come in, Chief, this is Ron Cunningham. Over."

"Ron, this is Chief Barese."

"Chief, we looked up the registration for the boat, and it is registered to Elizabeth Della Russo."

When they heard the news, Dan and Al looked at each other. They secretly knew it had to be Beth's boat but were hoping they were wrong. Al answered the harbormaster, "Thanks Ron, we suspected as much."

"Some other news—we called the Coast Guard, and they are on their way."

"That's good. We can use the help."

"I'm sure you can, Chief. Oh, and I called Beth's parents as soon as I found out. They are on their way here; I know that they are worried sick."

Al asked the harbormaster, "Ron, I've got a question. We found a sign warning trespassers about coming here, but there is no indication who put up the sign. Who owns the island, and who takes responsibility for it?"

"Chief, I've been on that island a number of times and explored it all over, and I've never seen a sign. I don't know who the island belongs to, or who is responsible for it, I just assume it's the county's or the state's."

"I guess that's a good assumption, but why would anyone put up a sign like this in the middle of the island where no one could see it." Al was just thinking out loud, but Harbormaster Cunningham answered him:

"I don't know who would have put that sign up without telling us."

"No worries. I was just wondering. We are continuing our search, so let us know if anything else happens."

"We will and good luck—over and out."

Dan and Al looked back at the sign and speculated about what they should do next. They had originally thought to start at the east end of the island, but finding the sign seemed to create more questions than it did answers. Al spoke first, "This killer has committed the murders of these women in pits, right?"

"Yeah," Dan answered.

"And this is called Pit Island, right?"

"Yeah, it is."

Now Al is becoming animated, "And what might you find on Pit Island?"

"A pit!" Dan yells.

"Now let's see if we can find an entrance to this pit." And with that, they began looking.

Chapter 51

As the demon legion comes toward me, I am terrified but reconciled to my fate.

I dropped to my knees and began praying, but as I do, the minions stop their movement towards me. I looked up, and the beasts began to move to either side of the pit in order to make a path for someone or something. The ground began to shake as the demons cower, trying to hide from what they fear. I had no idea what to expect, but Julian knew this. I heard his voice: "Christopher, I would like you to meet Asmodeus. He has special plans regarding your death that he would like to share with you."

I looked down the path that had been created by the separation of demons on both sides, and I saw him for the first time.

Asmodeus is enormous, more than thirty feet tall and at least that wide. He is a strong, powerful fiend that emerges from the darkness in hideous glory. The beast has three heads; the right is one of a bull, the center like that of a grotesque looking man and the left is the head of a ram. He has the tail of a serpent, and from his mouth, he is breathing flames. Asmodeus sits upon a dragon that can only come from the depths of hell. The minions are scrambling to get out of the way, trembling in absolute fear of this evil spirit.

"Oh, Christopher, you should know that Asmodeus governs seventy-two of my legions. I believe you see some of them here in this pit. They are of the lower-grade spirit variety but can prove quite effective in assuring that the task at hand gets done."

Asmodeus stood about twenty feet away from me as he looked down. Perhaps I was in shock, or perhaps I had got nothing to lose, but I summoned the courage to say to Julian, "Is that all you got?"

"No, Christopher. It's not all I've got, but I assure you, it's all I'll need—as you will soon find out."

Asmodeus looked to the ceiling way above where he stands and bellows a cry. Flames that burst from his mouth into the air above. I was nearly paralyzed with fear and stared at this creature, accepting the reality that I would die. I closed my eyes in prayer waiting for the end when I hear a shrill cawing from the crows above.

I opened my eyes to look above and saw thousands of small white crosses falling gently from nowhere at all. The crows began to take flight, circling above in mass confusion and fear. As the crosses touched the crows, the birds literally melted into a dark putrid slime that fell to the floor below and evaporated. This caused even more panic among the demon crows and, no matter how hard they tried, there was no escape. The crosses spelled their doom, and the crows seem to know it.

At first Asmodeus and his legions appeared bewildered at what was happening above their heads. Slowly, they realized, and as they did, their merciless hostility turned to overwhelming terror. Asmodeus looked back down from the ceiling and stared at me. The hatred in his eyes said that he would take vengeance for this blasphemy on me. The creature's three heads all turned to me as the dragon from hell that Asmodeus rode took a cautious step forward. My back was already against the rock wall—there was nowhere for me to go—it seemed that only a miracle could save me now.

Asmodeus reached for the lance that was by his side. The monster raised the lance, aiming at my chest, while he looked at me with a smile that chilled to the bone. What he failed to recognize were the crosses falling past them and onto his legion. The evil fiends began to run around, trying to find cover in the hollows of the pit, but it is too late. Impossibly loud screams and screeches filled the air in the pit as the crosses touched the demon hoard. With each cross came unbearable agony and pain. In a matter of moments, the beasts were reduced to slime, and the muck began to disappear.

Asmodeus now saw his fate and could not escape it. He looked up to see dozens of small crosses land on him and the devil dragon. Trying to scream but not even belching fire, his body and all three heads began to melt into ooze. Then, in one massive explosion, Asmodeus and the dragon vanished into nothing.

The cave was empty of all except Julian and Beth. They stood next to each other, untouched by the crosses, but dreading their fate. The crosses that destroyed the demonic crows and beasts lay all around them in a perfect circle. I moved away from the wall and walked towards where Beth and Julian were standing.

As I stood before them, I could see only fear. Julian spoke, "You think that your cursed Sainted can stop me? I am eternal; I am legion! I will triumph over the God of Heaven, and the souls of mankind will be mine!"

I ignored Julian and turned to Beth. "How could you believe him? How could you doubt your own life? You chose darkness over light, evil over good. You've condemned yourself." I was grief-stricken.

But Beth said nothing and just looked at me.

I needed to know. "Beth, say something!"

Julian stood behind her and put his arms around her waist. His hands went higher as he started to stroke her breasts. She closed her eyes as he let his hands find their way all over her body.

I screamed, "Stop it!"

Julian laughed and continued as Beth began to writhe against him in the utmost pleasure.

I needed to stop it, to try and save Beth from the demon that controls her completely, but before I got to them, a bright light began to fill the pit. The radiance found its way into every corner. Where there once was darkness, there was only light. I stared into the light, and in the center appeared the form of what I had seen before and knew to be the Sainted. It was a vision of St. Agnes. She stood before me.

She did not speak at first but turned and faced Julian and Beth. They stopped their sexual act and looked up at her defiantly, in spite of their failure to tempt my faith and the will of God.

"What do you hope to do here, woman? God will never defeat me, for I am the reason He exists! I am the true power," Julian screamed at St. Agnes who just stood there.

"Silence, you cursed demon!" St. Agnes held up her hand, and Julian stopped speaking. He tried to seem unfazed by the Saint standing before him, but there was genuine fear in him, and she knew it.

"You have turned away from God. Your pride has made you believe that you are like God, command the heavens like God, hold sway over men—but even with your lies, temptations and legion, you will never defeat the Lord our God. He is always, He is forever, and He is the way to the eternal light and everlasting peace."

St. Agnes then turned to look at me and said, "We must always trust that our Heavenly Father will hear our prayers and give us whatever is for our best."

"Please, forgive me," I said. "I thought that God and the Sainted abandoned me. I let temptation blind me to what I know to be true."

St. Agnes smiled at me. "It was your free will that caused your doubt, but it was free will, a choice of good over evil, which brought you back. God and the saints were always by your side, and you should take solace in that you were willing to make the ultimate sacrifice for your faith. You are forgiven."

Julian and Beth screamed in rage at St. Agnes and me, but they would not leave the circle for fear of the crosses that surrounded them. Having nowhere to go, they let me see their true nature. It was Julian who changed first, turning into the horrible beast I had seen before. His fury grew, and he roared a screech that shook the interior of the pit.

I was prepared for Julian, but I was not prepared for what Beth would turn into. The skin on her body turned into what looked like scales but were golden. Her hands grew to three times their size, with long tapering nails as sharp as knives. Beth's beautiful brunette hair fell out in clumps while protrusions resembling horns grew from her head; but it was the change in her face that I hadn't expected. Her eyes became large black circles; her mouth grew wide with protruding fangs and the rest of her teeth pointed.

She was no longer my Beth—she was a demon Beth. I just stared at her with an overwhelming sadness.

St. Agnes spoke to the devils trapped in the circle of crosses: "You have tried, and you have failed. There is no mercy for you, for you would give none back. God has condemned you to the fires of hell, and that is where you are to go."

The demons Julian and Beth began screaming and shouting curses and insults, but they were only words. Their threats were sapped of any power by the Heavenly Hosts who had battled them for ages. I heard a rumbling from above, and, when I looked up, a cloud formed amidst the sound of rolling thunder. I looked back at the devils in the circle and saw true terror on their faces. A moment later a bolt of lightning cut through the cloud and struck the demons Julian and Beth. They exploded into pieces and disappeared.

I looked at the place where Julian and Beth were, and they are gone; all the crosses are gone, and only St. Agnes and I were left.

I didn't know what to say, what to do. I told St. Agnes that I realized I loved Beth; I wanted her to know that Beth meant everything to me. I couldn't believe that she denied her faith. Now Beth was gone, and I knew I would mourn her loss for as long as I lived. I was in a state of total sadness, and I didn't know how to deal with it all. God and His Sainted had saved me—but for what? A lifetime of loneliness, of yearning for a love that I'd found, but now had lost. I was alive, but I felt empty.

"I know you believe in the goodness and mercy of the Lord, but you are in pain." St. Agnes looked at me tenderly, knowing the anguish I was feeling.

"I do believe, but sometimes it's impossible to understand why God allows things to happen in the way He does."

"Christopher, it was you who said you may not know God's will, but you know His will be done…a time for every purpose under heaven."

St. Agnes smiled at me as something miraculous appeared in the center of the pit.

Chapter 52

Dan and Al had been searching frantically for an opening that would lead them into the pit when the wind and rain suddenly stopped. The men just looked at each other in utter puzzlement.

Dan said, "How do you figure the rain and wind just stopped like that?"

"Who cares? This will give us the break we need to find the entrance. Let's keep looking."

Al and Dan decided that each would take half of the island and do a thorough search for the opening they hoped would lead them to Beth and Chris in time to save their lives. They created an imaginary grid of the area and began looking around every rock and under every bush. This went on for about ten minutes before they heard the sound of a boat fast approaching the area.

"It must be the Coast Guard." Al picked up his radio and called the Harbormaster.

"Ron, this is Al. Over."

"Hi Chief, I guess you heard the Coast Guard coming toward us."

"Yeah, we did. We'll go near to the shoreline and wait for help."

"That's a good idea, Chief. Over and out."

The Coast Guard anchored near the patrol boat. In what seemed like seconds, a group of men on board lowered a small craft into the water, climbed into it and began making their way to Pit Island.

The small craft approached, and Al could see that there were four men on board. They maneuvered the craft expertly through the rocks and shallows and onto the shore. As the men disembarked, one shouted, "Are you Chief Barese?"

"Yeah, I am."

"Chief, I'm Captain Warren Talbot." He held out his hand.

The men shook hands and climbed up the rocks to higher ground.

"Captain Talbot, this is Detective Dan Orello. I have to say we are really glad to see you."

"Glad to help. Ron—I mean, Harbormaster Cunningham—gave us most of the details behind the search, but is there anything else you want to add?"

"I suppose you know that we suspect a serial killer has kidnapped Beth and taken her here. Her boyfriend, my nephew, Chris Pella, went after her. We believe they both are near, given that his inflatable is up here and her boat has been sunk, as you can tell."

"Got it. Anything else?"

Dan said, "We were beginning to search the whole island. We believe there is an entrance to a pit somewhere hidden, and we hope that will lead us to where Chris and Beth are."

"Well, it's a small island, and we've got the manpower. Thank God it stopped raining. That should make it a little easier."

"One more thing—we found a 'Warning Trespassers' sign with nothing else written on it. Do you know who owns the island, Captain?"

"No, not really. I guess it belongs to the state or county, but I don't know for sure. I can always check."

"Thanks, Captain. That's not a bad idea, but in the meantime, let's get to work."

Al, Dan and the Coast Guard crew made their way toward the sign. The men spread out over a large area to begin their methodical search of every square foot. They looked around each rock, bush and tree to check to see if they hid some opening to an underground cave or pit. For about half an hour, they all continued, until one of the petty officers yelled, "I think I found something."

Al was the first to run to see what the seamen had found. Sure enough, not ten feet away from the warning sign, there was a small opening hidden behind a large rock with tall shrubs growing all around. The opening was small but could fit a man. Al took out a flashlight and shined it down the narrow hole, but it seemed very deep. The light did not penetrate the darkness.

"We've got to go down that hole, Chief. How about us getting a rope and harness?"

"Good idea, Dan. Captain, do you have any ropes and harnesses we can use to lower ourselves down this hole?"

"We sure do. I'll send one of the crew back to the boat to get us what we need."

The captain and crew went back to the inflatable while Al and Dan stood near the opening. It was Dan who spoke first. "Al, you know that it's possible that Beth and Chris, well, you know, they could be..." He trailed off.

"I know, I know. It is a possibility, but I don't want to think about it until I have to. At any rate, we need to get this resolved one way or another."

Chief Al Barese turned toward the hole in the ground and peered into the darkness. He shivered a bit and only hoped it was from the cold.

Chapter 53

Light had filled the pit with a wonderful brightness, and in the center of it all something began to emerge.

St. Agnes knelt in reverence and anticipation of what she knew was coming. I looked at her and did the same thing. As I went down on my knees, an image began to materialize. It became clearer, and I began to comprehend the overwhelming significance of the vision.

The Blessed Mother holding the infant Jesus appeared before us.

St. Agnes seemed to be in a state of complete and utter happiness that totally consumed her. The vision was so overpowering to me that I knelt, motionless and speechless, taking in all that I was allowed to see.

The Holy Mother Mary came and stood before St. Agnes. She knew of her love and devotion to all that is good and holy, and the mother of Christ smiled at her.

The Blessed Virgin Mary's voice filled the air as she said to St. Agnes, "You have done much through your miracles, prayers and kindnesses. You have suffered in the name of my Son, and for this you are blessed for eternity."

St. Agnes had tears in her eyes as she said, "Dearest Blessed Mother Mary, mother of Jesus, Son of God—I am not worthy of your praise."

Mother Mary replied, "You are more than worthy to be among the Sainted." The Blessed Mother opened the palm of her hand to reveal a golden cross. She took the cross and placed it around the neck of the speechless St. Agnes.

I was feeling like I was the last person who should be there experiencing this wonder.

The Blessed Mother continued smiling and said to St. Agnes, "The love of God and His love for all mankind know no bounds; you have given everything in His name." The Holy Mother Mary took the infant Jesus and handed Him to St. Agnes.

The saint could not comprehend the honor she had been given. She gazed lovingly at the infant Jesus and looked up at the His Mother as He was placed in her arms. I had never seen such pure joy and happiness on a face like I saw then on St. Agnes'. She gently hugged the baby and touched His soft cheek as He smiled.

The Holy Mother then turned to me and said, "Your trials have been most difficult, but you have shown your courage through faith in the Lord. You were told you would deliver justice, and through your faith, justice is done." The Blessed Virgin Mary then raised her head and looked toward the rear of the cave. She lifted her arm and pointed.

I looked behind me to see four apparitions beginning to solidify. They were the forms of four women, and as they become clearer, I saw both puzzlement and underlying sadness on their faces.

I turned to the Blessed Mother, trying to find a reason, an answer to who these women were, and then I realized. I turned immediately to St. Agnes, who was still absorbed with the infant Jesus. She had tears in her eyes as she looked up at Mother Mary. Reluctantly, she gave the child back to His mother and then turned to face the four women.

As she turned toward the women and me, I saw St. Agnes holding in her arms four infants—the four innocent victims of Julian's evil madness. The four women each stared over at the babies in St. Agnes' arms, and their sadness was transformed to complete joyfulness. They slowly walked towards their babies, instinctively knowing which one is theirs, and took the infants from the saint to hold them close in their arms. Each of the women then looked up at St. Agnes and the Virgin Mary holding her Son. The mothers were in such a state of absolute happiness, holding their babies and crying tears of joy. They looked at the vision of the Blessed Mother but could only say, "Thank you." And with that, they departed.

The Blessed Mother said to me, "Justice is done. It is the will of our Lord that the innocent live in His light and blessings for eternity." In an instant the vision of the Holy Mother and the infant Jesus became golden light as they were welcomed back through the gates of heaven.

St. Agnes and I watched as they disappeared and left us alone in the pit. She looked at me and said, "There is one more message I must give you before I leave."

"What it is?" I asked her.

"For Satan, it was all important that evil triumph. All that seems real, all the temptations, all the promises are illusions meant to prey on weaknesses in order to destroy one's soul."

"I know that now."

"What you do not yet understand is the power of good over evil, the power of truth over lies."

"Why are you telling me this? I don't comprehend..." Before I finished speaking, I heard sounds and words coming from a corner of the pit.

"Ugh, my head. Where am I?"

My eyes widened, and I looked at St. Agnes. She smiled as the glow from her halo got brighter and said, "May the blessings of the Lord our God be with you and yours all your days." And she was gone.

I had been frozen in place but was suddenly jolted back to reality. The cave was nearly in complete darkness, but I attempted to make it over to the spot where I thought the sounds came from. I felt my way around the rock wall and boulders that covered the floor of the pit.

"My head....Where am I?"

It was a voice that I knew, so I screamed, "BETH, BETH! Where are you, Beth?"

"CHRIS! I'm over here, Chris! Please, help me! Chris! Please, help me!"

I was overjoyed Beth was not the demon in the cave. Julian had tried to make me lose my faith in her, but it was just another one of his lies.

"I'm coming, Beth, just stay where you are, and keep speaking to me. I'll follow the sound of your voice."

"Chris, please hurry. This man, Julian, came to my house; he was there to work on my boat, but that's the last thing I remember. My head is killing me—it's like I've been drugged."

I was getting close, and I wanted her to keep talking. "Did that bastard do anything to you? Are you hurt in any way? Are you all right? Please, tell me!"

"I think I'm okay, Chris. My head is killing me, and I'm a little bruised, and I can't seem to get on my feet. But I think I'm okay."

"Just stay where you are, Beth. Just stay there. I'll find you." Her voice seemed to be getting louder, and I knew I was getting closer.

Beth was getting anxious. "Please hurry, Chris; I'm frightened. Julian could still be here."

"I'm almost there Beth—just hang on." I wanted to get her mind off the horror of the place and what she had gone through, so I asked her, "What did you want to tell me when we last spoke on the phone?'

"I...I wanted to tell you something."

"What was it, Beth? You can tell me."

"I...I wanted to tell..."

"What? What did you want to tell me, Beth?"

"I wanted to tell you that I love you." She said it as if she had to get it out before she lost her courage.

My heart jumped, and I yelled to her, "Beth Della Russo, I am so much in love with you that if I don't get to hold you soon I think I'll..." But I stopped speaking when I came around the side of a huge boulder and saw Beth lying on the ground.

I went down on my knees and lifted Beth into my arms. She was still very weak and a bit disoriented, but she held me as tight as she could. For two minutes we just held each other; then I said, "I love you, just in case you didn't hear me before."

"I heard you, and I'm not going to let you forget it," Beth said, with a smile that made me smile right back.

Then Beth looked up at me, "Where is Julian? Do you think he's here? My God, Chris; he's a maniac! What can we do? Is he still here?"

I wanted to keep her calm, so I told her that Julian must have escaped when he heard me coming down the entrance to the pit. I told her that she was safe and that, when she could walk, we would climb out of the pit and try to get help.

Now Beth just stared into my eyes. "You saved my life again."

I looked into that beautiful face and said, "Well, you're worth it." I smiled at her.

We sat for a few more minutes until we heard sounds and voices on the other side of the cave. By this time Beth was able to stand on her feet, but she was still a little wobbly, so I sat her back down on the ground. I heard another familiar voice, and I knew it was Uncle Al to the rescue.

"Chris! Beth! Are you okay? Chris, Beth—please, answer me!"

I shouted back, "We're over here!"

I heard a lot of talking—it seemed that Uncle Al brought a whole bunch of people with him. I was never happier to hear his voice and know that the nightmare was over. I sat back on the ground next to Beth and just held her hand. I said, "Well, looks like we've been rescued. Uncle Al seems to have brought the troops, and they can get us out of here."

"Chris, how did you find me? How did you know I was here?"

"It's a long story, and I will tell you over a bottle of my extra special Cabernet Franc."

Beth looked at me, "You came for me. You risked your life for me. How can I ever thank you?"

"Well, telling me you love me is a good start."

"That's true, but, seeing that we are way beyond our first date, what do you say we fool around—a lot?"

I smiled, held her in my arms and said, "Agreed!"

Epilogue

Uncle Al, Dan and the Coast Guard came to the rescue managing to get us out of the pit and onto the Harbor Patrol boat for the trip back to the marina.

The rain and wind had ended, and a beautiful starlit night helped guide us back. The boat motored steadily through the waters of the bay as Beth and I huddled together on a seat looking back at Pit Island. The terror we had just experienced slowly diminished the further away we got, but it never truly vanished.

The peace and quiet was most welcome. The only sound we heard was the rumble of the engine. I was enjoying the silence. Pit Island was getting smaller and smaller. But as I looked over the bay to the small rocky island, I noticed the trees swaying and what seemed like movement of the boulders in the water. I immediately stood up and called to Harbormaster Cunningham, Uncle Al and all else on board to look and see what I was seeing.

Beth said, "Chris, what's wrong? What is it?"

"I don't know, but there seems to be a lot of movement going on around Pit Island."

Ron Cunningham slowed the boat and everyone on board looked to see what was going on. First, we all heard the cracking sound, and then we saw a large fissure splitting the island down the middle. I stared as Beth asked, "What's going on, Chris?"

"I really don't know, but it seems like the island is coming apart." I turned to the Harbormaster and asked him. He seemed dumbfounded by it all and said, "I don't know either; I've never seen anything like it in my life."

The cracking sound grew louder, and we could see the trees and bushes on the island splitting apart. As the split in the island got larger and larger by the second, water started to fill it in. The cracking sound turned into a loud rumble, and the island shook as if there was an earthquake. The boat was far enough away so that we could see the entire event happening. In an instant, the island seemed to cave in on itself and disappear under the waters of the bay.

Everyone just stared at the bay where there once was an island and now was only water. Ron spoke first. "I've never seen anything like that. What could have happened?"

No one wanted to answer because no one could even guess. Ron called the Coast Guard, and they were just as puzzled. Captain Talbot said he would do an investigation and report back, but I suspected that nothing would be found.

As we headed back to the marina, there was a crowd of people anxiously waiting on the shore. Standing in the very front were Beth's parents, brother and sister. Beth jumped off the boat and into their arms. There were tears and hugs—all in all, a happy homecoming.

As we all were walking back to Beth's home, I heard the cry of an animal and noticed some movement on the side of the road near the woods. I stopped to see if I could determine what it might be, but it was too dark. Uncle Al, who was walking right behind me, asked, "What's wrong? How come you stopped?"

I continued to look at the wooded area and just said, "Oh, I don't really know; I heard a sound, kind of like a cry. I thought I saw something move, a deer or something large. Probably my imagination."

"Well, come on, let's get back to Beth's house and just try to relax a little. What do you say?"

"Sounds good to me." I turned, and Beth left the arms of her parents and ran back to me. She looked up and kissed my cheek, and we walked away with the rest of the group.

St Agnes of Montepulciano

Reprinted from
http://www.roman-catholic-saints.com/st-agnes-of-montepulciano.html
from *The Woman in Orbit* and other sources

Saint Agnes of Montepulciano was born into a noble family in the village of Gracciano, Italy, in about the year 1268. A miracle occurred to demonstrate that she was a predestined soul, for it is recalled that burning torches appeared to illuminate her crib on the day she was born. Agnes was no more than four years old when she began seeking solitude where she could pray privately for many hours to Jesus, whom she already loved.

At the age of nine Saint Agnes told her parents that she desired to enter the Dominican monastery at nearby Montepulciano. Both parents initially opposed Agnes' wish, so she prayed that God might change their opinions. In a short time she entered the convent and began living under the rule of Saint Augustine. The sisters she lived with soon recognized that Agnes appeared more like an angelic spirit than a human being. She lived an austere life, sleeping on the ground with a stone for a pillow, and fasted on bread and water.

To test Agnes' holiness and commitment to her prayer life, the sisters gave her difficult duties to perform in the convent. They were greatly edified to see that Agnes regularly completed her duties without complaint, and that she continued with her prayer life and regular acts of charity. In fact, it was about this time that Agnes could be observed absorbed in prayer while seemingly unaware that she was suspended nearly two feet above the ground, or violets, lilies or roses would be found growing up through the stones where Saint Agnes had just prayed.

Several of the residents of the town of Procena built a monastery for their daughters, and naturally desired that Saint Agnes should come with some of her sisters and become the prioress of the new convent. Agnes was only 15 years old, and feared for her humility should she accept the position. Pope Nicholas IV commanded her to accept the office, so she agreed to become the superior of the sisters there.

There are many miracles recorded at this time involving St Agnes of Montepulciano. She frequently multiplied loaves, as Christ did in the gospels, to feed those in need. She had also apparently reached such a level of sanctity that invalids and those afflicted with different types of mental illness would be restored to health just by being brought into her presence.

The Blessed Virgin Mary appeared to Saint Agnes and told her that she would one day found a large monastery based on faith in the Most High and undivided Trinity. She did in fact establish the convent under the Dominican rule, as she had been instructed by an angel, about the year 1300, as the citizens of Montepulciano had built a new convent there, hoping to lure Agnes back to them. She governed there until her death in 1317.

Agnes was known to have experienced several visions during her life. On the night of the Feast of the Assumption, the Blessed Virgin placed the Infant Jesus in her arms. She encouraged Agnes to continue suffering for the love of Christ – she had been sick practically all her life. The Mother of God left with St Agnes of Montepulciano a small cross to comfort and strengthen her. This little cross is still shown with great solemnity to pilgrims, especially during the month of May. Mary likewise vouchsafed Agnes a vision of Christ's suffering, which lasted three days.

To comfort Agnes, Mary appeared to her on the feast of the Purification while she was at Holy Mass. Mary told her this was the hour she had taken the Child Jesus to offer Him in the Temple. Our Lady smiled sweetly, and gave Agnes her Babe to hold and caress. Saint Agnes was also known to have received Holy Communion from an angel. She experienced repeated levitations, as noted above, and performed miracles for the faithful of the region.

Shortly before her death, Saint Agnes was sent to bathe in springs that were thought to have curative powers. The waters did nothing to help Agnes, though a new spring emerged close by which did indeed have curative power. It was given the name "the Water of Saint Agnes." While there, the saint prayed over a child who had recently drowned, bringing the child back to life.

St Agnes of Montepulciano then went back to the monastery, where she died on April 20th, 1317, at the age of only 43. Her body was found to be incorrupt, and a mysterious, sweet smelling liquid was observed to stream from both her hands and feet. When Saint Catherine of Siena went to pray before Saint Agnes' incorrupt body, the deceased saint lifted her foot for Saint Catherine to kiss. She also revealed to Saint Catherine that they would both enjoy the same amount of glory in heaven.

St Agnes of Montepulciano was solemnly canonized by Pope Benedict XIII in 1726. Her feast day is April 20th.

Acknowledgements

Unlike angels, most saints were, in life, real people like you and me. They have felt the same human emotions we've all felt, gone through the same turmoil's we've gone through, some have even been embarrassed by the same things we are embarrassed by, and some even learned to love in the same way we have.

While writing this book, I was able to reflect on my own Catholic grade school and high school religious instructions. In those teachings, I learned about some of the saints and their truly remarkable lives. It is amazing how a few of their names, life experiences and stories came back to me while researching information for this book. What is also instructive is to acknowledge how much more I have forgotten or never bothered to learn.

If you take the time, there are so many lessons about life, love, joy, learning, suffering and death in stories of the saints. Most of these accounts of the saints are real, taken from what had been recorded at their time and during the years that followed. Some are witnessed, and some are drawn from legend, and over time, their personal histories have provided guidance to many who are looking for inspiration, solace and reaffirmation of their faith.

I would encourage all who are interested to read about the lives of these truly remarkable people. With that said, I want to acknowledge and thank the following for their kindness, assistance, inspiration, visions and their miracles:

St. Agatha of Sicily
St Agnes of Montepulciano
St. Aloysius of Gonzaga
St. Anthony the Abbot
St. Augustine of Hippo
St. Barbara

St. Bernardine of Siena
St. Camillus de Lellis
Sts. Cosmas and Damian
St. Fabius
St. Francis of Assisi
St. Jude
St. Mary Magdalene
St. Michael the Archangel
St. Monica
St. Nicholas of Tolentino
St. Rita of Cascia
St. Thomas More
St. Valentine
Catholic Online (www.catholic.org)
Saints.SPQN.org
Wikipedia

Finally I would want to acknowledge two very important people in this journey of mine. John Colby, Founder and Publisher of Brick Tower Press who actually had the courage to take gamble with me, a first time author. I can't thank you enough John.

Next my last, and definely not least, acknowledgement goes to Alan Morell, my agent and President of Creative Management Partners. Alan and I have been friends for more than 20 years and when I asked if he would represent me he said "Of course, put it in an email." For those who have tried to find an agent you know how special this is.

CP

From the next exciting
Chris Pella Novel
THE SAINTED
Revelations

Preface

His screams shook the very foundations of hell itself.

Even the torture and torments of the souls of the damned could not quell the rage and hatred he felt. He should be exalted above all but he has been condemned and it shall be this way for eternity. He tried to take comfort in the knowledge that God held no power in his domain, but he had to admit that it was God whose judgment imprisoned him here.

It was happening to him now…when the fury became uncontrollable his entire figure grew and grew in magnitude. He was now the size of what the pitiful minions called a mountain. He looked down in anger and smashed his limbs into the swarm of the evil spirits and condemned below. The hoards screamed in terror begging for mercy but he was merciless…you would think they would know this by now.

He now screamed again, "I AM LUCIFER! I AM ETERNAL!"

God had condemned him to this fate. He sent Michael to vanquish me. Michael, my brother angel, how could he? God had condemned a full third of the heavenly host of angels to the lake of fire for eternity. The demon recalled how he could not understand what had happened, after all, was he not like God Himself? He remembered that he would not beg for forgiveness, after all, there was nothing to forgive. It was long ago, in the beginning of times, and he vowed that he would seek vengeance. He would destroy the souls of the pitiful creatures that God had placed on earth. Lucifer's sneer became full and clear as he thought of how easy it was to take advantage of the free will God had given these creatures. He knew what temptations best suited men; pride, envy, lust, depravity, heresy, hatred and so much more. There were many weapons in his arsenal and he would use them all.

He knew the minds and hearts of men were weak and many can easily be led to temptation. These temptations lead to transgressions and those lead to corruption and that leads to a sinful existence and the fall from grace. Many have found this out too late and all the damned in the hellish realm he rules are a testament to the weakness of men and the fate of their souls.

He would have his revenge against God, revenge against His Son and revenge against the cursed Sainted, especially his brother Michael. Yes, he would have his revenge. His rage grew as he thought of the encounter with the man and woman in the pit. He thought to himself, how could he have not seen how strongly they protected Christopher? How could he have not seen the power of the cursed Sainted and how their meddlesome interference would deny him the one soul he vowed to possess? How could he have not seen the strength of the forces of good? He had failed to be victorious in his battle against God, His Son and the Sainted but there must be a way to see that victory could be his...but how?

The demon tried to ponder these questions but he was so enraged that it blinded him to any answers he may have found. He hated that God had condemn him to this fate, he hated humanity and now he must wreak havoc on the earth so the souls of so many would be his. It was the only way to overcome the goodness of God and redress this greatest of injustices done to him.

This was his dream, his one overwhelming desire, but how would it be made manifest? It was then that a thought came to him and it was the first time in a long time the Devil smiled. God may have the Sainted but he had something far more powerful.

From the burning fires and molten pits that surrounded Lucifer they came... he merely thought it and they assembled. He commanded the princes of hell, the first hierarch of demons to appear before him and they always did exactly what he commanded. Satan looked over the unholy Seraphim at his feet and he began to feel better. He had been cheated of his rightful place in time without end. This cruel twist of fate had forced him to make many errors and miscalculations but that was in the past and that will change. Now the way is clear, now all his longings, all the desires he could only have hoped for will become manifest. These dark angels would assure that redemption would be his, that the forces that aligned against him would fail and ultimately the souls of men would, at long last, suffer at his hand.

One by one the hellish demon masters assembled in front of him, loyal soldiers before their leader waiting to follow his command. Lucifer gazed at the devilish legion that stood at hand and as he looked at each one, it gave him pause to delight.

First there is the ever constant Beelzebub who, with him, was among the first three angels to fall from grace. Beelzebub is able to tempt men with pride and that would be a great asset in the battle to come. Pride, Lucifer knew the sin of pride, but it is not the time to dwell on this, he will have his revenge and his pride will become his redemption, his victory over God Himself!

Standing next to Beelzebub there is Leviathan, an unholy prince of the Seraphim as well, who can tempt even the strongest souls into heresy. His special skills will be needed for the confrontation with the bastard faithful. For the first time those dedicated to the Son will know doubt, they will know fear and they will know the power of evil. Men and women will suddenly realize they are doomed and they will turn their backs on Heaven and curse their beliefs. They will come to this realization, albeit too late, as they kneel to worship the supreme master of Hell itself. As the pitiful creatures must confront the inevitable, then Leviathan will be triumphant and this will assure his ultimate victory.

Lucifer's gaze moved to Asmodeus, the third prince, with his burning desire to tempt men into depravity. Ever devoted Asmodeus would have prevailed in the battle of the pit if it were not for that bitch, Agnes. Satan assured Asmodeus that he would have his chance at retribution for the humiliation he had endured. The dragon Asmodeus rode on breathed flames as the demon roared in anticipation and Asmodeus bowed in appreciation.

This time it would be different, this time victory would be his and it will be Lucifer they will fear.

Standing behind the first three was Pesado, the keeper of chaos. It will be Pesado that will show men the true meaning of fear. This will happen as all goodness and honor are corrupted. It will come to pass when every one of these creatures abandons all loyalties in the vain attempt to protect themselves. Following behind Pesado is Berith, a prince of the Cherubim, who tempts men to commit homicide. Murder has always held a special place in the hearts of men and Berith would have a special role given the chaos that will follow.

To the left there was Astaroth, the prince of Thrones, who tempts men to be lazy. Lucifer's smile became wider as he thought that Astaroth had the easiest of tasks. When vigilance withers, laziness becomes the powerful force that takes over the mindset of men. Lucifer had so much understanding of laziness and he knew it was the easiest way to lead humanity to sin.

Next to Astaroth stood Verrine, another of the prince of Thrones, whose special skill tempts men to impatience and the demon knew that could lead to so much more. Lucifer's smile continues to grow as he stared and saw Gressil, the third prince of Thrones. Gressil who tempts men with impurity has captured so many of the souls littering the very foundation of hell.

Finally, there was dependable Sonneillon, the fourth prince of Thrones. He tempts men to hate and he is a particular favorite of Lucifer. He recalled how Beelzebub and Sonneillon inspired the temptation for Judas Iscariot to betray the cursed Son of God and seal His fate on the cross. Even now the screams and torment of Judas ring in terror as his punishment is meted out each and every measure of time immemorial.

How many souls have Sonneillon and the others sent to him? There were too many to count, especially in the last 100 years! Lucifer and Sonneillon took special pleasure in tormenting and afflicting horrendous pain and suffering on the most vile of men including the likes of Stalin, Mao, Pol Pot and new arrivals like Osama bin Laden. The demons took special delight and their enjoyment was boundless, especially when inflicting the cruelest of punishments for the likes of mass killers like Hitler. Lucifer and his demons look forward, with relish, to the torture they would inflict on Hitler and so many more souls that will be damned for eternity.

Lucifer yelled "Sieg Heil!", and he burst into laughter.

Nine in all! These were his princes, his weapons to strike at mankind and reap revenge on the self-righteous bastard Sainted of holiness. He was ready to reveal his plan but he needed to have his first hierarchy prepare for the inevitable battle and with that he spoke,

"It is time. The forces of heaven must not prevail and it is through you they will fail and the souls of mankind will be doomed and they will be mine. Go and assemble the 66 rulers and the 666 legions of 6,666 demons each and let them be ready to receive my command."

The dark angels looked up at Lucifer and as he looked upon their hideousness, he knew they were ready. If the battle were to be won these demons are all that would be needed. The epic confrontation between good and evil was inevitable. Dark versus light, hell versus heaven and the ultimately victory of evil over good was the plan he devised and it would be the path to his glorious victory. These devils, demons of the first order, would at last overwhelm the forces of heaven and then there would be nothing to stop the horror that mankind would confront. This would be his reward, his dream come true and the reason he exists. Lucifer, once ensconced over the souls of the damned, would derive such immense pleasure from the anguish and horror he would inflict that he will finally know true pleasure for the first time in his eternal rule.

Once cast into the lake of fire, Satan had tried many times to incite God and His faithful to conflict but it never came to pass. He knew his strength and that of the demon hoard. He knew his plan was perfect but he knew it would not be easy. The heavenly host had powers too and they would not be readily brought to battle.

The plan was all-embracing but there will need to be a catalyst for the impending conflict. The means to an end and it will all begin with a messenger, a conduit, and he will prepare the way. It will all start with the greatest of blasphemies and end with the victory of Hell itself. Satan would then have his revenge and this time the Sainted and their visions will not be able to save Christopher Pella and all of humanity.

For sales, editorial information, subsidiary rights information or a catalog,
please write or phone or e-mail
IBOOKS
Manhanset House
Dering Harbor, New York
US Sales: 1-800-68-BRICK Tel: 212-427-7139
BrickTowerPress.com
ibooksinc.com
bricktower@aol.com

www.Ingram.com

For sales in the UK and Europe please contact our distributor,
Gazelle Book Services
White Cross Mills
Lancaster, LA1 4XS,
UK Tel: (01524) 68765 Fax: (01524) 63232 email:
jacky@gazellebooks.co.uk

CPSIA information can be obtained at www.ICGtesting.com
Printed in the USA
BVOW06*1534151115

426717BV00007B/114/P

9 781596 874367